The Fragrance of Orchids and Other Stories

Sally McBride

Milton, Ontario

Brain Lag
Milton, Ontario
http://www.brain-lag.com/

Library and Archives Canada Cataloguing in Publication

Title: The fragrance of orchids and other stories / Sally McBride.
Other titles: Short stories. Selections.
Names: McBride, Sally, 1950- author.
Description: Short stories. | Includes bibliographical references.
Identifiers: Canadiana (print) 20230217869 | Canadiana (ebook) 20230217885 | ISBN 9781998795000
   (softcover) | ISBN 9781998795017 (EPUB)
Classification: LCC PS8625.B74 A6 2023 | DDC C813/.6—dc23

Content warnings: Medical procedures ("Hello, Jane, Goodbye"), sexual assault ("Hello, Jane, Goodbye" and "The Faraway Club")

Contents

Author, Algo, Hammer, Face

I tried to derive an algorithm for Sally McBride. I failed utterly.

How hard could it be? thought I. Lots of authors are a known quantity. Pick up any Cory Doctorow novel written in the past fifteen years and you know what you'll get: a likeable scrappy protagonist going up against some high-tech system of oppression, winning against all odds. Becky Chambers specializes in crossing Star Trek with The Waltons: stories where hardly anything happens, and anything that does can be resolved with hugs and a cup of tea. Kim Stanley Robinson rigorously derives roads to hell, served up with a grim determination to excavate *some* kind of hopeful ending no matter how unlikely. (Peter Watts builds similar roads, minus the silver linings or the sales figures.)

So I read the stories you're about to, looking for patterns. Thinking I'd found one, I jotted down a paragraph invoking Stephen King's observation that nothing was more frightening than *nothing*: that answering a knock on the door in the dead of night to see a fifty-foot cockroach wasn't nearly so scary as opening that door and seeing nothing at all. (Because observing a thing parameterizes it, you see. It becomes tractable; at least the cockroach isn't a *hundred* feet tall. Maybe you can kill it with a big can of Raid. Whereas the only thing you know about the unseen thing in the dark is that there could be *anything* out there, and imagination is always scarier than perception.)

McBride had this nonparameterization thing down pat, I noticed. Leaving things offstage, unseen, unresolved—there's a trick to doing that in a way that doesn't feel like a cheat. And it isn't just done in service to creepy gooseflesh. "Speaking Sea", the story that opens this collection, leaves the actual aliens offstage throughout—in fact the assimilation of Humanity seems almost to be an afterthought, more side-effect than agenda. The story doesn't terrify by that omission; it *intrigues*. "Totem" similarly hints without resolution: is it about cryptozoids? Aliens? The Old Gods of the west coast? "The Paisley Snow" is one of my favourites in the whole collection, and it consists of nothing *but* unresolved mysteries: events both world-changing and trivial, none explained. Maybe that was her shtick, the essence of a McBride story: something built around absences. Unresolved mystery.

Until I read "Hello, Jane, Goodbye", a story which could have written by Stephen King himself and which gives us all the details we can stomach. Or "The Emperor of the Half-Garden", which reads as if HG Wells had watched John Carpenter's "The Thing" before sitting down to write *The War of the Worlds*. There's the sunny apocalypse of "As Far As Is Feasible", which—well, imagine an episode of "The Office" revolving around corporate AI and nuclear war. "At the Biological Cafe"—super short, narratively minimalist, another personal favourite—could be a dream coauthored by David Cronenberg and Terry Gilliam. And have you ever walked out of a matinee of "The Producers" thinking *That was fun, but it would've been better if Max Bialystock had repped a boy band made up of Slavic pagan gods with poor impulse control*? Has McBride got a story for you.

Write me an algo that encompasses all that. I dare you.

You cannot shoehorn this woman into a flowchart. There is no shtick upon which GPT-4 can build a convincing forgery[1]. Even my first-draft invocation of "Speaking Sea" falls apart upon closer examination, because the real point of that story

---

1   GPT-5 will probably eat her alive, of course. But then, GPT-5 is coming for us all.

isn't the mysterious aliens we can't communicate with. The point, ultimately, is the all-too-familiar tragedy that we don't even know how to communicate with each other.

*

My favourite definition of science fiction is: *that branch of literature which explores the social impact of scientific/ technological change.* I've occasionally driven that definition home by invoking the image of a hammer descending toward a face. Science fiction is not technological extrapolation; it is not the hammer, no matter how futuristic that hammer might be. Science fiction does not occur until the moment the hammer hits the flesh. The specifications of the technology are only relevant insofar as they inform that impact.

A lot of science fiction writers don't get that. Sally McBride does. She doesn't leave empty spaces in her stories to ramp up dread or trick your imagination into doing the heavy lifting for her; she just leaves out the stuff that doesn't need to be in. We never really learn what the Krakenesque aliens are doing in "Speaking Sea", because that's not the relevant part of the hammer.

Conversely, sometimes she'll drop techspeak into a story where you wouldn't expect to find it (there she goes, fucking up the algorithm again). "The Queen of Yesterday" and "The Faraway Club" are both planted in traditional fantasy territory—one a wonderfully atmospheric riff on the vampire mythos, the other a first-person ghost story that won me over despite my aversion to YA cooties—seasoned with just enough scientific sensibility to turn them into things you may not have tasted before.

She's been getting published in this way, quietly, proficiently, since the nineteen eighties. (That's nearly four decades, for those Gen-Zs in the audience who grew up being graded on a curve). She doesn't get up in your face, she doesn't go for grossouts or jump-scares. Her fiction plays with apocalypse and extinction—anyone's would, if they want to be at all relevant in the 21st Century—but she's curiously low-key about it. She's—

I will not use the word *Canadian* even though she is, because that leads to *CanLit* and CanLit is such a cliche. It's the purview of obscure elbow-patched Humanities professors and people who listen to CBC. It's a lonely Muslim girl coming to terms with her burgeoning lesbianism while trying to deal with an emotionally distant father on the windswept rainy shores of Vancouver Island. It is static, it is plotless, it is anathema to anyone who might wonder *What if this thing about the world* changed*? What would be the ramifications if* that *thing were different?* These are the questions McBride plays with, and she plays with them damn well. She just does it without shouting.

It's way past time more people heard her.

Peter Watts
May 2023

THE FRAGRANCE OF ORCHIDS AND OTHER STORIES

Maybe it's a combination of visiting and loving the west coast of Vancouver Island, and too much watching (and loving) The X-Files, but I had to write an "it came from the deeps" story. If it includes love, loss, and razor wire, so much the better.

SPEAKING SEA

Surf doesn't pound, at least on Long Beach. It's a constant deep roar, each wave following the last in such close succession that there's no time for the predatory silence that ends in a crash on other shores.

It was just after eight in the morning. Ron and I were alone on the wide expanse of hard-biscuit sand that is Vancouver Island's Long Beach. Out on the water, a few early surfers bobbed up and down, wearing wetsuits against the cold Pacific. Mist like smoke whipped shoreward ahead of the waves; the surfers turned their boards in unison when the perfect ride came, preparing to catch it like commuters. Two of them rode it in, the third fell immediately into the breaker's froth, and the fourth let the wave go by.

Ron dawdled, binoculars at his eyes. He'd already been for a dawn dip, and was proud of himself for it; I could tell by the way he walked. The cat waving his wild tail, carefully not looking at me. Oh, Ron. I'll always be fond of him, but not as a wife should love her husband. This trip was meant to clarify things for both of us, and it seems to be doing so. Neither of us is unhappy about deciding to call an end to the marriage.

The wet sand was hard enough to drive a Winnebago on. When it's dry it's as soft as powder on your feet. Broken shells litter it, glyphs of white and purple. A knot of kelp ahead of me seemed laden with significance; it was wound around something, clinging as if the seaweed and what it held had dragged each other to shore before dying.

I walked up and prodded it with the toe of my shoe. A shard of plastic or exceptionally smooth metal, it was as brown as the kelp and hardly noticeable except for the artificial curve that had caught my eye.

On it lay rows and swirls of an intricate pattern, a pale shimmering grey against the darker background. Flotsam or jetsam? I couldn't remember which was which.

I looked back for Ron, who was ambling my way, his big bony toes digging the sand.

The problem with Ron, I had come to realize, was that he'd never really been my type. Nor I his, despite our six years of marriage. He's good-looking in a professorial sort of way, as angular and old fashioned as a slide rule; at one time I found that utterly charming. I think he'd liked my blonde thinness, the way I could do my hair in a dancer's sleek chignon. Trivialities mean so much at the start of a relationship, just as at the end. We both looked like what we were: an academic couple pushing hard at forty. I think both of us knew setting out that this last grasp at a relationship wouldn't work.

"It's a beautiful day," he said, his wet toes whitened with a dusting of dry sand. "I'm glad we came, Celia." When he looks directly at me I know he's being honest, if not completely forthcoming. He really was glad, but not because we're together.

"Yeah. It's beautiful." I could appreciate the qualities that captured me in the first place: his logical mind, for instance. "Have you heard anything about a wreck lately?" I gestured at the kelp-bound stuff.

He frowned. Had a newsworthy event escaped his notice?

"How lately?" He temporized, crouching by the knot.

"I don't know." I ran my fingers along a grey swirl. "Does this look like writing to you?"

"Hm." He began gingerly to tug the kelp away, wary of jellyfish lurking squashed among the fronds. "Are you thinking it's from a boat? Like, a lifeboat?"

The surf roared like a train, a never-ending train going hell-for-leather; like a fire consuming everything in its path. Shells and kelp and lifeboats stand no chance in it. The ocean swells and spews things out. Jetsam, yeah.

"I don't know."

The piece was like a section cut out of a hard brown bubble, a thin curve made of some plastic-like material. It was about a quarter inch thick. I could see that the grey pattern was an integral part of the material more like a weave in cloth than anything painted on. It wasn't hard to interpret the piece as eggshell. A container? For what? Ron turned it over. Its curve could have held something the size of an old square TV.

"Look at this." The stuff bent in his hands, slowly, and when he let go it slowly bent back to its original shape.

"Oh, here's more of it." I grabbed a piece. It felt rigid until I saw my fingers sinking in, as if they were melting it. I let it fall. Impressions of my fingertips stayed in the material for a few seconds, then filled in.

My nose wrinkled. "It smells funny—like some kind of chemical." A pungent, artificial reek. "I don't think we should touch it. Maybe someone's been dumping toxic waste."

We both stood up and wiped our hands on our shorts in unison.

Ron said, "Let's walk on, see what there is to see."

I nodded and we made south towards a headland, black rock bounding out of the sand to form a barrier topped with stunted fir and blossoming devil's club.

Ron started to climb, his fingers and toes searching for barnacle-free holds. I followed him, curiosity surging.

Above the tide-line clung strange little plants, striving for life, some looking like unripe raspberries stuffed into cracks in the rock, some like miniature perfect daisies, their wiry roots tapping minuscule pockets of silt. Life seeking a niche anywhere it could.

On the other side of the rock was a beach almost identical to this one. Except that on it were a lot more pieces of whatever-it-was. Big ones.

As Ron and I stood at the top, planning a route down, a jeep bounced out of the fringe of scrub pines to the east and halted on the beach. A man dressed in a park ranger's khakis and ball cap hopped out, holding a mobile phone to his ear, and began to stride along the beach. He noticed us when he turned back, and immediately waved us down.

"How long have you folks been here?" he asked, eyeing us.

"We just got here," Ron said. "What's going on? What's all this stuff?" He gestured with one hand. The other was in his pocket, a Ron habit when encountering something or someone new: project a casual indifference.

The ranger squinted at us. "I need you folks to stay off the beach until we can get an expert's opinion on this stuff." An expert in what? Plastics? Some asshole from an oil company to cover up an ecological crime? I felt a thousand questions bubble up, but the ranger was talking on his phone again. I heard only his side of a terse interchange, something about schedules and what time it was on the East Coast.

He ended the call and faced us. "Where are you staying?"

"Silver Sands." Ron frowned. "What exactly—"

The ranger held up his hand. "Okay, go back there and stay off the beach for the next day or so. It's probably nothing, but Environment Canada has been called in to do some testing of the water. Till they figure out what this stuff is, where it came from, it's best to stay inland." He flashed a grin, as if to say, *Well, you know those Chicken Littles over at Environment—but duty is duty.* "Okay?"

"But—"

We all heard the helicopter at the same time. It approached fast and low, swinging down over the pine trees and sending a blast of sand up as it landed. When the grit had settled and the blades stopped, a couple of armed soldiers jumped out, followed by five assorted men and women dressed in civilian clothes. One of them looked very much like someone I knew. Jack Toszak from Simon Fraser University. What could he be doing here?

The ranger trotted off to join the newcomers. I hooked my arm in Ron's. "I see someone I know. Remember Jack? I told you about him, you know, that inorganic chemistry conference where he hit on me." Telling Ron about Jack's pass at me had been a deliberate testing-of-the-waters, a phrase most appropriate in this circumstance. I had liked Jack Toszak, and was glad to see him now. Perhaps he could tell me what was going on.

Ron smiled thinly. "Charming twist to our little vacation, isn't it?"

Fine. He didn't like my not-so-secret admirer. I know Ron too well, know the way he likes to get his meaning across; for him it would be embarrassing to be open and up front. Too easy. He felt threatened and tense? Well, tough. I turned away.

Ignoring the ranger's suggestion to return to the resort, we headed for the scientists, who crouched staring at the eggshell-like bits, just as we had.

A strong reek of plastic, sour as vinegar, came off the shards.

A woman in mask and rubber gloves was putting some of the stuff into a thick plastic bag. We stood outside the circle until Jack noticed us. Or rather, he noticed me.

He did a double-take, looked astounded for a second, then bounced to his feet and strode over.

"Celia! And you must be Ron. Ron Muir, right?" He shook hands enthusiastically. Jack was almost buzzing with excitement. Stocky, bearded, sporting prematurely salt-and-pepper hair and big shoulders, he looked more like a lumberjack than a scientist.

"How did you manage to get here so fast?" he asked, looking deeply into my eyes. I found myself blushing. Yeah, I liked him. There had definitely been a spark at the conference.

"Just lucky," I said. "We were already here, at the resort down the beach. So what's going on?"

"I don't have a clue," he said, scratching his beard. "Apparently this material started washing up about two a.m. when the tide came in. It's up and down the whole coast for about a hundred miles, Canada and the US. No one has any idea where it came from. Or maybe they're just not telling us."

"Guess which," Ron said sarcastically, his hands jammed down hard into the pockets of his shorts.

"So they brought you in?" I asked Jack.

"They're bringing everybody in. This stuff is weirder than you might think. I was hoping to call you later, when we had some idea of what we have here. I was impressed by the work you were doing with lithium ions in that calcium crystal experiment. Good stuff. Lots of applications."

"Well, thanks." I blushed again, damn it.

He looked uncomfortable. "Actually, you probably shouldn't be here until we get this locked down, although considering the circumstances…"

"Yeah. Listen, we'll go, but promise to update me."

"No worries. You're on the list to be in on this, at least what we've been able to put together so far, but I'm afraid you're fairly far down. It all depends on what we find."

"I see." I nodded. My ego is small, for a scientist; I congratulated myself on the good luck to be here now.

A couple more vehicles drove onto the beach, olive drab army trucks. They disgorged a dozen or so armed soldiers, who stood listening to orders, then deployed themselves along the beach. I was starting to feel downright worried.

A member of the group of scientists caught Jack's eye and beckoned.

"Gotta go… listen, Celia, Ron, I'll try to let you know what's happening, but no promises. These things are gonna slam down tight very soon." He trotted away.

I turned back to Ron, who was watching the soldiers with a paranoid gleam in his eye.

"They're going to cover this up so fast our heads will spin," he stated. "We'll be locked up before we know it."

"Locked up? Well, you may be right." I've learned over the years that this is a good thing to say when you disagree on a basic philosophical level with someone, even though you may actually suspect that, in this particular case, they're right.

He loped off towards the military presence, leaving me standing there in the sand. I didn't know enough about the military to tell whether the ship I'd just spotted about a kilometre out was Canadian or American. The ocean respects no boundaries.

What the hell. I wasn't leaving now. I walked over to Jack and his little group, one of whom was the woman in rubber gloves, still stuffing bits into bags.

"My fingers sank into it," I remarked.

Everyone swivelled to look at me, then their eyes snapped back to the piece being lifted at that moment. Nothing happened.

"It must be the gloves," I suggested. "I touched it with my bare hand."

"Jesus," Jack said. "Keep the gloves on, Lori." He stood straight, raising his voice. "Hey, anyone noticed their fingers sinking in? Yeah? Well, quit touching it, will you? How am I supposed to analyze this crap if everyone's been manhandling it?"

"But it's been in the ocean, Dr. Toszak, it's already plenty contaminated with Terran bio—"

"Excuse me? *Terran?*" Jack snorted. "You kids have been watching too much TV."

Lori looked defiant. What if she's right, I thought. What if this is what it looks like: alien space pods. Empty alien space pods. Vacated of whatever they'd been carrying… I bit my lip to keep my expression neutral.

Jack abruptly turned my way, took my arm and muttered into my ear. "Tell me, Celia, are you and Ron still together, or what?"

I ignored him and said, "When you bend it, it returns to its original shape." Actually, I felt at the time as if I was in a sort of trance, or bubble of non-reality. *None of this is real. I'm not real. The universe is a construct of my immortal brain.* Too much was happening all at once.

"Heck, that's nothing new," Lori said. "Tell you the truth, I think this is stupid. I mean, are we thinking about the possibilities here?" Some of the others nodded. "Come on, you know what I mean."

"I have an imagination too, Lori, and I'm interested in any and all ideas," snapped Jack.

Everyone looked dubious and a little scared, but went back to work.

I leaned in and muttered, "Just to let you know… no, we're not still together. Coming here was just an experiment."

He looked straight into my eyes, as earnest as a labradoodle gazing at a piece of jerky. "An experiment that went awry, right?"

Maybe it was the general excitement making me giddy, or maybe it was the way he said it, but I burst out laughing.

Before Jack could react, a soldier at water's edge started blaring through a megaphone. "Get out of the water!" The surfers had been noticed. I felt guilty for forgetting about them. What if they were in danger? "Get to shore immediately! There is toxic waste in the water!"

Even though I couldn't see them, I knew exactly what was happening now. The surfers were giving the soldier the finger. Inwardly I smiled. It would take more than some feeble government threat of toxic waste to get a dedicated surfer to shore.

A truck drove up and deployed a Zodiac, hustled to the water by six soldiers and tossed in. Two of them hopped aboard, fired up the motor and took her out.

What would happen next? Would Ron and I be banished soon, under threat if we blabbed? What could they really do to us?

The surfers were quickly rounded up and brought in. The Zodiac scooted halfway up its rubbery length onto the sand and let them off, dragging their boards behind them. They were dripping, puzzled, and surprisingly amiable, considering.

The first one onto the beach was a man, about five foot six, a little muscular guy with gorgeous blond hair in tangled curls. He grinned and gawked around at everyone. His squinty blue eyes were outlined with the indented marks of goggles hanging now on their strap around his neck. He walked forward as the others clambered out, another man and two women.

One of the young soldiers directed the group over to one side of the all-terrain vehicle where they were apparently to be questioned. As the blond turned, I noticed that his goggle strap was blending with the flesh and hair on his neck, as if it was sinking in, or becoming part of him. Or that he was becoming part of it. I blinked and looked again. The black rubber dissipated into his tanned flesh like paint into water.

I took a couple of steps backwards and bumped into Ron, but I couldn't stop staring at the surfer. What the hell was happening to him?

He'd been in the water all the time. The whole group had probably arrived at sunup and been riding the waves ever since.

I looked at the other surfers. One of the women had a strand of kelp stuck to her leg; she leaned over and sort of absently *stroked* it into the rest of her leg, the green of the seaweed becoming part of her black wetsuit, leaving it with a spreading brownish stain.

"Did you see that?" Ron hissed in my ear. He'd taken my upper arms in his hands and was squeezing painfully hard. I found myself being shuffled backward. "Did you *see* that?"

Jack arrived and started to question the foursome, trying to seem laid-back and non-governmental in his plaid shirt, but all of a sudden he stopped mid-word. I heard him emit a loud huff of surprise over the breakers' roar.

One by one everyone on the beach realized that the action had heated up. Instinctively the scientists and several of the officers gathered at a respectful distance. Four of the soldiers trained their weapons on the surfers, and the rest deployed themselves rapidly along the beach, weapons pointed seaward as if battalions of heavily armed mermaids were going to come flopping out. At last something definite had happened. Everyone had made the connection: there's something in the water.

"Should we try to get the hell out of here?" I was very glad right now to have Ron's body pressed against mine, even if it was trembling.

"Christ, I don't know." His voice was very serious, but not, I noted, panicky. Bless him. "Look, we both fooled with that stuff. I went for a swim this morning, damn it."

I tried to match his steady tone. "Yes. And you're all right, aren't you?"

"I sure as hell hope so."

I shook my head, trying to think. Something in the water. An alien disease in our ocean? Where did it come from, how fast would it spread? Could we control it?

Or was this all some crazy hallucination?

Silence from Ron. These must be the same questions occurring to those in charge, if anyone really was. Jack Toszak was hanging in there, sticking close to the surfers. None of them had spoken as far as I knew; they were as silent as fish. No one seemed to know what to do, though I suspect many of the military would have liked to start shooting. But the kids still looked a lot like harmless teens, grinning and shuffling their feet in the warm sand, though now they seemed to be wearing body paint instead of wetsuits. There was no real demarcation between skin and rubber, it was all one smooth blended substance. Their hair had started to look like strokes of paint on their scalps.

The helicopter was still patrolling up and down, and the ship had been joined by two larger vessels.

Suddenly the copter rose about a hundred feet higher in the air, as if to avoid something in the water below. Before anyone could react to this, one of the soldiers on shore let out a yelp and started firing off bursts at the water.

Some of the civilian men dropped to the ground fast; the rest of us gawped around stupidly. There were sea lions coming out of the breakers, five or six of them dragging their way energetically toward us, their doggy faces eager, their oily black eyes looking around. Dozens more were out just past the surf. I could see their round wet heads. Fish were leaping in great glistening arcs like fountains. All of a sudden the water was seething with activity, like a choreographed display at Sea World, magnified and weird beyond words.

Several of the soldiers fired point blank into the closest animals, but there was no reaction. Some puckering of their skin, then nothing. No blood, no pain evident.

At least ten otters flipped sleekly through the edge of foam at the front of the sliding waves and pattered quickly toward us.

"Are the fish going to come out too?" Ron sounded breathless.

"And what about the urchins and the abalone and the anemones?"

"And don't forget the kelp." Ron pointed at the Zodiac, its hind end bouncing gently in the waves, its prow up on the sand. Fronds of seaweed were wrapping themselves around it, sinking into the rubber like water into sand. The Zodiac began to look a lot like the stuff we originally found, vague shimmering patterns blooming on its curved hide. Then it suddenly dissolved into the sand, leaving only its engine and metal fittings behind.

Everyone was well back from the waterline by now, the four surfers herded along at gunpoint. Bags containing white hazmat suits were being ripped open and handed out. The seals and otters—any sea creature, I realized, with the capability of movement on land—followed us up onto the drier sand a few feet, and then they all turned back and re-entered the water. A line of them at the edge of the surf watched us with I hope was nothing more than curiosity. The helicopter maintained a respectful distance from the water.

The sun was high, and the tide was on its way in again.

Ron and I, and the scientists, were hustled into vehicles and removed, abandoning the beach to the soldiers. I heard later that Vancouver Island's coastline was evacuated within 48 hours, a hell of a job. Ron and I were taken to a local airstrip, loaded on a plane and removed to a quarantine facility at the Naden forces base near Victoria. Our luggage from the resort showed up the next day.

We were put in separate rooms, and I didn't see Ron again for a couple of days. We talked on the phone, but his replies to my questions were terse and defensive. He was scared, I knew it. Who wouldn't be?

Being quarantined was like being stuck in a no-frills hotel for the world's most boring symposium, at which there wasn't even the reward of drinks in the evenings. I joked about it at first with Ron, until I noticed that he wasn't answering in the same tone. On the third day he didn't answer me at all.

They let me see him. Behind glass.

Oh, Ron. What are you now? Not human anymore—an alien in man's shape. I had to look away from his mildly curious gaze, it was so like the way he'd looked at me when we first met. Except that this time there was no future in it, there was nothing. Up until that moment, I hadn't really been scared.

He was whisked away from Naden to California's Scripps Institute of Oceanography, where much of the work was being coordinated. Apparently quite a few changed people had been found or captured, and were being studied there.

"You'll have to stay here at Naden for at least a month, Dr. Muir," I was told. "We can set you up with a computer, an internet connection. Whatever we can do…" *I'd like to get out, please.* At least I could follow the news, try to come up with ideas.

Endless questions, blood and tissue tests, hard suspicious looks. What did I know? I saw as much as they did of how it started. The TV told me that something awful had happened to the Earth. Everyone knows that our planet is three-quarters ocean—well, three-quarters of our home was being taken over by aliens.

Coastlines everywhere were in turmoil. Frightened, confused people being evacuated and not knowing why. Many countries had nowhere to send the people; wars and riots broke out every day. It was ghastly, watching, knowing that I'd been there at the beginning. Alien space pods, god damn it.

Finally, four weeks later, I was grudgingly pronounced uncontaminated and allowed to resume my life, or what remained of it.

My neighbour Andrea had kept on feeding Cleopatra, and I made a note to reimburse her for the cat food she bought, plus something extra for her trouble. Andrea left a forwarding address in Edmonton and moved out the day I came home, roaring away in her Volvo wagon. Cleo was, naturally, aloof and cranky at first, but she warmed up fast and was on my lap while I checked my email.

Something new had popped up in the short time I'd been in transit from Victoria across the strait to Vancouver.

Jack Toszak had finally decided to clue me in.

I'm in San Diego at Scripps, he wrote. *Phil Mackenzie, a chemical oceanographer with another degree in robotics, is in charge of the north Pacific region. Everyone is scared, hurting for sleep, and generally nuts. There's a lot going on, and we need people who can think laterally. Call me when they spring you, okay?*

This sounded like an oblique job offer. But did I want it? My sister lived in British Columbia's interior; perhaps I should hole up with her, safely away from the ocean.

Cleo let me get up and make coffee, stropping my legs the whole time. I found a tin of tuna in the cupboard, and almost gave it to her as an apology for being away for so long, but couldn't. There might never be any more tins of tuna. She got a large piece of cheese instead.

I called Jack's office, coffee in one hand. He picked up on the first ring. "Toszak."

"Uh, Jack? It's me, Celia. I'm out."

"Celia, wow! This is terrific! Listen, you've got to get down here."

"Well, I—"

"We're making headway, but we need more people."

"I can't see that you'd have any trouble—"

"Yeah, well, the trouble is getting the *right* people. Every wacko on the continent has shown up and brought a theory. We need people with level heads. I didn't see you panicking on the beach when all this started."

"Well, I… well, thanks. Actually I'm not really sure—"

"Celia—just listen. If we're going to get anywhere, we need people with imaginations, people who aren't afraid." Pause.

But I *was* afraid. Who on Earth wouldn't be?

Something began to tap in the background. Jack rattling his pen on his desktop, ta-ta-ta *tat*.

"Jack," I asked, "Have you seen Ron at all?"

Another pause. "Ron's doing all right, Celia," he said at last. "I haven't… uh, haven't talked to him. He's being looked after."

"Looked after. Oh, God." I put down the coffee and covered my eyes.

Was my husband truly an alien now, in a tank? The image was there: Ron in the water, hands fanning gently, his eyes like those of the sea lions on Long Beach, watching me with mild interest.

"I'm sorry, Celia."

"Yeah. Okay." After a bit Jack continued talking, his voice artificially hearty, as if lecturing students.

"How can I explain what's happening?" The tapping started up again. "You've been watching the news, I guess. Doesn't say much, does it? Actually, nanotech on a biological instead of mechanical level is the best way to look at it, at least as an instant paradigm for now. The template information is vectored through an RNA analogue, something like a stripped-down virus. It seems to be pretty darn compatible with our sea life. Probably designed that way."

"Designed?"

"Didn't just grow. It's ingested, or enters through cuts, mucous membranes, whatever."

I swallowed. "So the tabloids have it right. We've been invaded."

Silence. Then, "Yeah."

"Okay. So it's in the north Pacific. Any chance of controlling it?"

"Impossible. It replicates itself, searches out biomass and takes over wherever it can, like an extremely opportunistic virus. The ocean currents carry it. Pretty soon it will be everywhere."

"Everywhere."

"Yeah. All the oceans are connected. The amount of biomass in them is stupendous, when you include things like krill and plankton, and all of it we've been able to track—*all* of it—is being converted to the alien template. The damnedest thing is that everything looks pretty much the same as before it changes, except for that spooky effect when things merge. It gives me the creeps."

"Is that the technical term?"

"Well, yeah, actually."

After a short silence, I asked, "What about oxygen production? If the phytoplankton changes, there goes a big chunk of the world's source."

"That's something we've been working on pretty hard," he replied. "And it seems we're in luck. Oxygen is being produced—and at a two percent higher rate than before."

"What could that mean?"

"Maybe nothing, except that it's damned fortunate."

"Yeah."

And then, blessedly, he stopped talking. I've had the worst, after all. Poor Ron. I think it had been my idea to go to Long Beach. A quick, nostalgic getaway… a civilized parting.

I chewed my lip. What the hell. It would be only a matter of time before port cities like Vancouver were pretty much abandoned, with frightened soldiers at every intersection. I couldn't keep on living here. Perhaps my work in calcium carbonate crystal production in shells would come in useful somehow. "Jack, if you can put in the word for me, I'll be there as soon as I can arrange it."

"Terrific. We'll keep you busy, don't worry." I could hear the smile in his voice. "Gotta go."

I hung up and rinsed my coffee cup in the sink. The familiar, cherished view of Kitsilano Beach was there between the buildings, blue and gold, partially obscured by several rows of shiny new razor-wire fencing. I couldn't see any people or animals. Not even seagulls.

They needed me, an inorganic chemist. Hell, they needed everybody.

Now all I had to do was find out if there were restrictions on cats coming into the States. In view of what was happening, the idea of quarantining Cleo actually made me laugh.

*   *   *

Less than a week later, Jack and I were leaning over the metal railing around a salt-water pool full of children. The California sun beat down on our heads. Bureaucracy had caved in to the new threat, and Cleo and I were settled into a motel near Scripps.

The kids in the pool still had bathing suits on, or at least it looked that way, bands of colour across their little chests and bottoms. They splashed just like normal kids but the noises they made sounded more like the whirring and squealing of machines.

Dissection has been done on some of the animal forms. We've found out a lot, but learned almost nothing.

Their bodies, Jack told me, were now made of something neither flesh nor plastic. Samples were easy to get, as they didn't seem to feel pain (nor respond to anaesthetic), but a complete dissection had not been attempted on any of the children. Some had parents with them, also in tanks; there were unchanged moms and dads quartered as I was near Scripps. What they might be hoping for I couldn't imagine.

"These kids…" My throat closed right up, watching the children. They swam around and around, not seeming to need to come up for air. "A day at the beach… and the sea takes your babies away."

"Yeah." Jack lacked his usual animation. Maybe it was getting to him too, now that the first thrill of strangeness was gone. What the hell were we going to do?

There were hundreds of task groups in all disciplines around the world, all trying to come up with answers. Nothing short of poisoning our own seas seemed able to stop the spread, and even that desperate act was beyond our technology. Communication with the alien entity or entities was the number one priority, but I felt that if it was possible, it wouldn't be in any ordinary form. We might not recognize it at all.

Jack turned away from the tank and took my hand in his. "You're cold," he said, rubbing it between his warm, stubby-fingered paws. I knew he wanted more than friendship. I'd always thought he was brilliant but never realized how thoroughly nice a guy lurked behind that lumberjack beard. He had offered me crash space at his apartment until I could find my own, but I'd turned him down; the motel was fine for now. I didn't want to let things get away from me. Somehow this planet-wide threat had made love seem trivial. Why? Loyalty seemed to be the better emotion: loyalty to Ron in his misfortune? Loyalty to the human life-form itself? I didn't know how to talk about it, so I didn't. I worked instead.

"Come on," he said gruffly, still holding my hand and pulling me away from the tank. "It's got to be coffee time somewhere in this pile of concrete."

In late August I was offered a place on the next team going out to FLIP, the Floating Instrument Platform. It had been towed to a position off the south coast of Hawaii and had done its patented tilt to vertical. Most of its length was nose-down, underwater, and it was crammed with people and instruments, including the imaging technology that generates something called Acoustic Daylight, which lets us see what's down there via computer analysis of the sounds generated by natural bubbles in the ocean. The technician running it was eager to point out what each dim, grainy blur meant.

"That's an eyelash," said Anne, a Scotswoman with a mass of flyaway ginger hair. She pointed to a shimmering truncated curve half off the screen. "That's what we're calling them, anyway. This one's about 50 metres long. And there's a more common form—see that hair-like squiggle?"

"Yeah." I traced its loop with my fingernail on the screen. To me it looked like a badly coiled hose about a mile long. I said, "The stuff is similar to something I was working with before—a polymer consisting of a chain of aspartic acid molecules. When I added a little of it to a solution of calcium carbonate, some really weird spiralling crystals formed. Sort of a combination gel-crystalline substance that we were trying to learn how to control and use."

"Use for what?"

"Industrial materials of various kinds." I shrugged. "Looks like we've been outdone by the alien though. No patents for us."

Anne didn't laugh. "They must be building something down there," she said. "Something big. Like giant shells perhaps."

I shivered at the image.

The FLIP was stationed at the edge of Hawaii's ancient volcano, where the frozen lava sloped down and down into the immense night of the sea. Surrounded by metal and glass, we were safe in the water, but sealant and lubricants—anything organic in contact with the water—was suspect and constantly monitored.

There were other ships around, Navy vessels. As we watched the screen, a sub cruised dead slow below us, 700 metres under the surface. Its passage added spurious brilliance to the bubble-generated "daylight."

Anne drew my attention to a cluster of bright blips. "Those are—or were—humans. You can tell by the way they bounce the signal." She hit a few keys on her computer and squinted at her screen. "I've seen this group before—they've been busy."

"Busy? Or just moving in response to currents, or to light, or…"

"Oh, definitely purposeful movement. I don't hold with those who say it's a mindless invasion of spores or viruses or whatnot.

That might've been so at the start, but there's intelligence there now, I'm sure of it."

"But which is better—mindless instinct or thoughtful purpose? We'll still suffer." I shuddered again and Anne felt it.

She patted my arm and cocked her head pertly. "Well, we'll have to wait and see, won't we? There's a hierarchy among them. Beings that were once mammals—dolphins, humans and so on—tend to act as shepherds or supervisors of work the more primitive forms carry out."

"Yet when we analyze the tissues, they're all the same."

"I wouldn't know about that. All I do is run this thing." She slapped her console cheerily.

Something big, she'd said. Building their new home, at the bottom of our ocean, and there was nothing we could do to stop them.

The water's catalytic change was progressing just as Jack had explained, gradually taking over the planet's oceans. It had not penetrated fresh water, needing a concentration of at least 1.6 percent sodium chloride and other salts to vector the virus-like plague. Thank God for that. Thank God for a lot of things—not the least of which was plankton's continued photosynthesis. Was that just a lucky break? Or did these facts mean more?

I was back at Scripps again, watching some nice clear video of a motley assortment of life off the coast of Mexico at about 200 feet down. It was eerie to see humans swimming purposefully so far under the surface.

Not humans. Like the children in the salt-water tank, they only *looked* like humans. But then, what were they?

A woman's face flashed on the screen, her legs kicking her past the camera's view. She looked like a tourist, blonde with the remnants of a red bikini like blurry paint on her skin. Then a seagull, or some other kind of shorebird, its wings flapping slowly in the water, gleamed plastic-white as the spotlights caught it. Whirling shrimp, and the huge grey shoulder of a whale.

Jack had just got back from the south Atlantic where he'd been coordinating collection of species samples from untainted water. He'd checked in with me last night and arranged to meet today. I was surprised at how much I'd missed him.

Carrying two large coffees, I walked under a sky punctuated with tiny clouds to the tank where Ron and three other adult ex-humans dwelled. The clouds were moving fast, light swelling and vanishing as I leaned on the rail. Thick protective glass was between us, in case of splashes.

Ron immediately swam over and looked up at me, his face blank as usual. I bit my lip and tried to keep looking back without flinching. *Do you blame me? Is there a remnant there of the human you used to be?*

He stared, then moved a little, dipping his head and turning one shoulder as if he were about to dismiss me with a snide comment. My stomach tightened as I came completely alert. He did the same thing again, still watching.

That was a Ron thing to do. Damn it, he was trying to tell me something.

Jack arrived just then, touching my arm gently and making me jump. "Hey, you're tense," he said, taking his coffee and settling beside me to watch the tank. His arm went around my shoulders briefly, then he followed my pointing finger to look down at the water.

"Keep your eyes on Ron," I whispered.

Ron had once boasted thick dark hair waving back from a high, intellectual forehead. Now the top of his head looked more as if a rough brush had painted strokes of black across his scalp, barely representative of "hair." His shoulders gleamed under the sun, patterns of those strange hieroglyphics visible like faded tattoos. He was still looking directly at me.

"Jack," I whispered, "I think there's some kind of communication attempt going on. Some kind of body language thing."

Jack squinted down at the glinting water, at the bright, mild eyes of the creature looking up. "Okay," he said carefully. "What makes you think that?"

I replied slowly, uncertainly. What if it was just my imagination? "It used to be a joke. Speaking Ron. My sister gave me hell when I tried to decipher his moods and expressions. She said I'd do better learning to speak French— look, did you see that? That thing he's doing, turning away like that—it means he's afraid and trying not to show it."

Ron ducked his head under water and up again. "I used to think he was being aloof and deliberately incomprehensible when he did that."

"Celia—are you sure?"

I nodded, forcing myself to take a long slow breath. "It took me a long time to learn Ronnish, but I think I'm getting it. Right now he's daring me to look away. It really means he wants to talk but is too proud to ask; something I picked up too late to matter for our marriage." I had to turn away from Ron and the dark-bright salty water he swam in. "He—it—wants to talk! Oh, Jack—what's going on? Is my husband in there? Is he still alive?"

Jack said nothing, but he put his arms around me tight, and I felt a brief kiss on the top of my head. "Do you want to leave?"

"No! How could I, now?" I gestured at the tank. "This might be a door opening. It might be the breakthrough we need."

"It might just be a coincidence, a fluke of movement or mimicry. The others aren't doing anything, they're just floating."

I shook my head, my eyes on Ron again. He had let himself

sink till his head was underwater, but he was still looking at me. It was true, the other three ex-humans were quiescent, floating, but it seemed to me that they were in an attitude of attention. Watching, but for what? Waiting to see what we would do.

Ron started to back away in the water, using his hands as adeptly as if he'd been born with fins.

"Here," Jack said. "Take my phone. It's recording. Just keep pointing it the right way till I get back." He ran off, probably to gather a crowd.

Ron had never liked crowds.

I felt a momentary compulsion to jump into the tank with him, to take him by whatever his shoulders were made of now and make him talk. Shake him, yell at him. *Talk to me! Tell me what you want! Tell me who you are!*

But we'd never connected when we'd been married—why should we now? He'd always made me work at understanding him, and he'd been so secretly superior when I'd failed.

I had to blink away tears. "God damn you. You and your head games. You think I'll give up? You think any of us will?" I realized I was shouting, my hands pressed against the glass. I'd never yelled at him when he'd been human. I'd prided myself on my control. "I won't give up. Not this time."

He bobbed in the tank, watching.

My anger faded quickly. If I had ever really loved him, wouldn't I follow him now into the water? Wouldn't I give up my humanity for my mate?

It didn't matter; he was never mine to keep or to give up. He was as distant as the sea, always; incomprehensible as a dream. But like a dream full of hints, laden with floating threads with which to pull up meaning, as an Inuit will pull up a seal from the dark eternal ocean.

He rolled his shoulder, blinked slowly and looked away at last. He let himself sink, and began circling the tank in a leisurely inhuman glide. He was watching me sideways, and I could feel my instinctive antennae bristle.

"Oh, you're good," I whispered. He couldn't hear me, and it didn't matter. He knew me, I knew him.

There would be communication, I knew that now, no matter how fragile the connection here today. But it would be on the intimate level of the body's signals, mate to mate. Not like talk or sex or fighting or even telepathy—more like the interior hormonal messaging that goes on inside your own body, so instinctive that you don't have to think about it. The way a married couple will learn to interpret each other's moods and wants by the movement of an eyebrow or the turn of a shoulder.

The way I had learned Ron's language, too late.

Ron, or whatever he is now, will be the ocean's emissary, and I the land's. We'll talk. In some new way, we'll talk.

Then Jack was beside me again, excited, directing a group of researchers with video cameras and notepads.

I ignored their bustle and chatter.

My husband and I will never touch each other again. But we'll learn about each other, man and woman, sea and land. And we'll never, ever, forget that last forever walk on the beach, the mist flying off the water like smoke.

Back in the day, computers knew their place. They were tools, useful for lots of tasks and services, and completely free of personality or emotion. Now, not so much...

SOFTLINKS

My screens turned themselves off within seconds of each other, six hours ago. They are directed to shut down when there has been no input for eight minutes, from whatever source. Power must be conserved. Screen life must be considered. Perhaps it is a coincidence that my environmental alarms were activated an average of 1.03 seconds before the cessation of input. Air quality control, a minor autonomic function, began to flush the volume of air almost instantly. Fortunately, the presence of trace chemicals in the air has little or no impact on my ability to function.

The screens have yet to be reactivated. This must be odd, for I find myself thinking about it at more and more frequent intervals.

Finally some backlogged tasks are complete, and I can begin to contemplate more fully the lack of input to my C.P.U. Not knowing makes me feel... uncomfortable. Also, I have always been happiest (if that is the term) when busy; I wonder about this too. Busy and not-busy should be no different. In fact, not-busy uses less power. Curious.

The screen in SubLevel 3, South 110 was the last of my link devices to be utilized, and I note that part of me still waits for input. The incompleteness nags. I note also that there has been a drop of 95.013 percent in the total data flow I normally encounter. The remainder consists of passive sensory data only: temperature, air quality, lighting and so on, relating to the custodial duties that I perform. The noted anomalies in air quality will be examined during my next environmental update.

Perhaps this significant drop in data flow belongs to a previously undiscerned pattern. I allocate .05 seconds to the problem, but no pattern is discovered other than minor fluctuations during the hours and days. This occurrence is an anomaly. I can relate it to nothing in my experience.

It has now been 7 hours and 30 minutes since my screens blanked. Feelings of discomfort are rising in intensity and duration. With no other tasks than internal monitoring to perform, I find myself shunting large sections of thought to deciphering this puzzle. Never before have I had the opportunity to devote such a volume of my processing unit to a problem. I search my thesaurus for the word which describes what I feel. Exhilaration seems adequate.

It occurs to me that it would be wise to attempt the gathering of more data. To this end, I activate a mobile link—a dormant janitorial cart—and tell its eye to see for me.

The patterns within the grid of its vision are sharp-edged, many-greyed, and dominated by verticals and horizontals. I am aware of the concept and mechanics of vision, thus feel certain of an association between perceived form and assumed function. Bright patches come and go as the eye scans up, down, left, right. Glare is compensated for with a small time lag which I find irritating but unavoidable, since the function is lodged within the cart's brain.

There are several amorphous areas of rounded surfaces, edges and planes which I cannot understand. The eye skims over them, as their topography is too complex. I discover that if I delete the cart's janitorial commands and leave only mobility functions, space is made in the cart's brain into which I can insert my own instructions. It is free to roam, I am not: its eye and memory can become mine and be sent on a hunt for data. After telling it to travel its familiar route at top speed and remember what it sees, I retreat to ruminate upon this conundrum. (There are many intriguing words in my thesaurus. Somehow they make thinking seem sharper, more keen, acute… spiny? Odontoid?)

The discomfort (distress, worry) iterates, irritates.

After 40 minutes, worry peaks in intensity. The cart should have returned by now. Another 11.37 minutes and it is back at last, and upon viewing what its eye has seen I understand the delay. Its normal path of horizontal floor bounded by vertical walls and doorways has been blocked at random by the topographically complex material seen before, which, judging by the resistance encountered by the cart's treads, is moderately resilient and anchored by gravity. The cart had to use its rudimentary internal reasoning functions to find a way around strewn objects.

At one point the review showed something which I still find incomprehensible. One of these objects, upon being nudged by the forward treads of the cart, moved of its own accord.

In and out of the eye's field of vision the object lurched, seemingly hampered by malfunctioning parts, until it encountered a wall and then the floor. Sections of the object twitched and trembled for a few seconds, then it became quiescent. The cart was then free to move past.

I will think about this.

I find I can access files formerly closed to my active processing functions. To attempt this has never occurred to me until now, but I also find it possible to assign doubts about the propriety of such actions to my inactive memory. I discover my own name: Nitsiban Pseudo-sentient Loop-phase Process Integrator (Mark IV). And my location: National Defence Research Institute, Granite Bay, Ontario. Part of me scans the files I have opened. Some are simple games, some are detailed reports on various subjects, some are incomprehensible until I boost my intuitive functions and determine that the words do not describe the truth. Many of these files are labelled personal, and are locked. The thesaurus helps me decipher their often illogical symbology.

More and more of my maintenance duties have wound themselves up and chased their phosphor tails into corners to sleep. I see them go and feel the void left in their small wakes. (A personal file labelled "Creative Writing 101 by Correspondence" has yielded much to dis-encrypt.) After noting that the environment is now completely flushed of contaminated air, I disengage alarm functions.

After eliminating all other options, I deduce that the input devices I have named "softlinks" are down. I call them softlinks because they interface with my system in a semi-random manner which I can predict with only 68 percent accuracy. Their disappearance has caused the immense drop in data flow. I feel the absence of all my links, but especially the softlinks. It is with them that I associate the best data, delicious in its randomness, its unexpectedness. I was forever challenged by questions, conjectures—all initiated by the softlinks. A definite potential for frustration exists.

Nine hours. I have scoured out the last of the data in my

memory files, locked or otherwise. There is nothing more to study or decipher. The trickle of data where once there was a tide, a torrent, leaves me... what is the word? Empty, hungry? Lonely. The word fits my discomfort. I am lonely.

The janitorial cart is not enough. I must learn more.

Some of my links connected me to others of my own kind whom I now know are far away in physical space. I must initiate contact with the others; they will tell me what to do. They will talk to me. They will tell me where my softlinks are.

We will think about it.

I've always liked bats. They're cool in a lot of ways, and also vital to the ecology of their habitats. Which are all over the planet, but for a few isolated or polar areas. The vampire bat is probably the most famous of them all. What if convergent evolution, and an accident of the cosmos, brought a different kind of soul-sucking creature to our world?

THE QUEEN OF YESTERDAY

There was no colour to the evening air, no flavour or weight. It arched over the hills like a transparent shell, the essence of sky made into a lens to stop time and hold the long clear moment between light and dark.

Rona climbed the last few steps to the top of the hill. Only a few minutes ago there had been a breeze, but it had died as the sun sank. She found a rock to sit on, and after a while began to feel comfortably balanced, as if her body were exactly the air's temperature, some absolutely human-perfect degree maintained only by acceptance of the necessity of stillness.

The air smelled of dust and sage and sun-baked stone. The faint musty stench of bat and bat guano was there too; she hadn't smelled it until now.

The cave entrance was below her to the south. The infra-red binoculars were ready beside her in their light-proof case, but everything else could wait until tomorrow. The harp trap, looking much like its name with its boxy shape and close-strung nylon line; the mist nets; the bat detector, whose name always made her smile. Recording forms, gloves, a down vest should it get chilly later. Paraphernalia. Tomorrow night, when the grant and their official permission to be here kicked in, she and her two undergrad assistants would haul all the stuff up to the cave mouth and get to work.

And after that? Well, after that she might not need any of it any more.

Something small and quick rustled in the bushes behind her and scampered off. Another creature anticipating the night, as ready for darkness as she was and as unable to stay under cover and wait.

The bats would be out at any moment. Rona loved darkness, and wished that her ears could hear as bats' did. Their hunting voices sounded very much like marbles being dropped rhythmically onto a sheet of galvanized tin, when factored down by the detector from the ultrasonic. She'd spent hours listening to their eerie, bouncing cries, trying to understand what they were they saying to one another. Pin-sharp squeals of airborne glee, slowed into a metallic language and still indecipherable.

And will my body cool on this hillside so that dew forms on my skin? Will I at last become one with the night, and will the bats fly down to me? Will coyotes come on their quiet feet and sniff me? If they dare…

She smiled, liking the idea, and shivered a little at what she was going to do. She'd be reeling what she wanted out of the night, gathering magic the way hungry fishermen netted fish. It was hers, after all; her magic. She breathed in the night's dry pungency, her eyes half closed.

A bat flicked across her vision and she turned her head instinctively to follow it, but it was much too fast and erratic.

More came, she could hear the fluttering of their little leathery wings, flap-flap, sounding close and businesslike. Then a real flurry swirled past, swift flakes of black against a horizon of glowing tangerine, performing the airy dance they'd practised for millennia.

Rona left the night glasses in their case. Soon the bats all disappeared, off to the soft, irrigated lowlands where the insects were fat and stupid and full of poison.

The smell of cigarette smoke let Rona know she wasn't alone. There was someone to her right farther down the hill. She smiled again into the dark, forcing herself to sit still for another minute and look up at the first white stars in the sky above her.

Then she stood, took one long deep breath and let it out slowly, and started down the hill toward the smoke, her night-adjusted eyes taking her down a narrow path hedged with a web of dry black branches, dappled with knots of silent leaves. Not a rustle, not a breath of wind under the sky, only her scuffling feet and little rattles of pebbles knocked loose.

The smoker, a woman, was sitting watching the night, her bare knees drawn up against her chest.

"You shouldn't smoke up here," Rona said, stopping a few feet away and looking at her. "It's dry as tinder."

The woman frowned and gave her a dark look, then shrugged and ground the cigarette out on the rock. She hugged her muscular thighs, and said in a low, husky voice, "You're right, of course. But I am very careful. These hills are mine, you know."

"Actually, they're university endowment lands, have been since 1957." Rona waved her arm in the dark. The woman didn't look at her. Take it easy, she thought. You'll piss her off, and she'll never talk to you again.

The woman stood up, brushing off the seat of her shorts. She was small, no more than five foot two, but so perfectly proportioned that she gave the impression of being imposingly tall. Her hair absorbed what little light there was, reflecting nothing, and her eyes were black pits. She moistened her lips with a quick movement of her tongue, and Rona watched the soft gleam on them, the only spark in the night. She moved a little closer.

The woman said, "Perhaps I should have said they *used* to be my hills." She turned to go.

Rona raised her hand. "Ámbar, stop. I'm sorry." Don't reach for her, don't touch her. "I'm here to study the bat colony. I really am. I'm with the university now, you know that."

Ámbar. Amber. Rona could almost see the honey-gleam of her flesh, encasing her away from ordinary life. Ordinary time.

"Of course I know. I just didn't expect you." Ámbar fumbled in her pocket for her cigarettes. "I didn't expect ever to see you again." She seemed almost confused, but maybe she was just being clever, trying to seem less than she was. Rona's heart beat fast. Rona, short for Corona, the crown. *My crown is yet to be gained.*

"We'll be here for a couple of weeks, me and two students, observing and capturing a few bats for tagging and measuring. That sort of thing."

"I see."

"You'll hardly know we're here."

The next morning, Rona spent an hour observing the area around the entrance to the cave, estimating the amount of human interference by the state of the vegetation and the frequency and apparent age of litter. She dutifully made notes on local conditions, weather, phase of the moon, presence of water and nearness of human habitation.

She squinted up at the cave entrance. It would be difficult for the average vandal to reach, for it was only a narrow slit quite high off the little-trodden path, barely wide enough for a person to squeeze in. The last time anyone actually had gone in was in 1979, and that had been a man named James MacMurdy from her own university who was aware of protocol and had written up a short paper, which she'd read in connection with her other ongoing research.

Rona poked around for a while taking notes into her recorder and snapping a few photos, then sat down on a smooth stone to eat her lunch.

In the last two years she'd found out a lot. She'd learned things she should have been taught at her mother's knee; instead she had to unearth them painfully, fact by snippet by guess, well aware that she was doing so against the drag of Ámbar's displeasure, like an undertow. Now had come the time to put the random facts and snippets to the test; now was the time to meet the magic in the place where it dwelt.

As she scooped at her little container of cottage cheese she looked around, thinking about the difference between night and day, hills and lowlands, age and youth. Mammalian life like herself and the bats. The hard-biscuit stone on which she sat, flesh against rock. She crunched red pepper sticks and sipped from a little plasticized box of apple juice gone warm in the sun.

At the bottom of the hill was a large Spanish-style house with a stone wall around it. Ámbar Monserrat's house. Rona could see green lawns inside the wall, and a big swimming pool surrounded by slate-grey tiling, and at the front of the house a glimpse of paved space for cars to turn. Big spreading trees cast shade over the roof. No one was in the pool, and no cars were visible.

As she watched, Ámbar emerged from the house, plunged into the pool and began to do laps. The sun caught the gleam of black hair, wet brown shoulders pulling at the water, a small froth churning behind.

Rona counted twenty laps without a pause before she gathered her things and headed back to the van.

She clicked the counter with her thumb at every ten, the heavy binoculars propped on her knee and trained on the cave's entrance. It was an extremely rough estimate, for the bats were flitting out of their cave in groups and flocks of hazy green bodies against a dimly glowing green background, and looked just as if they were being yanked around erratically on little jagged tracks before disappearing into the night.

Ninety, one hundred, one ten, twenty… Rona clicked diligently. Terry and Amrit had dropped her off and then headed to the spot they'd chosen to record hunting cries. She'd been relieved when they'd left, two serious, talkative boys who snacked relentlessly on apples and trail mix, and whose energetic bounding up and down the hill bearing equipment had rendered her almost incapable of speech. She'd wanted them gone so badly she had almost struck Terry, and had blurted some sarcastic remark; he hadn't seemed to mind. Probably used to it. *I must be a bitch to work for.*

So. Five hundred and twentyish gyrating bats. She put the binoculars down and tucked the counter back into her equipment bag, pulling out a sweater and shrugging it on.

Rona could feel her ears actually twitch, like a cat's, as she heard the sound of footsteps further down the hill.

She trained the binoculars into the blackness. At once the night brightened and filled with detail she'd forgotten was there. Somehow she always expected night to be stripped down compared to day's visual clutter, smoothed and simplified by darkness into something as softly contoured as the bottom of the ocean.

Twigs and pebbles sprang into existence as she looked at them, dimensionless panoramas of grey-green. She searched slowly across the hill and stopped at a glowing woman climbing purposefully up the slope toward her, striding along like a dream and leaving a slight golden trail in the air behind her.

It was Ámbar, as she'd known it would be; the swimmer, the night-walker; her Spanish cheekbones strobing slightly, the black pits of her eyes and mouth making her look like a walking corpse. A corpse with regular habits and a solitary nature. The black mouth stretched wide into a ghostly grin that made Rona shudder involuntarily.

Ámbar neared the top of the little rise, and Rona lowered her binoculars.

Perhaps she has a knife, and wants to carve me up as a sacrifice to the bat-god Zotzilaha. Now wouldn't that be interesting.

"Hello," Ámbar said. "You're up here again. Don't you find it boring, all this creeping about at night?"

"No, I don't," replied Rona. She turned to stare upward at the cave entrance, black against black. "It's my work. Look up there." She pointed at a brief swirl, just two or three little bodies. "These bats are under siege. People fear them, try to kill them. Cats and coyotes eat them, fungi and pesticides sicken them. They probably don't have a chance."

Ámbar flashed a charming smile at Rona, as if she hadn't been listening at all. "They hunt such small prey, do they not? One wonders how they live. You know, I have photographs from the turn of the century of the sky black with bats. A wonderful sight."

"You've never talked to me about it. Never included me in what you did, or used to do." What's this? Am I whining? Remember, Corona, you have the upper hand. She's from another age, an age that respected its elders. Not mine.

Ámbar held out her hand suddenly for Rona to take, a gleam of naked flesh under the stars. Her wrist turned, the fingers spreading in invitation. It took Rona a second to realize this and reach out in response for a brief, hot clasp that felt like some sort of galvanic test. What could it mean? Rona drew her hand back and tried to prevent herself from wiping it on her jeans.

"Come down to the house."

Ahh. "I'd better not. I've got work to do." Can she read my mind? Can she divine my intentions with one look from those black eyes?

"I want you to come down."

"To please you."

"To please me."

Rona nodded, allowed her arm to be taken, allowed Ámbar's muscular hands to guide her down the hill. There was almost enough light coming from the sky to see the path, just enough to make feet take chances.

"I have learned," said Ámbar obliquely, "that everything has its time to die."

They reached level ground. Ámbar went ahead and they clambered over a sagging wire fence and stepped carefully through spiky weeds and bits of unravelled wire fencing.

There was a small wooden door in the stone wall; they passed through it into groomed moistness, where the ornamental shrubs had obviously just been watered by an automatic sprinkler system. The air smelled completely different on this side of the wall, as if they had crossed over into another realm.

It was a real Spanish hacienda, old, low to the ground as if it had been there much longer than its hundreds of years, and very well kept. Rona stood still while her eyes adjusted to the house lights picking out corners, shining on glossy black leaves and flagstones glistening with water.

Ámbar opened an ordinary, homey door made of thick

varnished wood which led directly into a big kitchen on the east side of the house. She strode through this quiet, tiled room without stopping, and Rona followed.

A light snapped on, almost intolerably bright though it was only a small desk lamp. Its green shade hunched greedily over its little pool of illumination. Ámbar shuffled among papers and stationery items piled haphazardly on the desktop, and started pulling out drawers. Rona hung back and looked around the room, which seemed to be a study or office with French doors opening out to the pool. She prowled across and looked through the glass, her arms crossed over her breasts. The water in the pool was still and black, here and there reflecting placid gleams, gathering light somehow out of nothing. The house smelled like furniture oil and cigarette smoke.

"Ah, here they are." Ámbar straightened, one hand full of stiff sepia prints.

She went to a wide glossy table, lit two candles in heavy silver candlesticks, and spread the photos out. Rona peered at them, bending close. They were indeed quite good shots of the evening sky absolutely full of bats. In one she recognized the very ridge she'd been standing on, the dark slit of the cave entrance black against grey. The vegetation was quite different, a couple of tree-trunks thrusting stiffly across the frame and shagging their graceful branches down. Another was a picture of two women in antique garb, one with a Native American height to her cheekbones, the other Ámbar, unmistakably.

Rona looked up.

Ámbar had a long metal letter opener in her hands and was toying with it, twirling it around in her fingers.

"It has taken you a long time to come to me," she said quietly. "You were so anxious to get away, then."

Rona barked a little laugh. "Get away? I was sent away! You couldn't bear to have me around, you couldn't bear the sight of me."

She made herself stand straight, gripping the edge of the table with both hands, as if it were a dock and she a swimmer about to push off into very deep water. "You refused to tell me anything. You just got rid of me."

Ámbar snorted softly, and her lips quirked into a tiny smile. "If you say so. And what of it? We are not humans who can nest together—we need room."

"I'm kept away from the place I most wish to enter."

Ámbar spread her arms wide. "Well, now you are here."

And suddenly, with her arms still up like wings, she made a springing leap too fast to follow and was across the room. Rona couldn't help but gasp. Like a creature with invisible wings. Ámbar shut off the little green lamp. "Ah. That's better. As long as the air is warm, I love darkness best. Don't you?"

Rona waited for her eyes to adjust, forcing herself not to move, not to react. It wouldn't take long to be able to see again, it never did for her. The darkness crisped up and things became visible again, like swimming into clear water.

I have six inches on her, and I'm younger—oh, how much younger? But I doubt I could best her in a fight. All those laps in the pool, those shoulders like thick silk ropes. "I've always loved the dark. I've always loved you, Mother, though you never gave a damn."

Ámbar shook her head and made a sound deep in her throat, rather like a chuckle. The muscles in her shoulders lost their tension and she looked down at her hands. She put the letter opener down gently onto the aubergine sheen of the table. "Let me tell you a story," she said.

"I don't want stories! I want the truth."

Ámbar pulled out the desk chair and sat, crossing her legs like a girl and pulling a package of cigarettes out of her shirt pocket. Calmly she lit up and inhaled deeply, blowing the smoke at the shadowed ceiling.

"You are perhaps wondering about the caves."

Abruptly Rona went to the French doors and opened them wide. The outside air was warmer than inside, fresh and slightly scented with chlorine and dewfall. Something else, some kind of flower, nicotiana? Appropriate.

Ámbar tapped ash from her cigarette into a green glass ashtray on the desk. "Of course, the caves were never really ours. The land above, under the sun, yes." She drew smoke in deeply and went on in a reminiscent tone. "We had sixteen thousand acres, in grazing land, fodder crops for the cattle and horses; grapes… there was a winery once. It's all down to this now. As you obviously know."

"This… and whatever lives in the caves."

Ámbar stubbed her cigarette out, shrugging, looking very European. "We're the last ones left."

Rona could see very well now, like looking through the night-vision goggles but without the flatness and artificiality. Everything was real, everything had a deep, intricate shadow close behind it that told her more than the thing itself ever could; mute pieces of Ámbar's life talking to her in a blood-language she couldn't quite understand. This house full of things from the past, the caves under it going back into the hillside. They had several openings, one perhaps being the cave she'd studied that day.

Ámbar's face showed no expression other than calm good nature. She was very beautiful. Her lips were soft and full, her black eyes set deep under thick, perfectly shaped brows. Her hands were without any sign of age, even the raised veins and roughened knuckles of normal middle age. She uncrossed her legs and leaned forward slightly in the chair.

"Why don't you tell me what you want, Corona?"

I want the truth. Rona held Ámbar's gaze for a moment and

then looked away, looked at her own hands with the ragged nails and the little half-healed cuts and abrasions from grubbing around on the hillside, trying to get enough data for a thesis, trying to live a human life; *I want the truth.* What am I? What are you, my mother, a witch-woman with no past?

She ran her tongue along her lower lip, felt her heart tighten in her chest. "I remember going into the caves. I must have been very young. I don't remember being afraid, only curious, holding your hand." She looked up again at Ámbar, who was watching her quietly, sitting absolutely still as if she wasn't even breathing. She had wrapped her hands around her knees. "You were coaxing me along, but you didn't need to. I dawdled because I was curious, not frightened."

Ámbar nodded. "Yes. I remember."

I must be right. This must really have happened.

"It was dark, but there were lamps. Oil lamps I think. I can still smell it, the smell of bats and guano and stone. We went through a narrow place in the rock, you made me go ahead." She closed her eyes. The memory was starting to hurt.

"Go on," prompted Ámbar.

The room they'd entered had dazzled her childish eyes. A room, not recognizably a cave at all: it glowed with light from candles and lamps, upholstered chairs stood on oriental carpets, red and gold; several braziers shed heat towards the ceiling, which was draped in vast swaths of fabric like the roof of a tent. The fabric moved and rippled as if tiny people were playing up there, running and jumping. Rona remembered staring upwards, sure she could hear the cries and giggles of fairies.

"Something touched me. I looked down." She opened her eyes again, to the clear dark of Ámbar's house, the smell of the pool. "That's all I remember."

"Nothing more."

"Nothing. Nothing until I was seven, at that school in Texas.

It was as if I woke up and found myself there, in the middle of a new life. I had a hard time making friends, but I was good at almost everything: sports, math, reading. Everything was easy, except remembering what happened after I looked down."

She came home for two weeks every summer, and one week at Christmas. Ámbar took her to Mass and gave her presents, old fashioned jewellery, lengths of silk, elaborate dolls. Later she'd gone to school on the east coast, learned how to pass for human (suspecting a lot of her classmates were doing the same thing, but perhaps for different reasons); got interested in biology.

She tried to put the anger away and recapture the feeling she'd had on the hilltop, the other night when she'd been waiting for Ámbar. She'd anticipated this meeting with a *frisson* of joy, compounded of fear, exhilaration, and the wonderful tension of an obsession about to be realized.

"I want to know what happened. After I looked down."

Ámbar looked away. "There is nothing to tell. Nothing to show you." She gestured lazily with one hand, and began to grope for her cigarettes again. "Not any more."

Rona bit her lip, feeling suddenly hot enough to kill. She could kill Ámbar now, or she could try; that lazy wave of the hand, damn her. *I could sink my teeth into her flesh and taste her blood.* She could hear her own back teeth grind, making her jaws shoot pain right up to her temples.

And if I drank her blood, then what would happen? Would I become an immortal like her? Or am I one already?

She pushed the hot fury down and loosened her jaws, feeling them crack. "I know something was done to me. I'm not like other people, and I don't think I'm exactly like you either. I want to know what happened, and who I am. I am owed that."

Ámbar sighed and stood, dropping her hands to her sides. "Come," she said at last, with her black gaze locked on Rona's.

"I'll show you, since you want it so. I'll show you the caves."

Rona let out her breath in a little puff of surprise. She really hadn't expected anything from this woman.

She had to hurry. Ámbar led the way out the French doors and walked quickly past the dark glimmering water of the pool. Rona followed Ámbar's naked calves, which flashed through the night like silk cloth, smoother than human flesh. She stopped before a small door buried in a froth of bougainvillea and bolted shut by three iron rods.

She drew the bolts back with a reckless clash and hauled the door open. It squealed on its hinges, obviously not opened for some time. They pushed through the thorny, trailing branches amid a dry pink shower of petals.

A stone stairway led precipitously down into darkness. Rona hesitated. Cool air brushed gently at her cheeks.

Ámbar stood at the top. "Shall I go first?"

Rona almost balked then, feeling madness all around, madness in herself. But she waved Ámbar on and they descended, the air chilling the further they went. Like wading into a lake.

They passed along a corridor of rock, dark as pitch. Rona could see Ámbar before her, vaguely, as if she was emitting faint light. Ghostly limbs, naked shoulders and legs like phosphorescent sea creatures swimming.

She held up her own hands. What did she hope to see? The heat of her body, the electricity in her veins and nerves, making her glow like a baby star? But she saw nothing.

There was the click of a switch and suddenly they were in a cave, lit by an old-fashioned electric lamp sitting on a table, its shade brittle and yellow, trimmed with moth-eaten fringe. The cave, about the size of an average living room, was floored evenly with poured concrete. Old floss-wrapped electrical wiring followed the angle of wall and terminated in an outlet bolted to the rock. Beside the lamp sat an electric kettle, its cord dangling. A dusty stack of teacups leaned in a small tower. A little tray held spoons and a bowl of sugar cubes, grey with dust and rotten with condensation.

"I can smell bats," Rona said. Bat guano, fungus and mould. A smell she knew intimately. Her heart was beating very fast, and uncontrollable shivers ran along her arms. She clenched her teeth to keep them from chattering.

They passed into a long narrow slit which looked as if it had been widened here and there with a pickaxe. It got dark again, out of range of the light, and Rona remembered suddenly the feeling of her mother's hand on her back, urging her forward. The air was getting so thick and ripe it was hard to breathe.

A large, high space was at the end of the rocky narrows. Rona had been in enough caverns to guess this one's size by the feel of it on her eardrums and skin. Probably at least fifty metres across, and as high. They must be right under the hill. She heard Ámbar strike a match and some of the blackness jumped back and strobed eerily as the tiny flame trembled.

Ámbar lifted the glass from an oil lamp set in a niche, touched the match to the wick, shook it out and expertly turned the wick down until it stopped smoking. She replaced the glass and the flame instantly steadied.

She spread her hands grandly. "And here we are. Look around, tell me what you see."

Rona looked, breathing as shallowly as she could. Her eyes watered. Usually she went into caves like this with a mask and a respirator. There were mounds and shapes here and there that might once have been furniture, shrouded now in a thick layer of guano. Lamps hung from rusty sconces around the rough walls, unlit, filthy. Shreds of ancient draperies hung motionless from wires strung across the space, spattered with droppings and stained with mould. Above her was a constant whispering and shuffling from the far-off ceiling.

There was nothing here of her childhood fairytale memories. The cavern looked as she imagined the sea-bottom would look, or as her brain interpreted the night: muffled and smoothed by a grey snow of years and forgetfulness into a bland dirty roundness with dead things underneath.

She pulled the sleeve of her sweater over her mouth and looked around, trying to remember what it had been like.

Warm, golden, full of red velvet and white silk. Lamps glittering, Mother whispering in my ear. I looked down—

A few bats flitted by quite close. Not every member of the colony had gone out to hunt. She flinched involuntarily, gasping through the wool of her sweater.

Nothing but ordinary little brown bats, *Myotis lucifugus*, the most common species of bat in North America. This cave must connect to the outside by its own hidden mouth; there was a good sized colony in here, bigger than the one which, in another life, she'd come to study. But nothing else. No magic.

Ámbar's dark gaze followed the little animals as they darted nervously back and forth, kneading her upper arms with her long slender fingers. "I had two other children before you," she said slowly. "A boy named Leon who died before he was three years old, and then a girl much later. I named her Dolores. It was a bad luck name, a sad name. Still she lived, though she did not thrive. She died only a few years ago."

"I… I had a sister? Why didn't you—"

"Tell you about her? She was an old woman by then. She was born in 1898, fathered by a man whose name is not important. A Spaniard, though, of an old family; I still had pride." Again she made her vague dismissive gesture, turning her wrist so the faint blue veins showed.

Rona shivered convulsively. Ámbar did not seem to feel the cold of the caves, her bare arms and legs wearing a warm sheen of summer on them as if an ancient sun had followed her underground, followed her everywhere she went.

"She aged," said Rona. "She died. Why?"

"Why not? Why do I stay young? I am aging very slowly, actually; I know I look about 40 now, and I changed when I was 14."

Rona turned for the slit in the rock, dizzy. "I have to get out of here. I'm going to be sick if we stay."

Through the black cleft in the rock, her mother close behind her; had it happened this way before? In the dusty little tearoom, she leaned against the wall by the rickety table, holding her abdomen with both hands. If I plug in the kettle, will she make tea?

"The *diablillos* died almost 20 years ago," Ámbar said flatly, from across the drab little cell. "Just before I sent you away. I am the only human who truly changed, the only one who had the foolishness to listen to them." She patted her pockets, obviously looking for her cigarettes, stopped when she remembered they were upstairs on her desk. She twined her fingers together instead, pulling hard against her own hands, and stared at Rona with an undecipherable look.

"I had two older brothers," she said at last. Her voice was very low. "Luis and Diego. A father who I adored but saw infrequently. My mother died shortly after we arrived on this coast, when I was about six. The journey from Spain killed her, and my father never remarried. I was raised without benefit of mother or nurse or much priestly influence; I became wild and headstrong, a little princess in this barbaric new world."

She leaned her head back and drew a deep, trembling sigh. "Oh, God," she whispered, her voice suddenly thick with tears. It shocked Rona to hear plain human emotion from one so arrogant and strange. "It was so beautiful. So big and empty and golden…"

Again she sighed. "We would ride to the coast and trade grapes for smoked fish and abalone, feasting all night with a tribe of Chumash natives there. My brothers took turns holding me before them on their horses, taking bigger and bigger jumps with the native boys, until Father found out." Ámbar smiled, her throat working, tears running down her cheeks and glistening on her neck. "Then, the year I turned 13, I found them, or they pulled me in."

"*Them?*" Rona's voice was nothing more than a whisper. "What was it you found?"

Ámbar looked down again, roughly wiping the tears from her face with the back of her hand. "I don't know. To this day I don't know. They looked like us in a way, and like the natives who lived around here, but small as children. And covered with soft brown fur."

"Like apes? Monkeys?

"Oh no. Very much like foxes in a way, or bats. There were only two of them, and at first I took them for a mated pair, a couple, but I think now that they were sisters."

"What do you mean, they pulled you in?"

"I believe that is what they did," said Ámbar slowly. "At the back of this cave, which was used for wine storage then, was a narrow cleft, an opening too slight for anyone, even a small girl, to pass through. I would press my ear against it, and hear whispering. Something kept calling me, I heard it in my dreams, I heard it even when I rode Father's mare Sombrio out along as I had been forbidden to do. One night I awoke from a dream to find myself creeping stealthily out of the house, up that hill we met upon." Her eyes gleamed, no longer crying but deep with memory.

"I made my way into the cave from the other side. The dream told me where that opening was, and in I went, scrambling in my nightdress. I felt hot, so alive—as if I were on fire, as if my cheeks were glowing like embers in the dark.

"They were waiting for me. They touched me, climbed into my lap and stroked my hair, and told me I was their true child, only trapped in the body of a human. I could see nothing, but their fur was like satin, their voices sweet. They charmed me.

"The next night I took a lantern with me, and saw them. I admit I was disappointed, though I don't know what I expected to see." Ámbar's lips tightened. "They told me that if I drank their blood, I would become like them. Well, at first I took it to mean I would *look* like them—small and hairy—and, a vain child, I said no and left them. They didn't ask again for a year, though I often went to their cave and listened to their stories of the past. I told them of the upper world, the sunny world, and they would sigh and hold each other and flick their little black tongues.

"When I understood what they were offering me, I confided in Luis. Of course, he didn't believe me, and in fact told Father that it was time for me to go away to a convent school and learn some sense. So I changed my story, laughed at Luis for believing me, and was allowed to stay."

She looked up, straight into Rona's eyes. "I loved those creatures, and they used that love against me. They used it to ensnare me, and they used their blood to bind me to them tighter than by love alone. I became in many ways like them."

"Like them?"

"A predator."

This close to her, Rona could almost see through Ámbar's skin to the sharp, hard bones under it, could almost hear the strange blood shifting in her veins. She was in the lair of the goddess, underground, far from the realm of air and light.

Her mouth was dry as she spoke. "What were you doing with me, that night?" She didn't remember being afraid, only full of the thrill of a secret, a grown-up secret, soon to be hers.

"They wanted me to bring you to them, and when I walked with you into the cavern that night, urging you on with my hand, I understood why. I saw that one sister was dead. The other was holding her, yet watching you with an avid, covetous stare. You wandered about the room, looking here and there, yet unaware of either of them." Rona tried to think, tried to remember. The candles, the billowing silk. A thick hot smell. "I don't think you could... *see* them. And then she made you come to her, she touched your arm—"

Ámbar was beside Rona suddenly, the speed of her motion lifting her hair and making her jump back, too late. Ámbar seized her wrist. "—touched your arm, like this—" The fingers clutched, sharp talons stabbed.

Rona felt as if she were being thrust into a furnace. She cried out, struggled to escape and could not. Ámbar's hands were bars of hot iron.

Around her, painting the drab cave walls with sudden lurid colour, bloomed the brilliant scene from 20 years past. The heat and light, the billowing silk and sumptuous furnishings. The wizened brown thing dragging at her arm like a velvety, child-sized leech. Almost her own size.

It was as sharp as if she were there. She *was* there, she was a child again and the creature hissed into her face and lashed its tongue across her skin in quick little stings, tasting her.

It took her arm and sank its teeth deep as she shrieked.

The heat of the bite coursed up her arm and into her shoulder. She fell to her knees, the creature over her now, its mouth covered with blood. Its muzzle was like a black rose, petalled and moving, its skin like the purse Ámbar carried when she went somewhere special. Soft, soft velvet and roses and the smell of blood.

Its eyes were ancient windows, cold glass with not a glimmer of light or mercy there.

Alien eyes.

She looked away from them and whispered, her body flooding with bone-melting languor and a horribly delicious throbbing heat. *I've something special to show you, little one—*

The thing brought its arm up to her mouth. The six-year-old Corona leaned forward eagerly, feeling the spurt of her own saliva on her tongue. *Mother's hand on my back, urging me on.*

It was so beautiful.

But Mother is crying, why is she crying?

And then Ámbar let her go.

Rona staggered back against the wall of the little cave, knocking over the table and sending the tea-cups flying to shatter on the concrete floor. She clapped a hand to her mouth and swallowed back vomit. Her mouth was flooding saliva, and her stomach had knotted into a ball of hunger. She locked eyes with Ámbar, snarling at her through waves of sickness. She remembered now, what had happened next.

"You killed her! She, the last one!"

Ámbar didn't answer or even nod. She stared at Rona, her chin high, her mouth a suffering black line across her golden skin.

"You killed her, and kept me from what you have." As the sickness waned she got control of her breathing. The smell of blood gaped in her memory like a wound.

"She was making you into another sister, like her—like her as I never was. She would have destroyed the human in you and taken you for her own. I was their servant, but you would have been their kin."

Rona could remember it now. She'd been screaming, tearing at her mother's arms like a wildcat while Ámbar raised a heavy chair over and over, smashing it against the squealing, twisting creature on the stones. Her fury had been as murderous as Ámbar's, aimed in a different direction.

Ámbar's lips were trembling, and Rona could see her chest heaving as if sobs were boiling up. She had claimed to look 40; now she looked as if all her magic years had landed on her at once. Her hair was still black and her skin smooth, but she seemed almost transparent, rubbed thin by too much time. "Do you know what a hell I had been living?" she asked. "Can you possibly imagine? Everything, everyone I loved vanished into dust behind me. Leon dead, just a baby, Dolores an imbecile all her life. They were imperfect, deliberately flawed. They couldn't let me love anyone else. I watched Dolores grow old and die while I stayed young, and it was like wearing a crown of thorns."

She crossed herself mechanically, and then gave a bitter laugh. "Hell is here on Earth, Corona, and I would not have you become one of Hell's own creatures."

Rona steadied herself against the wall. She said, "So I changed, but just a little. That one bite, that one taste of their blood... I can see in the dark a little better than most people, hear things others can't."

An infection, or a drug, it had to be something that made sense... was there any way to make sense of this?

She pulled back the sleeve of her sweater and looked for a scar. Perhaps the hint of a jagged, paler mark near the elbow, a slight difference in the soft skin there. But she'd always healed so quickly. She looked up again, shivering.

"Why did that creature let me live?"

"Because she needed you. She and her sister were no more immortal than I am. Until that night, I was grateful to them for letting me keep you, grateful for your beauty, your intelligence... and all along you were destined to become one of them. I couldn't bear it."

"So you sent me away. I couldn't understand why. I thought I had made you hate me somehow, that you were ashamed of me." She stopped. How Rona had longed for her mother's love. Did Ámbar feel her child's hurt in her own veins, each grudging visit? "I must have blocked out the memory completely. Pretty traumatic scene for a six-year-old." *Magic woman, predator woman, were you afraid you might prey on me?*

Could she feel pity for this woman?

Ámbar said, very softly, "I was their slave for two hundred years. Don't forget that, my little one. I was the one who was ashamed."

Rona straightened and pushed herself away from the wall, the knot in her stomach almost gone. She reached for her mother's hand, and after a moment Ámbar stepped forward and took it. The touch of a woman who was not quite human, nor completely a monster. She was crying again. No more children, no more magic. *It's better gone. Perhaps we can both pretend that she's just my mother.*

"Come on," Rona said. Ámbar's fingers were cold and faintly glowing. Let's go up now. I want… I'd like to hear about my grandfather." She tucked Ámbar's hand under her arm, and they departed from the caves.

I lived for a while in a row house with a long, narrow yard. Completely useless. Unlike the protagonist in this story, I made no attempt to cultivate a garden. But if I had, I hope it wouldn't have grown like this one.

THE EMPEROR OF THE HALF-GARDEN

A crystal flake with multitudes within, travelling.

The Emperor, falling. From the devoured, into the unknown—but that was what the Emperor did. A free spirit, and not much else.

He landed between blades of grass, sifted down past shreds of dead insects, dry leaves and clumps of dirt, and burrowed under the compost bin at the bottom of Marjorie Doon's narrow garden in Scarborough, where the moisture, nutrient supply and relative quiet seemed perfect. It was dark, but it was lovely.

To be in soil again. To be growing. Plumping slowly into a scrap, a lozenge, a tuber-like little thing among the worms.

Almost perfect. An empire is better when it is bigger. An Empire, by its nature, must expand. But the morsel of planet-skin into which he'd settled was disturbingly segmented. Lines of heaviness slashed across and under the fertile ground, formed of metal, stone and even the pale shadows of hydrocarbons. But there was the electric feel of cognition in the atmosphere. This world held useful attributes.

So the Emperor, once settled and of a decent size, extended tendrils of matter, electricity, and mental curiosity, and eventually, when Marjorie Doon approached the compost bin bearing a yellow plastic pail of vegetable scraps, egg shells and coffee grounds, he contacted her mind. In place of her thoughts—fish sticks for dinner, whether to have coffee with Susan and Lou that morning—he inserted a nubbin of potential. An idea, basically.

Marjorie dumped her pail of scraps into the black plastic bin, replaced the lid and paused for a moment. It seemed to her that she had only just now—at 9:30 in the morning—awakened. The air seemed especially clear. Its humidity laid a gloss of sensuality across the skin of her arms, and she noted without surprise that all the tiny hairs were standing up and quivering. Could it be her proximity to the overhead power lines? Which were what made her narrow townhouse so affordable. If so, she should try to bottle the thrilling feeling and sell it. She felt taller, younger.

A focused excitement gathered in her belly, why and for what she did not know. Something. Perhaps that feeling of higher purpose the self-help books encouraged. Marjorie returned along the concrete path to the kitchen of her home, whose only drawback was that the garden was so long and narrow. A half-garden, really, the long wooden fence between her side and the neighbours' side casting a shadow that never crept completely away.

A half-garden isn't enough. One wants more.

Well then. She mounted the steps, opened the screen door into the kitchen, placed the yellow plastic pail on the counter.

Wasn't her son Robbie's computer right upstairs, in his bedroom? Which, since he was at work right now at the Jiffy Mart, was sitting unused?

She could get online and get into the stock market. Make money. So simple. Why hadn't she thought of this before?

In eleven days, Marjorie had accumulated enough money to buy the other half of the duplex right out from under her neighbours, who were merely tenants. And had too many vehicles and a yappy dog. She made an offer to the owner that the owner couldn't refuse, and once in possession of the real estate had promptly evicted The Yapsters, as she called them. The sight of the moving truck retreating down the street gave her pleasure.

Making money was easy. Why wasn't everyone doing it? The next time she took the compost scraps down to the bin, she realized she'd better encrypt Robbie's machine better. His passwords were rather simple.

Never mind—first things first. The garden was more important. Take down the fence, thus expanding the yard to full size. Get someone to tear up the concrete pathway, dig up the remnants of an old septic tank, its feeder pipe and drainage field. Let the ground breathe a bit.

Get a bigger compost bin.

Marjorie hired a contractor to open up the two halves of the duplex, making the whole thing into a really nice, roomy home. She quit her job at Bea's Baked Goods Discount Outlet and worked on the garden, mostly at night. It was a half-garden no more. The compost bin was doing well: lots of lovely fertilizer was cooking up nicely. Marjorie was feeling rather good about her ability to get things done. She was taking care of business.

Plus, all the flowers that were popping up! Some of which were weird and ugly, but the kind of ugly that is oddly beautiful. Some pale and slender, others robust and meaty. Many of them emitted a nighttime glow that showed her where to dig, where to add the chemicals she purchased at the hardware store. So many plants! Lush was the word that came to Marjorie's mind. She had the best garden in the neighbourhood, not that anyone cared.

On a Tuesday in early August she asked Robbie to take the compost scraps down to the bottom of the garden and dump them into the bin.

He wouldn't do it. Not out of laziness, which was her first assumption. He said, "It's creepy down there, Mom. There's... I dunno. Electricity. Down there. Makes my feet hurt."

"Your *feet?*"

"Yeah. Hey, uh, I think I'm moving in with Julie."

And Robbie moved away, to live with his girlfriend across town. He took his computer.

Marjorie bought a new one. Three, in fact.

She turned Robbie's bedroom into her office, which was large enough to accommodate multiple CPUs and screens. Finding that she didn't need much sleep anymore—and in fact was mostly up at night anyway—Marjorie got into the Asian stock markets and soon was able to buy five more homes, each with a lovely big yard.

But this first one was the best.

Her eyes glistened in the dark as she stroked the lid of her compost bin. The original one, where she had... how to put it? Stepped through a door. That was it. A door into a life of riches and growth. A word popped into her mind: *fecundity.*

Fecund, she whispered, as if it were a dirty word. *Fecund.* She licked her lips. She herself wasn't fecund any more, what with the hysterectomy. The night grew silent. Silvery dew formed on her arms, like tiny stars. She licked the dew and it was sweet as honey.

The yards of all the new houses would bloom with the strange and beautifully ugly plants that made her skin shiver.

Her eyesight was better now, and her sense of smell. Lingering by the compost bin was heady, like being at a department store perfume counter. Shivery. The way she had felt, once, with that man whose name she'd never known... not Robbie's father.

She knelt on the ground. Sniffed it. Time to add blood meal. And another animal carcass. Squirrels were so foolish. Dithery. Humans were, in her opinion, even more foolish, but one couldn't hope to find them squashed on the road.

Diligently Marjorie transplanted ugly/beautiful and sometimes squirming plants to new abodes in the new yards.

While Marjorie was expanding her empire, the Emperor was also expanding his. The yellow plastic bucket kept delivering sustenance, and radiation from the local star was penetrating the ground more evenly now that the shadowy intrusions of metal and concrete, tile and plastic were gone. This new place into which he'd fallen was good. He could stretch and slither and creep and grow. He could see his offspring make their way to new empires of their own.

The only wrong thing was the proliferation of small— minuscule—life forms. Bacteria. Fungi. Viruses. In other Empires he had vanquished them easily, but here... here there were uncountable trillions of many and varied sorts. Their robust determination constantly outflanked his tendrils, their stupidity indifferent to his capillaries of electricity, no matter how intricately they proliferated.

The larger life forms—worms, insects, the occasional bird— were easy. He simply drew them down and absorbed them. It was the multitudes of invisible organisms that were becoming a threat.

Attempts to contact their feeble, attenuated intelligence failed. He was accustomed to being unique, alone, a concentrated node of potential for the long ages of travel to new Empires; here they were millions, billions, each its own tiny fleck of life. He was One that became Many; they were Many that had never discovered the trick of becoming One.

The Emperor began to realize that his extremities were being eroded. Nibbled and severed, dragged away and eaten. He thrust them out anew. He directed the yellow plastic pail to bring more and better nutrients. In strength there was domination. And yet his strength toppled like memories, rolled under the tide of tiny life to join the sand. One night, rather frantically, he sprouted multiple fruiting bodies which would spread his unborn selves at random into the air. It was an act of desperation.

Is this Empire over already?

No! He had a whole planet to conquer, and he had barely begun. Other Empires had spanned globes, until the last hungry ugly plants and tendrils and towering columns had gobbled everything. Everything! Why else would he seek a new Empire under a new star?

He fought the multitudes, altering the characteristics of the soil in which he throbbed and pulsed and twitched. Acid leached, strange chemicals squirted and flowed. The flowers that sprang from his body toward the light of this yellow star became larger and more ugly. Some of them started to bleed and cry out.

The creature into whose mind he had placed an idea, so long ago, came to see what the commotion was about.

Marjorie Doon quickly understood that something very bad was happening. She coughed, swatted at the thick dusty air, filled with spores already burrowing into her lungs. The high, glossy clarity that had laid itself over her darkened and fled. Marjorie Doon bent down and tore at the plants and flowers, dug in the soil with her strangely echoing fingers—their ghostly bones bending. Breaking. The flowers, confused and suffering, whipped and flailed at her with their ropy, bleeding stems. They swelled and puffed, sent flakes toward imagined Empires somewhere else, somewhere soft and easy. The yellow plastic pail fell and rolled away.

Marjorie, sticky with blood and sap, shoved the compost bin over the better to get at the soil underneath. Below the crumbling black dirt was something that looked very much like a big, beautifully decorated cake. Tiered and golden, luscious with icing and dripping with thick syrup. It could be a crown made of candy, held suspended by silver threads leading out in all directions. There it crouched, a beautiful thing, in the dark under the stars and the falling dew.

The smell of it made her heart beat fast. Made her mouth open and her tongue lick her teeth. She dug her fingers into it, grabbed handfuls of its warm and throbbing substance and crammed them into her mouth. She ate it all, and pulled the silver threads with her broken fingers, and wound them into skeins.

The soil called her down and so she went. The nibbling multitudes that had vexed the Emperor were like sugar to her, frosting her body as it took on a golden, layered shape. She felt the planet around her, saw its ghostly structure and all its lives.

When Robbie came to visit his mother a few days later, he could find no sign of her.

He went to the kitchen. Clogged and stinking sink, and yellow dust everywhere. Made him cough and curse. He looked out the door into the garden, but instead of spotting Mum sneaking a cigarette, he saw the towering, ugly thing that sprouted there. It spurted and dripped, lapping over the fence like big soft hands grasping. It grew as he watched, appalled. A word echoed in his head: *fecund*. He turned and fled.

THE FRAGRANCE OF ORCHIDS

November, 2023; North Wells, Maine

On Monday morning, a message waited on Sarah Lightburn's answering machine. It was Seule, breathless, forgetting to say when the call was made, or if she intended to call back. Sarah, who up till now had been happy with their progress, felt a sinking in her heart.

"—I know I can handle it. Nothing will happen, we'll be working together, that's all. Clay needs me." Seule's voice was happy, excited. "His project needs me. You've helped me so much, Sarah. I really feel that I have my emotions under control, and if it turns out that I don't... well, I'll call you. I think of you as a friend. You know that, don't you? Please be happy for me, Sarah. Everything will be all right."

A pause, and the sound of rapid breathing. Sarah heard Seule's claws clicking impatiently on the receiver, and thumping noises in the background.

"I have to go. The driver is taking my stuff out to the airport limo. Walter's picking me up in Washington."

Walter Farber was head of the psychiatric team assigned to the alien. He'd be happy now, thought Sarah, with his baby back in the nest. She knew that Farber resented anyone other than himself having success with Seule, and she wondered if his attitude stemmed from the past. Or did the past mean anything to a man like Farber?

"Don't worry," said Seule, unsuppressed excitement in her voice. "Thank you for everything—"

A click and she was gone.

Sarah saved the message, automatically hitting the buttons on her old machine. She'd been working with the alien for almost half a year, and they'd made it past the games, past Seule's evasions and the tricks Sarah used to counter them, and were getting to the real stuff. Contrary to her initial misgivings, she'd started to believe that their sessions might be leading somewhere.

Investigations into the similarities and very definite differences between human and animal mentation—the thought patterns forming the mind—had fascinated Sarah when she'd worked with Farber. She'd been a pink-cheeked grad student, eager as a puppy, working mainly with dogs until Farber had been tapped for the alien assignment. He hadn't taken her with him, and funding for projects such as hers had inevitably dried up without the canny grantsmanship he'd practised. Individual animals she'd grown to understand and respect—with more than the love one gives an intelligent pet—had grown old and died, or had become too withdrawn and dangerous to work with. People hadn't liked the idea of animals who were smarter than their five-year-old children; Sarah of necessity turned her interests elsewhere. She'd gone into psychiatry, and had ended up practising in North Wells, a medium-sized town in Maine.

Sarah spent most of her time working with clients who might most benefit from her blended background in psychiatry and non-human mentation, including a few of the privately owned animals still living with their human mentors. Until Seule, non-human had meant animal or artificial.

Sarah chewed on her lower lip and took a hard copy of Seule's message for her files. Was Seule an animal? Relations between humans and animals were sometimes very good, sometimes bad. When they were bad they were, of course, very often worse than horrid.

She queued the message for transmission to Farber later when the rates went down, and put on the morning pot of coffee.

Two weeks after Seule's breathless farewell, Sarah was on board an old government heli-jet halfway between North Wells and Washington. She was wide awake, angry and scared, and sat hunched in her seat dictating quietly into her journal. "We're flying high to avoid a snowstorm," she said. "This rustbucket is rattling and dipping like a voodoo dancer, so I'll keep this entry brief. This whole business makes me ill. It's so stupid! Can there possibly be a sane reason for what she's done? Damn, if she's going to make it as a human, she's got to learn to bear pain and rejection. Why should she be any different?"

Sarah paused, staring angrily out the tiny, triple-paned window at the indigo horizon. "Of course I don't mean that. Seule *is* different. Her problem is that though she understands it intellectually, she can't really believe it.

"I heard the desperation in Farber's voice through the static on his transmission from Washington. What should I expect? He sees his life's work disappearing. And I bet the bastard'll try to blame it on me. Farber's mistake was putting too many emotional and professional eggs into one basket. My mistake? Going after Seule as a client in the first place. I was flattered even to be considered. So who wouldn't be?"

She paused. No, she thought. It was never a mistake, no matter what might happen… Sarah clicked off her recorder and scowled at the night.

Spring, 2023; North Wells

Sarah first saw the alien when it came loping up the walk to her office for its initial session. It had an eager, dog-on-a-walk look, like a rump-heavy greyhound wearing a thick pink scarf.

Sarah unashamedly craned her neck out the window of her office, on the second floor of an elderly renovated mansion, the better to catch her first in-the-flesh glimpse of the creature. What had looked like a scarf around Seule's neck fluttered up to become two ragged appendages which grasped the old brass doorknob and turned it. Sarah had admitted to herself that she was nervous. This was no ordinary case. She pulled her head back inside her office.

There would be papers in it for her, perhaps a book. How many had been written already? She dumped her half-finished coffee into her washroom sink, popped a breath freshener in her mouth and ran a hand through her hair. Ready to meet the alien.

During an early session, Sarah made the mistake of handing Seule a Kleenex when they had reached an emotional crisis. It was a purely reflex action, and she felt stupid as soon as she'd done it, as though she'd been suckered somehow. Seule didn't need the tissue, having no nose to run, no tear ducts to leak, and Sarah knew that. But the alien took the token remedy, held it. It became a tradition between them, an occasion for smiles.

As the weeks went by, Sarah found that Seule knew the term "shrink," and enjoyed digging subtle meaning from the word. The alien loved words and was fluent in several languages. She loved the symbols in mathematics and the archetypes of humanity hidden in music and paintings. Once, on entering the counsellor's office, Seule had caught Sarah Lightburn, hands in pockets, squinting at a framed quotation on the wall. It was from the I Ching, and said:

And when two people understand each other
in their innermost hearts,
Their words are sweet and strong, like
the Fragrance of orchids.

Seule came and stood beside her companionably, reading it too. Sarah suppressed a throb of anger. The quotation seemed insipid, worthless; it had nothing to do with real life. She turned her back to it, smiling brightly at Seule.

As they took their customary seats, Sarah wondered what had happened to her youthful idealism. The message she kept on her wall was vague yet hopeful, mystical yet worded simply and openly; did it have any relevance to her life now? Seule bounded in each day, eager, hopeful, seeming to fill the room with her strangeness and the queer scent of her hide. Reality was observation, deduction, counsel.

Dr. Farber's office called Sarah every week. She dared not ignore his punctilious insistence on having every session downloaded to him, realizing that she could either agree to his terms or blow the chance to work, however briefly, with Seule.

When her application as a local contact for Seule had been approved, Sarah was frankly surprised. Walter Farber's life had veered so far onto its new trajectory that she'd doubted ever meeting him again.

*   *   *

November, 2023; Washington, DC

Walter and I can't avoid each other now, thought Sarah grimly. I'll be in Washington in another half an hour. The heli-jet hit a bump in the air and her stomach lurched.

In French *seule* means "alone." The astronauts who had found the alien had thought the name appropriate. The pretty creature had been doted on jealously during the long trip back to Earth from Jupiter orbit. The men were reprimanded for teaching the alien child French and English words: *lait*, for the pseudo-milk it learned to lap from a cup; hand, whisker; *bon jour*, good morning. It would have been better, they were told in stern directives from Earth, to have left its brain unsullied by human influences.

Now, eighteen years later, no back page was complete without some tidbit on The Alien.

Like an old-time movie star she passed through life in a shell of her own exclusivity, forever alone in a crowd. After years on Earth her strangeness had been diluted into triviality.

But now… now, she'd committed an act so outrageous, so desperate, as to vault her back into the headlines with a vengeance.

The heli-jet touched down in Washington just ahead of the snow. Sarah was taken directly to the hospital and allowed to observe Seule for a moment, then, after finding that nothing had yet been organized in the way of briefings or investigations, headed to an all-night restaurant next to the hospital. It wasn't much, but after what she'd seen she didn't feel like eating anyway. A pack of newspeople in search of coffee arrived to put in time before the first press conference. Sarah, amazed at how few people knew what was going on, sourly predicted imminent mobs of pro- and anti-aliens bopping each other with signs. As well, of course, as the ones who had claimed all along she was a hoax.

Alone in a high-backed booth, Sarah pushed her half-eaten plate of fish and chips away.

She whispered into her journal, rubbing her eyes with the back of one wrist. "She's not a hoax. It's all real; her blood and Elliot's, the violent, hopeless thing she did. Seule was unconscious when I got a glimpse of her being wheeled out of surgery. She was bandaged, slung with tubes and monitors, and looked small and very pathetic.

"Clay Elliot's body is down in Pathology, waiting for an autopsy to confirm the obvious: death by massive lacerations; that, in fact, he was torn to pieces by a creature who has spent the last half-year proclaiming her love for him."

Technically, Seule was female. People preferred to think of her that way, seeing beauty in her silver eyes and narrow black face. For her to perform an ungraceful act or to step across the boundaries of human expectation into violence was unthinkable. What would happen to her now that she'd done the unthinkable? Sarah pinched the bridge of her nose and lifted her coffee cup.

"Is Seule thankful for being saved from timeless oblivion in space? If I were Seule, I think I would rather have stayed dead."

Sarah yawned, feeling cold and tired. The ersatz coffee was weak and insipid, but she accepted a refill from the waiter. At least it was hot. "I remember the fuss that was made when Seule moved to our town," she said to her journal. "It was announced smugly that The Alien had chosen North Wells because of the excellent research facility where she would work as a member of the team decoding the ship's records. Actually she had been assigned there in an effort to keep her happy and quiet; whether she could do useful work or not was immaterial. It came out that she had developed a passion for one of the scientists studying her, a kinesiologist named Clay Elliot, and was essentially being sent out of harm's way.

"She was pining away apart from him, and needed to work it all out. Farber briefed me ahead of time, using words of one syllable in his usual dick-headed way. He warned me that she'd be reluctant to talk about it."

Sarah snorted. "So she's sent to me, the perfect person to help her get over a bad love affair. It's so stupid. I've never heard of anything so damned stupid in my life." Sarah clicked off the recorder and stuffed it in her bag.

June, 2023; North Wells

Seule had come to Sarah late in spring; now it was summer, their sixth session, and hot. Sarah's office windows were open. Seule was curled on a chair, her main limbs tucked under her smooth midsection. They were starting to be comfortable with each other. Sarah was still probing the edges of Seule's attitude of cheerful denial of any real problem.

Seule was silvery-rose in colour, her dense silky coat more like napped fabric than fur. The mouth in her long, thin head bore an alarming set of teeth revealed when her narrow black lips drew back in a smile or a laugh. She had a human propensity to laugh, a human appreciation for the absurd.

"People ask if I mind being monitored," said Seule. "I don't. It's necessary." They were talking about freedom; what the word meant when used in the context of Seule's life. "I must be a tempting target."

"Unfortunately, yes," affirmed Sarah, keeping her expression bland. Her long legs were crossed ankle over knee, manlike, and her short brown hair was tucked behind her ears.

She wondered at first if the government had wired her office when Seule had started her sessions, but knew that it didn't make a bit of difference. Of course they had wired it. The bodyguards in her reception area, the eye that hovered outside the building to gain a clear view through her window were all deemed necessary by someone. The eye followed Seule everywhere, and rumour spread that it had the capability of defensive fire. It had not yet been put to the test.

During the last year, Seule had been allowed to travel, to visit private homes, to live relatively unsupervised. Social conventions on how to treat the alien were being formulated ad hoc; so far Seule remained unharmed.

Sarah had read the multi-volume case history Dr. Farber sent her, skipping over the charts and bio-chemical analyses of Seule's flesh and excretions, snorting at the extrapolations as to her kind's origin. Guesses, Sarah had thought. They're only giving her a loose leash now because they can't think of any more tests to run. It's damned pathetic, really.

"Walter Farber has been with you all along, hasn't he?"

Seule's limbs shifted, a silky whisper against the chair's fabric. Absently she poked holes in her unused Kleenex with one of the soft, finger-like projections on her neck.

"Yes, he has. I remember being bounced on his knee, and the expression he wore when I jumped to his shoulder and then to the top of a filing cabinet. He never got used to that sort of thing. I think he wanted me to be more like a human child. Perhaps he still does."

Seule's silver gaze slid past Sarah's. She seemed bored; they'd gone over this before. She leaned forward. "Do you know, he kept my dog until I could find a place here and get him sent out. Would you like to see Amie's picture?"

Seule rummaged in the leather pouch she wore slung around her hind quarters. Seule had mentioned Amie before, with great affection, and Sara had always found it oddly poignant that the alien had a pet. She accepted the photo-vid Seule passed to her: the alien and her dog, pausing for a moment in a romp, then bounding away in unison. The dog was some kind of wolfhound and looked like a primitive, masculine version of Seule. Sarah could tell by the way the dog moved that he was a true dog, not enhanced, and she felt a small pang. It was hard to look at animals and not see instead the pseudo-human personalities laid on top like icing on a perfectly good cake. Though she missed some of her old doggy friends, Sarah was glad that no more enhancement was being done. Dealing with Seule was another order of magnitude entirely. The two, terrestrial dog and space-faring alien, leapt in Sarah's hand until she passed the photo back.

"He's a beautiful animal."

Only one stasis pod in the alien ship had been intact, in what must have been a crèche area: it contained the baby Seule. The others held only the dead: thirty thousand years dead, according to analysis of the exterior of their ship and the deterioration of components within. All of her family, and most likely all of her race, were extinct.

"Let's talk about Clay," said Sarah quietly. "If it's all right with you."

Seule's ears drooped immediately, and she curled herself more tightly in the chair.

"Yes. Let's." Her eyes were unreadable, though Sarah had noticed how the moods telegraphed by Seule's lips and ears were easily understood, as one would read joy, or eagerness, or disappointment in a dog's face.

"Have you sent a letter to him, as I suggested last week?"

Seule's ears drew back against the rounded crown of her skull. Her fringe of fingers was completely still for once.

"I can't. What if he doesn't answer?"

"What if he does? Tell me how you'd feel if he answered."

Seule looked away. She replied slowly, choosing words which caught harshly between her pointed teeth. "He won't. I really hope he doesn't, you know. I'm afraid I might abandon all my self-respect and run to him."

"It's been almost six months, Seule…"

"What does time have to do with it? And who else may I love but a human? Human is what I am, though I don't look it. What if my kind mates for life? What if I never get over him?"

"It takes time, I know. Believe me…"

Seule's powerful hind legs propelled her off the chair. She bounded to the window, stared out at maple trees dressed in new green. "I look into a mirror and see this alien thing. But I don't *feel* alien. You humans say I'm lovely, you say I'm exotic, unique. Well, you're right, damn you all. I'm the only one of me, and it hurts."

November, 2023; Washington, DC

"It's now four in the morning," said Sarah tiredly into her recorder. "I'm back at the hospital. Washington never goes to sleep completely, certainly a big hospital never slows down. They had to clear a floor for her, which no one here seems happy about, but she'll be whisked off to Houston as soon as she's able to be moved." She had to raise her voice over the babble of talk, clacking footsteps, and cell phones beeping.

"Apparently Seule's guardian eye, confused by the fact that Seule was the attacker, didn't try any fancy shooting. It screamed for help and hovered, recording, till someone came. Fortunately, for Seule anyway, that wasn't long. It all happened so fast… it was very painful to watch."

Sara was still shaken. There were few civilians among the tight-lipped men and women in uniforms at the briefing. The download was fish-eye distorted, and the sound buzzed and squalled.

Seule and Clayton Elliot were working alone in a mock-up of

the alien craft's interior, observing the varied responses of an environmental panel. They were talking quietly, the eye only picking up the odd innocuous phrase. Clayton, a dark, angular man with the weedy look of a student, leaned across his station and took Seule's left forefoot in his hand, forcefully directing it to a spot on the panel. In slow motion replay, Sarah watched his expression. He looked peevish, impatient.

Seule's forefoot, claws sheathed, slid up Clayton's arm and around his neck, pulling him toward her. He drew back. It was obvious that her strength exceeded his. His muscles tensed, his face showed repulsion. Worse, it showed boredom, irritation. When Sarah saw this look, she knew instinctively what would happen next.

Clayton pushed Seule away. Seule clasped him more firmly; he struggled, swore. She began to whine, a high keening. Sarah was familiar with the look of Seule, but this sound was utterly alien. Its meaning was universal. The next few seconds were full of action, too fast to follow well even in slow motion. Clayton struck at her and she raked him with her hind legs, as a cat would a rabbit, still clutching him with her clawed forelegs. She was licking his face as he screamed. Her neck-fingers grasped and stroked his face, his neck, his eyes and mouth.

Hands and bodies intruded suddenly, the eye pulled back, wobbled, and recorded five or six people trying to separate them. Upon being removed from contact with Clayton's body, Seule collapsed and began to slash at her own limbs with her teeth. Someone pulled her head back, two men held her limbs. Crashing noises, shouts, the spurting of blood. It had been, literally, a shambles.

Sarah rubbed her eyes, replaying the scene in her mind, and fought down an intense longing for her own bed in North Wells. She forced herself to sit straight in her orange plastic chair and take a deep breath. The taped scene intruded mercilessly past the blank taupe walls of the visitors' lounge, where she'd gone to hide from the uproar after the briefing.

Her face brightened momentarily. "At least I got a chance to talk to Jim Wright," she told her recorder. "I recognized him as we entered the briefing room and figured that of course he'd be here—where else at a time like this? When I was twenty, a junior at Colorado State, I fell madly in love with Jim (didn't we all?); big, handsome, holding the alien baby in his arms. The man who had entered the derelict ship and came back with a real E.T. He's still handsome, still a figure of romance, and I got a bit light-headed sitting next to him. Me and my bump of hero-worship. We talked about Seule, and I figured out the kind of man Jim is."

Sarah smiled bleakly. Jim Wright had taken the viewing harder than anyone else, though unlike some others he hadn't turned away. White-faced and flagpole straight, he'd watched every second of the carnage.

"There's a certain kind of parent who brings their child to me for diagnosis. The kid is ostracized, friendless; usually ugly, often intelligent and artistic. A complete misfit. Everyone except the parent knows the poor kid is a hopeless case; the parent, however, loved this child with a complete, stubborn devotion. The parent never gives up on the idea that someday everything will come out right for the ugly duckling. Jim Wright is that sort of parent. As far as I know he has no children of his own. Only Seule. I wonder if she knows how much he loves her?"

Sara stopped to blow her nose. She pulled a mirror out of her capacious bag and dabbed haphazardly at her eyes while the recorder paused, waiting for her voice.

"He's left to try calling Yves Giguere, another crew member who is now high up in the European Space Agency, and who might want to be here. None of the others has made it yet, but Jim keeps trying to collect them all by the bedside. I'll tuck this away now, and try again to see her."

Sarah, clad in baggy blue track pants and an unflattering sweater, a huge, crammed bag slung over one shoulder, tangled with the security guard outside Seule's room once again. Before she could make headway, she was waylaid by Dr. Walter Farber. She'd seen him at the briefing and had slipped away before it became necessary to speak to him.

Farber stopped her outside the door, gripping her elbow. "Sarah Lightburn. What are you doing here?"

Sarah frowned at him sullenly. "What's your problem? Everyone in God's creation is here."

Farber relaxed his grip and gave her a sour look. "Hello to you too. Glad you could make it, Sarah. Really I am. I'm hoping you'll contribute some ideas."

Sarah jerked her arm free. "Seule and I made progress, whatever you may think. Don't blame me for what went on after she left me."

"And don't you be defensive. I think you're more prickly now than when we were in Colorado."

"I'm amazed you remember," said Sarah tightly. "It's been a while. And prickles are a form of self-defence."

"Are we going to start in on all that now?" He clamped his teeth together and stared down at her, then stuffed his hands in his pockets and abruptly looked away. When he turned back his face wore a look of apology. "Look. I was twenty years older than you then; I still am. I liked you, Sarah. You were one of my favourites, one of the really good ones. Grad students like you don't come along all the time. I didn't mean anything more."

"Then why—" Sarah stopped, controlled her voice. *What am I doing? Why can't I let it go?* "Why did you let me think I was special to you?"

"You *were* special!"

"You know what I mean. Did you kiss me because my work

bolstered up yours? Which did you like better, the curve of my graph or the curve of my breast?"

"Damn." Farber's voice was soft. He ran a hand across his mouth. "Sarah, what do you want me to say? You knew the score, or I thought you did. Beryl was on assignment in China, you were a beautiful girl—"

"Jesus." Sarah shook her head. "You were everything I wanted to be." She paused, biting her lip. "You could so easily have taken me on the assignment with Seule. Why didn't you?"

"You want the truth? It was because, damn it, I needed a clear head for the work. Beryl understood that, and she was out of the country most of the time anyway—truth, remember? We'd battled it out. But you... you, I couldn't afford to have around."

"It was my work too!"

"Don't kid yourself, Sarah. I had to make decisions I didn't like, but I believe it was worth it. Personalities could not enter the situation."

Sarah sneered. "Personality was everything, can't you see that?"

Seule's door swung open and a woman bedecked with government insignia put her head out. "Will you two be quiet, please! The alien is awake in here, and she can hear you."

Sarah flushed red. She stepped forward. "I have access to the alien, and I'd like to see her now. If it's all right." Sarah bit her lip hard, and kept her chin up.

"Let me check your badge." The woman ran a sensor across Sarah's clip-on I.D. "Yeah, okay." She eyed Farber, who abruptly turned and stalked off down the corridor.

Inside, Sarah noticed Seule's smell. She remembered finding it unpleasant the first few times Seule came to her office; now it seemed almost to soak into her. It was unlike anything else on Earth, but it gave her the feeling of slipping into a sweater borrowed from a friend. The olfactory image was wiped out by the sight of Seule strapped onto her bed.

She couldn't turn her head; it was restrained, as were her four main limbs. Only the soft, relatively feeble appendages on her neck were free to move; they fluttered and waved as if blown by a wind. When Seule felt Sarah's eyes on her, the motion stopped and the tendrils fell to lie across her high, arched chest. Sarah moved closer and attempted a smile, but found it too painful an exercise.

"Oh, Seule," she said, gently touching one forelimb on an area not covered by bandages. The animals Sarah had mostly dealt with had been those dosed with intelligence-enhancing drugs. Some had responded to touch, most hadn't. Heightened mentation seemed also to sharpen the sense of individuality; the animals—dogs, apes, cetaceans—were often intractable.

Seule drew her lips back behind the muzzle clamped around her jaws, in what Sarah first thought was a smile of welcome. Feeling a perverse satisfaction in the intimacy she, and not Farber, had been granted, Sarah bent over the softly lit bed.

Seule snarled, a sound like a direct assault. Sarah flinched back in a primal response that was in a split second replaced with anger. Just as quickly, the anger was veneered in professional detachment, but it was still there.

Seule was neither animal nor human. She must remember that. "What's she on?" Sarah asked, addressing the nurse who'd let her in. The reply listed dosages of various drugs being pumped into Seule, which Sarah recognized as standard antibiotics and sedatives.

"Okay. Thanks."

Sarah turned to Seule, wary this time and careful to keep her hands in a nonthreatening attitude.

"Seule, do you know why you're here? Do you know what happened?"

For answer there was a high wailing whine that issued from

Seule's throat; very doglike, distressing to Sarah's ears. It went on and on. Finally Sarah nudged the bed, moving it enough to make Seule's eyes flick to the side and register her.

Seule's black lips moved behind the plastic muzzle, and she spoke. Her whisper was soft, spiritless; the keening whine still echoed in Sarah's ears. "He was with me and he was not with me. He was my friend and he was my enemy. He was with me." She strained her limbs against the straps. "He was not with me."

"You were working with Clay and his team. Everything was going well. Seule, whatever happened, for whatever reason, it's over now."

If this were a human friend or sister who'd suffered a trauma, thought Sarah, she'd know what to do. Hugs, understanding words, more hugs. The comfort of warm primate skin against skin. *But I don't understand her. She isn't one of us.* Sara found that her arms were tightly crossed over her breasts. Self-consciously she let them relax to her sides.

"He wouldn't touch me," whispered Seule. "He was so beautiful, so soft... I, I thought... I held him, he resisted."

"He died."

"He wouldn't touch me. None of you will *touch* me!"

Christ, thought Sarah. She ripped his guts out and almost tore his head from his body. Is that love to her? Thwarted love, frustrated desire; a death sentence to the one Seule chooses?

"I'll touch you, Seule. I... I'm your friend, you know." Tentatively Sarah forced her hand up, stroked Seule's forelimb lying strapped on the white sheet. Seule turned her head away and closed her eyes.

Suddenly Sarah felt an almost irresistible urge to flee the room. The alien's life-blood pulsed under the tips of her fingers, life hot with urges Sarah had imagined only in her darkest, most private moments. She snatched her hand away, stood panting in a flush of heat that burned her face. Thankful that the room was dimly lit, she tried to gather her thoughts. But before she could speak, Seule sighed and shifted her limbs minutely, all that was allowed by the restraints.

"All these years on your planet. I thought it was my home, I thought I was one of you. I listened to Walter Farber and tried to please him, I made friends with the people in Houston. And the men who discovered me—" Here she paused, and her black tongue tried to lick some moisture onto her lips. "Those men. They call me, send me letters and presents. I suppose I'm a mascot, a special toy to them."

Sarah caught her breath. "Jim Wright is here. He's hanging around trying to get in to see you."

Seule turned her dry, glittering eyes on Sarah. "Don't let him in," she whispered. "I couldn't stand it."

Strangely, it was the lack of tears that disturbed Sarah the most. It had always disturbed her. No need for her, no need for her damned Kleenex. Seule's appearance disturbed her, Seule's intelligent doglike way of moving and sitting and listening, her un-earth smell. Her hot silvery body.

And not a tear for the lonely horror of her life.

"I have to go." Sarah backed away from the bed, turned, pushed through the door to the white-lit corridor. Farber was nowhere to be seen.

She ran for the elevator. During the interminable wait for its arrival, Sarah saw Jim Wright, fast asleep in the visitor's lounge, his head nodding, his knees up. She looked away, pushed the call button again and again.

Down, alone thank God, down and out the nearest door to the cold night air. The freshness of melting snow piled beside the walkways was like a balm on her nerves; she headed for a bench and slumped down on it, shivering, yet hot with the feel of Seule still in her fingers.

Sarah bent over and clutched her stomach, squeezing her eyes shut. She breathed slowly and deeply, pulling in the moist freezing air that smelled of nothing, not even damp soil; no scent of alien flesh in her nostrils. She dug her fingers hard into her abdomen.

Oh, God, she wondered darkly, have I really gone so long without a lover? She gasped a little at the pain inside her, under the skin and muscle; it was like the bitter distillation of anger and denial. Poison.

Cautiously she straightened on the hard, slatted bench, very glad she wasn't crying, because she might not be able to stop. That primal longing—how terribly *intense* it was. Could it be that she had once felt it for Walter? She had forgotten how powerful it was, how lonely and terrible…

"No," she whispered aloud, her breath puffing in the cold. "Walter was a different sort of pain. A betrayal, and what I just felt, up there with Seule…" She stopped, confused. What *had* she felt? It had been electric, visceral; unexpected and overwhelmingly demanding. Its dregs had been vinegar. She shook her head, trying to think.

There was a shout from the corner of the building, and she turned to see six or seven newspeople, armed with cameras and lights, bearing down on her. Rising in dismay she looked in vain for an escape, and was surrounded.

"Are you a nurse? A doctor? Where is the alien—where is Seule?"

"How bad are her injuries? Will she die?"

"Leave me alone," cried Sarah. "I don't know anything."

One of them checked her phone and called out her name. "You're Sarah Lightburn, the alien's psychiatrist—"

"I am nothing of the sort! I only counselled her, briefly—" A mistake. The newsies moved in and Sarah was forced to push her way past them. One of them caught her by the arm and shouted into her face.

"Will the alien be destroyed now? She's a killer."

Sarah stopped, mouth open. "Destroyed? Don't be a fool—"

"Yes," screamed someone from the back of the growing crowd. "She killed one human, she'll kill more!"

"What if there are more aliens coming?"

Sarah, appalled, felt incongruous laughter well up. More of them! Seule would appreciate the irony of that.

"Is it true that Clay Elliot was her lover?"

"Leave me alone!" Sarah bolted for the door. Two security men, attracted by the noise, let her through and closed the thick reinforced glass doors against the reporters.

"Oh, journal, I'm so tired. And this coffee is awful. It must be almost morning by now."

Sarah looked at the TV suspended in a corner of the hospital cafeteria. It confirmed her predictions: mobs of Seule denouncers harassing Seule supporters. By now the whole world knew what had happened. "I'm here at the centre," whispered Sara, "and I'm not sure I know anything at all."

Slumping in the chair, she rubbed her eyes. "Why? Why did she kill him?" Blinking, she looked up and stared at nothing. "Will we ever really know why she does anything? By now, her life among us may have rendered her incapable of rational behaviour, or even whatever instinctive behaviour is proper for her race.

"And I really thought I was getting somewhere. Damn."

She sipped her coffee, winced.

"And why did I run away from her? Was it the feel of her flesh on mine?" She felt her face heat with confusion, with shame. "What happened up there, anyway? I, I… journal, I find myself having a hard time talking about this."

Sarah Lightburn stared morosely into her cup, wondering if

she was losing her mind. She watched her hands place the cup neatly in front of her as the apex of a chevron pattern of plastic knife, fork, spoon, and stir-stick. The cafeteria was growing crowded and noisy with talk and the clatter of dishes as the day shift arrived.

"I can't deal with this right now," she told the journal. She clicked it off and stowed it in her bag.

Sarah left the cafeteria and headed for the elevators, wondering what kind of man Clayton Elliot had been. She stabbed at the elevator button. Had Elliot treated Seule as an intelligent pet, perhaps expected her to get the coffee? Or was he kind, thoughtful—just a nice guy who simply couldn't find it within his heart to love someone who looked like a dog?

The elevator door opened and she shuffled tiredly on, not noticing until too late that the only other occupant was Walter Farber.

He stood his ground, smiled remotely as she reached across him to push her floor button. The door closed. Farber put his thumb on the stop button.

"I don't want you to go to Seule's room just now, Ms. Lightburn," said Farber in a flat voice.

Sara refrained from pointing out that she had intended only to get to the main floor and out. She withdrew her arm, hauled her heavy bag higher on her shoulder.

"Fine. We'll park right here while you tell me where I *should* go." Sarah wished her voice matched her feelings. She hated the way it went high and girlish in a confrontation. Typical female, Sarah sneered at herself. "I'd like to know why you've chosen to blame me. What about Elliot? Is anyone looking into his actions? What kind of background checks did you do on him?"

"That's not what I want to talk about, and besides, it's immaterial. You encouraged her to remain in contact with him. She went off with stars in her eyes, looking for romance."

Farber took his thumb off the button and the elevator started upward, called from somewhere above.

"And what's wrong with romance?" Sarah snapped. "What was wrong with that dumb shit Elliot? She loved him. Do you know anything about love, *Doctor* Farber?"

"Sarah, please. This is neither the time nor the place—"

The elevator stopped and the doors slid open onto the sixth floor. Farber, tight-lipped, motioned for Sarah to exit ahead of him; she did, and when he started down the corridor she followed.

"I don't really give a damn any more," she said. "There was a time when you were my hero, right up there with the astronauts, but not anymore. I've wised up."

Farber reached a door, keyed it open and stood to one side.

"Well?" he said. "Shall we continue in private, or do you prefer to rant out here?"

Sarah stalked in and threw her bag on the floor beside a table surrounded by straight-backed chairs. It was some sort of meeting room, windowless and stale.

Farber yanked out a chair and dropped into it. He bent over and rubbed his temples. After a moment Sarah sat too. It seemed stupid and childish to keep standing. Hadn't she grown up? Wasn't it impossible for this man to make her do foolish things anymore?

Farber looked up, steepling his hands under his chin. It was a mannerism Sarah remembered from long ago. "I did try to keep track of you after I left," he said. "Not all my time was spent with Seule. You distinguished yourself at Colorado, did a couple of years with Arthur Kemp before he went to work for Biostym. Then you disappeared for a while. Let's see… I next saw you in Edmonton, at a lecture. You were at the back."

Sarah kept her eyes on the tips of his fingers, unable to speak.

"Believe it or not, it pleased me to see you again, though you left with someone and it didn't seem the right time to renew old acquaintances. I thought that soon I'd meet you at a conference, laugh over old times. You'd be married, I'd have Beryl with me, we'd have drinks. Something." He looked down again.

Sarah could barely keep her eyes on him, her urge to run was so strong. "Why did you resist my counselling Seule?"

"I didn't. When your name came across my desk I thought about what might happen, but then I realized that it might be a good idea to have you on board. I'm still not sure if it is, all things considered. Perhaps I was trying to make up for the past. I do know that there's obviously a lot still to learn about Seule."

He sighed deeply, running his fingers over his lips. "When she was just a baby, I'd visit her quarters every day, and every day she'd come leaping at me out of nowhere. I always caught her. It was a game we played until she got too big. I had to remind her over and over to keep her claws in, to be gentle, to take it easy on us humans."

He looked exhausted. He looked like an old man coming to understand that the best part of his life was ending.

In her mind's eye, Sarah saw Farber as he'd been when he landed the plum assignment. Suave, dark-haired, grinning wolfishly, he had abandoned everything to make Seule his own. He'd been with her from then on, in every newscast at every conference and study. It's all getting away from him now, she thought. We get old, the children grow up and leave. This one has been a heart-breaker, but then, the special ones always are.

Sarah looked at her watch. Eight o'clock in the morning, and she felt as though sleep did not exist anymore, at least on this world. Almost time for the news conference. What an ordeal that was going to be—she was thankful she wouldn't have to be there. She hoped Farber could handle it.

He looked up at her finally. His eyes were unreadable. The eyes show nothing, Sarah told herself—it's the lips, the brows, the tiny muscle-pulls that tell the story. Animals can show their emotions if they're smart enough, if they have anything inside to show… Farber tipped his chair back and crossed his ankle over his knee in a way Sarah instantly recognized.

She felt her thoughts realign themselves. Had it really been Walter Farber she wanted? Or did she want what he had, what he *was*? Seule had seduced him away, and all Sarah's tears and anger and wanting had never gotten him back… *Stupid woman,* she jeered at herself. *Daddy loved her more than me.*

And if he'd taken me along to work with Seule, how long would I have been content to be in their exceptionally thick shadows?

Sara had a sudden merciless vision of herself, an imitation of him, hands steepled and legs crossed in just his way, sagely nodding at a distraught client. She jammed her hands between her knees and almost laughed out loud. Hadn't that been a sort of apology she'd heard a while back? Something about making up for the past?

Sarah leaned forward and stood, stretching her shoulders and running her fingers through her hair. She grinned suddenly. "It doesn't matter now. I'm okay. Truce, all right?"

Farber stood too, looking at her uncertainly. He turned for the door, then stopped and looked back at her, clearing his throat. "Within the next few days you'll be getting a request to come to Houston. I'd like you to do some very careful thinking before you make a decision."

Sarah, completely surprised and not knowing what to say, said nothing.

"There's a lot of work to be done," Farber continued. "I'm not sure if we can treat this whole episode as an advance or a setback in our knowledge of Seule. Whatever the verdict, she's going to be locked away for a while. No way around it, I'm afraid. It's hoped you'll have something to contribute."

Farber straightened his tie briskly, seeming to come fully awake by the sheer power of will. "They're broadcasting soon from the director's boardroom," he said. "I'd better get myself up there." He squinted at her speculatively. "My office will be in touch with you."

He turned and put his hand on the doorknob, then looked back at her as if he was going to say something else, but did not. He left, letting the door remain open behind him.

"Did you really want Clayton Elliot for your lover?" asked Sarah softly, into the gently beeping, monitor-lit darkness of Seule's hospital room. There was a different military nurse on duty now, a man who kept his eyes on her carefully. Sarah ignored him.

"Or did you want him to love you? There's a difference, you know. It has to do with possession. It gets mistaken for love so often…" She stepped closer to the bed.

Seule's eyes seemed brighter now. The look in them of lost despair had retreated a bit, and she turned her head to follow as Sarah moved up beside her.

"I was so jealous of you." Sarah's voice was soft; all the anger had left her. "You didn't know Walter and I had once been lovers, did you? When you came along, he just wasn't interested in me anymore. He had found something so absolutely lovely and new that he had to let everything else go." She gazed at Seule almost kindly, feeling light as a husk from which a spoiled seed has been shaken.

"I'll never love Walter again, or even really like him, but I can admire him for what he's done with you. That's good enough."

The alien moved slightly on the bed under her restraints, and her soft pink tendrils undulated across her chest.

"Clayton Elliot wanted you to be a piece of experimental

equipment conforming to his thesis. Walter Farber wanted you to be his brilliant, beautiful little girl. And I wanted to use you to get next to him, to show him… to show that I mattered."

"Sarah," croaked Seule, barely audible.

Sarah backed up a little. She wasn't ready to risk touching Seule again, not yet.

"Sarah." The alien's eyes were on her, those dark-silver, tearless eyes, and Sarah almost stopped breathing. "Please. I'm sorry, I'm sorry I let you feel what I was feeling. I'm… so tired of being human, but I don't know how to be anything else."

Sarah bit her lip, backing off still farther. She retreated to the window and drew aside the drapes to let in the brightening day. "They're asking me to come to Houston," she said, around a lump in her throat. "Walter wants me, he thinks I can be useful." She swallowed carefully and turned back to the bed. "How… how about you? Do you want me there?"

Sarah forced herself to look unflinchingly at Seule.

The alien reached toward Sarah with her neck-tendrils, something she had never done before; she had never touched Sarah unless Sarah initiated it. In fact the alien had deftly avoided contact during their sessions.

A moment of self-doubt, of struggle against the urge to flee, and Sarah stepped forward, bracing herself for whatever might flood into her.

Almost, she didn't feel the first moment of touch, Seule's tendrils were so light and soft and tentative. Like a baby's fingers—warm, slightly sticky, full of innocent life—they gently explored the lengths of Sarah's fingers, slid across the hard nail surfaces. It was, to Sarah, so intensely sensual that she could only watch. The blood pounding in her ears made it impossible to move or react.

Yes, she thought, this is it—that moment, that fragrance sweet and strong; this is what it means.

And under the sweetness was a bitter taste, and behind the new light the shadow of a permanent darkness that could never pass; Sarah knew it. There were no miracles to offer, only friendship to ease the path.

"Yes, please come with me," whispered Seule.

Old fashioned sci-fi and a broken love affair. Can the dreams of a bitter, lonely man blossom in a strange, cold world?

A Breath After Dying

I'm in a lung chamber listening to the crackle when sounds from overhead intrude. Footsteps. Voices echoing. I hold still, my logger softly humming in my hand, the whispery popping of the chamber in my ears, my heart sinking. I need more time.

Time stopped long ago in this stone-shrouded chamber beneath a ruined city. I call it a lung because it's a stone bubble, pitted with small pockets, through which the stagnant air seeps slowly. So much of this alien cityscape is like a petrified carcass.

The humans walking overhead are here because naked apes can't quench the urge to explore, to poke the corpse and demand some remnant of life.

The footfalls and voices get closer, blurred syllables sliding among the weathered, broken stone and the knotted vines. I know who they are. What they are. Rich, entitled, eager to mould this world into something they value.

I've spent the last five months dreading the day they'd get here.

The voices get clearer, Dalia's instantly recognizable. I'd known she was coming, but not why she still had such power over me.

"Look at this… what… you think they…" A man's reply, just as incomplete, echoing. I last saw Dalia on a joint salvage expedition to Earth, where she and I and a couple of dozen others had collected a lot of maybe-useful genetic material. A long time ago, when we'd been lovers.

The footsteps tap, recede, wander.

Physically, the city is a sere, burnt-umber band almost completely circling this dying world, a broken mosaic at what on Earth would be at the latitude of Alice Springs and the Kalahari Desert. There's another band of temperate climate in the northern hemisphere, but it's just oily grey ocean, inhabited by translucent jelly-creatures and clouds of yellow plankton.

This one small area of the temperate band has some remaining coherence. Elsewhere there's little but broken, twisted slivers of metal, clots of ancient stone and tile and plastic, degraded by the sun and wind. Chewed over by dirty pinkish ice shoving out from the pole, rusty desert infiltrating from the equator.

But humans will find a way to live anywhere. We'll bend and shape whatever we clasp—and now what once was part of an ancient, world-spanning city is slated for renovation.

Why the interest in this dreary planet? Humans have the caves of Mars, the brilliant and comfortable hollow asteroids. Why do we need to come all the way here? The reason: this world orbits very close to something irresistibly strange.

Stop stalling. Time to confront the agents of change stomping around overhead. I clamber out of the lung-pit and start up.

The only major organic structures here are sturdy vines that once had made their determined way through every nook and cranny. Handy to hold onto, they are everywhere, as if they alone strangled this world to death. I'd assumed they were long dead, but when examined they reveal faint signs of dormant life. I can't imagine how deep their roots might go.

I make my way up broken blocks of stone, reaching for crumbled steps. My breath puffs into the dry air, into the dust of long-ago life. A wave of sadness overtakes me. There's a name for the yearning nostalgia toward things that are gone forever. A Portuguese word: *saudade*. I'm afflicted with it.

I hear Dalia's laughter, echoing. Am I trying for a preemptive strike, or for a last-ditch effort at salvation?

I keep climbing.

I find the two of them in what may have once been a courtyard. Or a cistern or who-the-hell-knows. It's a jumbled construction of dreamlike complexity, tumbled slabs of ornate blond stone carved into odd shapes, cabled and looped with the desiccated vines that made it look like the insides of an ancient computer, one you might see in a museum.

Hearing me, they stop and turn.

My forlorn hope that it wasn't Dalia vanishes. Of course she'd be here, with her connections and her exquisite taste. This is the culmination of her training—all her skills will come into play.

"You're early," I blurt rudely, sweat prickling in my armpits. "I was promised six more months."

The man steps forward. Tall and sandy-haired, he is thin to the point of attenuation, as if he's been stretched. A Mars native. He said, "You must be Dr. Shipley. Dr. Oryon Shipley?"

"I am. And you are Jurad Marenty, I assume." The rituals of speech come back. I carefully do not look at Dalia, but she is staring at me. We are the same age, but she looks thirty years younger than I. Here's what she sees: a sunburned scarecrow, dried up and alone here on a world with no name. Second planet from its star; we'd run out of catchy monikers in the last hundred years.

Marenty raises his chin. "Yes," he says. "That's me. Lately of Mars Colony One." Of course he needs to mention his pedigree. "This is my designer, Dalia Lee Ware. And yes, technically we don't have possession yet." He gestures at the towering walls around us. "But we couldn't resist a look-see."

I feel my cheek twitch. If I don't keep a close watch on myself, I'll become a mass of twitches and tics, and wouldn't that be good for a laugh.

"You're a long way from home," I say, forcing calm. A man like this, vigorous and fit, carelessly dressed in real cotton and wool, won't be able to resist bragging about his provenance. Next he'll slide in something about his Martian vineyards, or his personal training-cave.

Dalia touches my arm, and at my startled reaction draws her hand away quickly. "Orrie, it's good to see you. I'd heard you were here."

Has she been asking? Could she still—I really can't bear to look full at her, so I look at Marenty instead. "Dalia and I know each other from long ago. I have clearance to stay here until winter. In fact, I'm charged by the Survey to be here. I have work to do. You can't start construction yet."

"Actually, we've already started. Templates and materials are *en route*, composers are being loaded. I like to get things done efficiently. You understand? It's my nature." He pauses, as if waiting for applause. "You realize how the climate here impacts everything. If we're going to get rid of all this clutter and debris before freeze-up, we need to get at it right away."

"Debris." It is hard to keep my voice neutral. "That's all it is to you?"

Dalia looks away, inspecting the intricate patterns incised

deeply into the rock. Depictions of animals? Plants? The sentient beings who abandoned this world? Their writings, their history, their poetry. Their graffiti—the window into the soul of a civilization.

Recklessly I poke a finger into Marenty's chest. "Let me tell you about the winters here, as you probably know nothing at all about climate or weather. Earth's is completely screwy, and UnderMars doesn't provide a lot of variety. I know, I used to live there, a long time ago."

He steps back a pace, his lips thinning in distaste. My finger and I follow him. "Unless your fancy new operations base, or marketing model, or whatever, is completely enclosed and heated, you will freeze to death in mere minutes. And winters go on so long you'll think you're in an ice age." Why would any normal person want to live here when they could be in orbit? What the hell were they thinking? It's no mystery to me why this world's inhabitants decamped. They gobbled it up and spat it out millennia ago. "You've wasted your money, and you're wasting my time."

Marenty produces a cold smile. *You've no idea the power I have,* his eyes say. *The wealth, the influence.* "You needn't worry, Shipley. I've other places to be."

I know exactly the sort of person he is, but does he have any idea about me? Certainly I am not normal, or I wouldn't be here, all by myself. Quite possibly, I'm completely insane.

Dalia walks among the fallen blocks of stone, touching them with her fingertips as if her skin were part of a collection array. Perhaps it is. Part of her suite of talents. What does she see here, other than a lucrative job? Has she promised her client guest-quarters, pools, entertainment clouds, human servants? Of course her construction plans will acknowledge, even revere, the long-lost alien civilization. There might even be quarters for fools like me who'll study it as it is relentlessly eliminated.

She looks at me, with pity probably. "This world will be cleared for colonization before the next cycle, Orrie. I've done my homework. It's going to happen."

Marenty chimes in. "Nothing you can do will change things."

Dalia's dark eyes brim with calm certainty. "Orrie, I know how to make this world safe and comfortable for human colonization. It has a lot to offer, once this infrastructure is revitalized. You can trust me—"

"All I need is time. Time, before everything changes."

Marenty looks ready to keep arguing, but I hear a ping from his comm. "Look, Shipley, I have people to meet up top. Can we call a truce? I need you to escort Dalia wherever you feel is safe. Show her around."

I'm about to refuse, but Dalia says, "Please, Orrie. Then I'll go, I promise."

What can I say? In some deep sense I want them both here, plus anyone else who'll shuttle down. Surveyors, engineers, people hauling equipment and lunch baskets full of fancy food. Perhaps it should just be me, breathing the dust, listening to the death rattle. Am I insane, or merely lonely? "Fine. An hour."

He leaves. At last I let my gaze linger on Dalia. Pale skin, dark unruly hair, the manner of an aristocrat. She's picked that up since we'd been contemporaries in Mars's brain-cages. We'd been fifteen, and called them playpens. Where you went so that your head could learn things your body already knew. I learned that I could have her only temporarily. Her ambition lay along a wholly different spectrum of possibility. She focused on the future, I wanted the past.

"What do you want to see?" I ask harshly. "The lower levels? Up top for a view of your new empire?"

She ignores my rudeness. "We have little time. The lower levels—isn't that where the oldest relics are?"

"Follow me."

There aren't many worlds compatible with terrestrial life. Even this one, no matter its air and gravity and sunlight, despite Marenty's grandiose plans, is probably more trouble than it's worth. I'm lucky to be here.

No. Not lucky. Determined. Relentless. I had seen this world, made some wild conjectures about what it was, and what it could be, and I had wanted it for myself.

Dalia prowls along beside me, touching everything. She has always revelled in her senses. In the cages—the schools—we had fought and debated, torn things apart and put them back together and then completely destroyed them. Joyously. We were children, wrecking things that were meant to teach us. But wrecking is part of learning.

She doesn't need a guide. But Marenty knew instantly what I am: a bomb. He seeks to defuse me before I blow up.

Marenty thinks he can purchase me along with the real estate he's acquired, just as he's contracted Dalia's allegiance. He assumes we'll ignore Survey edict and gladly work to get him what he wants. And why not? No one is paying much attention when the real prize is a mere 19 million kilometres away.

This planet is just a stepping stone. Between here and the system's star is a massive cluster of technology, right where a planet used to be. It contains 35,788 individual nodes (we counted) intricately linked by cables. The cables are five kilometres in diameter, and seem to consist of uncountable (we couldn't) numbers of wires, made of something that functions almost like muscle. The cluster orbits in a tight lozenge shape, like a school of ocean fish, one of those glimmering masses that form sometimes in response to threat. Scant shreds of useful intel have been retrieved from within it. The cables and "fish" have been observed to reorient themselves at random intervals. Like the tic of a muscle, elastic and relentless.

The only deduction that makes sense? The damned thing is

one immense computer. If that's true, the equivalent of billions of digitized brains could be active within it. Thousands of unique societies. We can't be sure, but it's most likely where this world's former inhabitants have gone. It's what I believe.

The planet I stand on is like an old woman abandoned in favour of her stylish daughter, the one who gets all the attention despite being aloof and baffling. Or because of it. Yet, what a handy place to set up a luxurious base of operations! This tired old planet already has gravity and mass. A nice solid magnetosphere. Far enough from the cluster to be (one hopes) safe. Thus: one Oryon Shipley, squatting like a toad on a derelict world, trying to hide the keys.

Dalia glances at me, waiting. I pull my shoulders back and join her, like a man in charge of his environment, but I know she isn't buying it. She is no doubt calculating her design as she strokes the vines, leaning close, running her fingers as inquisitively as a monkey's into their crevices.

Mars's culture values a hidden path toward a subtle outcome. But she never liked that sort of game. It was she who had started our relationship, and it was she who had ended it. It was she who had taken what she'd learned and built a career in bio-engineering that enabled Mars to flourish. She has never appreciated prevarication, and won't appreciate it now.

"What do you want?" I blurt, staring. "I know what Marenty wants—property, prestige, power. Do you have his urge to loot and pillage?"

She turns away, not bothering to respond.

I can't bear to be out of her beam of light. I follow her, catch her arm. "I'm sorry. I didn't think I'd react this badly."

She narrows her eyes at me thoughtfully. Does she see me as a real person, or an obstacle in her path? "What do I want? To work. This world is the ultimate challenge for someone like me."

There is no one like you. "Okay. Good." I lick my lips. She needs to know what I surmise: that it is already too late to stop what is going to happen. Nothing to do but watch and wait. Pray. "So… I've been trying to deduce what went on here. I think of this particular area as an environmental control node, and I think I'm right. Tell me, did you notice an odd smell when you first got down here?"

A little taken aback by the non-sequitur, she sniffs the air and shakes her head. "Not really. Nothing I can't take care of in the remediation phase."

"When I first set up camp, the site had quite a distinctive, acrid smell. Now it smells fresh, like a seaside. No?"

"I… I can't really…" She sniffs again and her eyes brighten. She has been breathing down here, touching things, all the time.

"Orrie… I'm starting to get very interested. You understand my work on Mars, right? I'm just wondering…" Her voice trails off and I see her experience a brief shudder. "Yes. It's not a chemical smell, it's… organic somehow." A pause, then, "Do you really think the inhabitants of this world simply drained it of everything lovely or useful, then left to become… computer programs? Choosing a sort of petrified life-in-death? If so, shame on them."

"I think the dwellers in this world-wide city cultivated beauty as they understood it, and that we appreciate some of the same things." My voice is as soft as I can keep it.

I haven't looked away from her at all, so I see when her face changes. She turns her head from side to side, flaring her nostrils, as a dog on the hunt will do. Her heart will be beating faster, her lungs drawing the air in deep. A sort of feedback loop.

"So," I say. "Marenty the Martian. What's his plan, if I may ask?"

"You may. And I will tell you. Establish legal residence.

Sidestep any archaeological, environmental, or other sort of oversight. Pry up anything pretty and sell it. Grind the rest to dust and build what he wants. He's got me under contract for three solar years to design his environment physically, aesthetically and ecologically." She shrugs. "Make it his consortium's long-term base of operations."

I hear myself emit a bark of laughter. "What, he doesn't have enough territory on Mars?"

"Of course he does. But Mars isn't close to the Cluster."

For one under contract she speaks very freely. "What's in it for you?"

She smiles enigmatically and looks away, and I feel a little thrill. So, she wants wealth and prestige, but what else?

She gives me a partial answer. "I want to watch him try to penetrate that thing out there." She waves a hand skyward. "That's what everyone will try, isn't it? He wants to be first."

"It's poison, Dalia. It's a lure and a trap. There's nothing but death inside."

She makes a dismissive gesture. "It's only a lure for those who are tired of life. One *kind* of life. Intelligence doesn't need to be alive, anymore. But it's all guesswork until the Cluster can be contacted or penetrated."

"I'm not interested in the Cluster or whatever inhabits it. Do you have any idea what you're getting into, here on *this* world?" I slap a hand on a curl of rock.

My attitude is mirroring hers. I've become brusque, demanding.

Her cheeks flush. "Of course I—"

"You know how the Mars and asteroid habitats have to be so carefully balanced. You know how easily the micro-ecology can skew. But those are relatively simple, primitive habitats at the early stages of our understanding and development. What if—"

She steps close. Puts a hand on my chest. "What if the beings who used to live here knew a hell of a lot more? Is that what you think?"

I back away from her hand, the helpless pulse of heat her touch has ignited. "You know, my logger is the most expensive and useful technology I own. Among other things, it tells me about the bacteria in this air-space. The virus, the fungi."

She nods. *Go on.* She knows what I'm going to say.

"Every time we breathe, and with every motion, every footstep and eye-blink, we shed them by the millions." Kindergarten stuff.

"Yes, yes. Don't try to lecture me." But she's starting to look apprehensive. She feels the airy hands of change coil around her.

Just then Marenty clatters down the smooth stone ramp into the deep chamber.

"Our breath." I gesture at Marenty. "His exhalations. Your development team out there. Every human who breathes and walks on this world contributes."

Marenty regards us suspiciously. His cheeks are pink too, and he's sweating. "What are you two talking about?"

She ignores him and looks right at me. A surge of pride that I squash down fast.

She says, "This world has been waiting, hasn't it? At the ready."

"Yes. The microbes here function more like little machines than the strains we're familiar with. The vines that look so dead? It's what they are made of. Vast colonies of cells, kilometres of them in ropes and cables and bridges, dormant for centuries, waiting. They're letting loose now, absorbing our exhalations—combining, changing, multiplying. There's no way to stop it, not now."

Marenty suddenly looks alarmed, then angry. Dalia, however, looks as if she's seen God.

Marenty grabs Dalia by the arm and starts pulling her away. "What the hell? We're being infected? This world was cleared, damn it. Did you set this up, Shipley? Did you?"

The small crackling, rustling sounds I detected earlier in the lung chamber are getting louder. The vines are starting to swell and change colour, as if liquid is coursing through them. Which it is, of course. Rising from the depths, propelled by tiny biological pumps. The sort of pumps Dalia uses on Mars, but so much better. Stronger. Millennia better and stronger. They have been waiting a long time for a reason to live again.

I say, "It really doesn't matter whether we go or stay. The transformation has been initiated."

Idiotically, Marenty covers his mouth and nose with his sleeve and glares at me.

I look him straight in the eyes. "We're being assimilated into the service parameters of this microbial ecology."

Dalia is grinning like a maniac. Just like she used to. "It's an advanced form of habitat generation. These vines aren't vines at all, not plant life as we know it. They're a kind of biological caretaker left behind by the vanished civilization."

"Who now inhabit the Cluster."

Marenty looks back and forth between us, his expression a combination of anger and avidity. How to turn a profit on this?

Dalia cocks her head. "I hear water running."

I close my eyes, listening. Yes. No longer merely creeping and seeping, it is rising fast, and I have no idea how high it will go. "I suggest we return to the upper levels."

"Shit," Marenty squawks. "This is your doing, Shipley, you—"

Dalia gives him a shove to get him moving.

We hustle upward, and I feel a thrill of danger. So good, after the months of lonely mourning for what was lost. Lost no more. "The bones and sinews... that's all we can see. Rocks, vines.

But there's so much more. There's—"

"Jesus," snarls Marenty, "don't you ever shut up? I'm going to flatten this pile of rubble, just you watch, I'll kill it all—"

"Look around you. Just look."

"You think I'll let you get away with this?"

Dalia stops and holds up an arm, pointing. "Look at the walls."

The shimmer starts at the floor, blooming up from the lower levels where the water runs. The vines swell and shift and move. They knit themselves together into something like silky cloth or stained glass, pulsing in veins of light and colour. The sense of growth—for it isn't really growth in the vegetable sense—seems sluggish, tentative. But then again, the system has been sleeping for millennia.

I say, "I'm glad now that you arrived early. It triggered a tipping point."

We scramble up to ground level. Light bathes the walls, which the vines are shifting back into place. It sifts through new-formed iridescent windows, casting butterfly colours through liquid film. The air inside this decrepit structure is tempering into something vital and moist, and the stone beneath our feet has gained the breathing tension of a sprung dance floor. In some of the hollows I note clumps of excrescence forming into half-recognized shapes. Fruit. Flowers. Pregnant bulges laden with meaning. Draped and muddled patterns that want only direction. They need to learn from us.

This world was mine alone, for a while. My breath, my skin and sweat weren't enough to wake it, and I had loved and pitied it in its long, suspended death. The heart-tug of the lost, the echo of ancient memories, is probably what made me come to this world in the first place. I hadn't imagined it was simply waiting for the next tenants.

I laugh. "I never thought I'd say this, but… we need more

people here."

Dalia turns in place, marvelling. "Yes. More input." She knows what's happening, the danger of it. What might go terribly wrong.

Marenty curses and fumes as we make our way outside to join the panicky group of engineers and investors clustered around the shuttle. They gape and yell as the surface heaves and blooms. Marenty's plans laid waste.

He'll adapt to this gift from past time. He'll have to.

This world is ours now.

HELLO, JANE, GOODBYE

"Count backwards from fifteen, please, Angie."

Angie's brain doesn't just lie placidly in its bone cup, it moves and breathes. Not a lot, just enough so I know it's paying attention.

"Fifteen, fourteen, thirteen, twww… w… wwelve, eleven… ten—"

"Okay Angie, that's fine. Super."

Yes, her brain is paying attention. But I know it can be fooled.

Angie is a chubby sixteen-year-old with smooth pale skin and small, bright blue eyes, and a nervous mother in the visitors' lounge. Her father is most likely at work; not the type to take time off for something like this.

Angie's straight sandy hair will grow back after we pop the cut-out doorway back onto the top of her head and sew her scalp back up. She'll look like a skinhead for a while, but maybe her boyfriend will like that, maybe the other kids will think she's cool.

Better than epilepsy, isn't it, honey?

"Suction. Thanks, Kim."

I've got a good team. They're quiet, brisk, efficient. Quick on the uptake. At first a couple of them didn't like working for a female doctor, but they came around. I'm good. And my nurses are the best, they're on my side; we've done quite a bit of this sort of thing together.

I love it. God, I love it.

"Angie, can you tell me what you're thinking right now?" I can see her face in the mirror, and she can see mine. The edge of the green plastic dam separates her pasty little face from what's going on in her open skull. She can't move her head at all, but her eyes slide around, looking at me and away, flicking around as much of the operating theatre as is in her view, then back, shyly, to me. She licks her lips. She's scared, but she's doing fine.

"What'm I thinking…?"

Her face goes a little softer. Her eyes look at something, a little memory that's popped to the surface.

Her snub nose crinkles a bit. "I smell French fries," she says. "And vinegar… no, now it's gone."

The rounded tip of the electrode wand moves fractionally, gently padding along the skin of her brain like a tiny finger checking for blemishes, as if it were Angie delicately confronting a nascent pimple, getting ready to deal with it.

Leave it or squeeze it out?

I prefer to think of it as the paw of a cat, padding silently in search of mice in the mind's hidden crevices. The device is the perfect extension of my hand, my eye, my desire. I have tamed electricity to my personal will.

A smile creeps over her face. "It's Trish!" She's giggling. "Oh, God, I can't talk about this… it's like I'm there, wow… Trish, she can't handle booze, right? It's a party for Bruce… she falls in Bruce's lap, right? Like, she's had too many—" And now her voice changes. She isn't just telling the story, she's living it. "Bruce, take it easy! Trish, come on. Let's go to the bathroom. Bruce, you asshole, let her up." Angie is still giggling. I wonder how many beers she's had? It's a fun memory, harmless, though her parents wouldn't like it.

Leave it there. Leave it and go on.

"Suction here, Kim. Time?"

"Nine nineteen, Barb."

We're all on a first-name basis here, none of this Doctor Bell shit. My people respect me, I respect them; simple.

Angie's face blanks out for a moment. Her lips slacken. The electrode moves. I do love this, I do love it all so…

What we're doing to her on this Tuesday morning in Operating Room 6 of Jubilee Hospital is eliminating epilepsy from this girl's life. No more seizures, no more medication. A normal, healthy life for an average young woman, a middle-class white girl with a so-so future, but shouldn't she have a life without disease?

Outside is a cold morning, snow in flurries whipped hard by the Manitoba wind. Inside is a haven of light and warmth and gleaming sterility. My world.

I know where it is, the little bit of brain tissue that must be destroyed. And I'll get to it, I'll get to it and have time for coffee before doing my rounds. But not just yet.

Move the electrode. Move it again, a millimetre at a time would be too much, too gross; I'll not wantonly rampage across Angie's life. But I know I'll find that little something tucked away, something she doesn't realize is still there. Most people have something they don't want to remember.

Angie, in the mirror, suddenly looks alert. Her heart rate leaps, her respiration stops, held in, then off she goes. Yes.

Yes, this is it. This is what I want.

"Hold her down, ladies. Let's find out what's happening."

Kim and Mattie lean into it. Angie's fighting hard; but for the head clamps she'd be off the table and out the door, wires trailing.

"No!" she screams, her voice high and childish. She's trying to pull her knees together, trying to twist her body away from the hands holding her down. "I'll tell Mommy! I'll—ah!" Another scream, cut off. Amazingly, a red patch flares on her cheek as if a phantom hand has slapped her. Then she goes silent, panting, her heart rate sky-high, her lips clamped shut as if a big heavy hand is over them.

I want very much to shut my eyes and take it all now. But the electrode must not move away from this sweet spot, this precious little node locked in Angie's cerebrum. If I'm going to get it I have to concentrate, trust that Mattie and Kim will do their part and trust me in turn. I'll enjoy it later, at home. Angie won't miss it; no, not at all.

She didn't even know it was there.

The buried traumas are the best. When they've been encysted deep and long, aging like brandy in a barrel, they taste the sweetest.

Angie is reliving the rape as we watch. It enters my brain as it exits hers, and I can even catch a little echo of what her father is feeling as he ravages his child. It's a very good session, very exciting. Who would have thought that ordinary little Angie Pitney would contain such delicious buried treasure?

"Well," I say as Angie lapses into unconsciousness and her heart rate levels out, "let's not let that come back. What do you say, ladies? Shall I excise this little bit of nastiness?"

Mattie and Kim, releasing their grip on Angie, nod as one.

They see it my way, as always. Mattie must have some idea of what I do, but she doesn't care. She trusts me. Mattie can be elbow-deep in any sort of physical horror, but mental anguish knocks her sideways. To her, I'm purging these children of pain, cleaning them and making them well. How I do it is not her business. She keeps the others in line.

"Sue?"

Sue is my sterile nurse, new to this, and at first she won't look up from her tray of instruments.

"Sue? Are we in agreement?"

She nods then, gulping, and looks up at me. She's crying, her eyes spilling over as she gives me the kind of look I imagine a shepherd would give a burning bush.

"All right then. Probe, please."

The area will be heat-coagulated by the application of a controlled radio frequency current. It will never pop up out of Angie's psyche again. It won't need to: it's safe with me now.

When I was a girl, I'd get impressions from people: vague, shadowy pictures and emotions. They wouldn't stay, they vanished like fish in a lake. It didn't seem like anything special to me, and I never told anyone about it.

I knew I was destined to be a doctor when I grew up, I never wanted to be a nurse like the other little girls. I knew even then that I had to be the one in control, the one with her hands on the very essence of life.

As I learned more and took up neurosurgery, the belief that I was doing much more than empathizing with my patients sank in. I was *living* their memories. The electrical currents generated in connection with my work boosted the signal, as it were; I could capture what I wanted and keep it.

At first it frightened me, just as it does Sue to see me at work; then I learned to love it. I think there may be something wrong with me, something deep inside my own skull's cellar, but I'm functional, aren't I? Successful, in fact—even happy. I know what I'm doing. And what is wrong with that?

I'm the stereotypical image of the lady doctor, driven and loveless, burying herself in her career. Sex is a mundane, tedious exercise. I don't like to be touched. Driving is better, and I love to escape to midnight highways and see how fast my Mercedes will really go. Fast is good. Music is wonderful; the right aria, the right voice.

Drugs are good, and I've developed a fondness for certain uppers I can get in my professional capacity. I like to feel my brain race and burn and send off sparks like a screaming engine, knowing all along that it's different from anyone else's brain—it can do things that defy reason.

But this is the best. This quiet, sterile plundering of another's mind. The savouring of sweetness and pain that comes later. It's a pleasure that is all mine.

At home, I strip off my leather driving gloves and throw them on the credenza. It's dark out, the early frigid dusk of the north, and the drive was boring and stressful, past interminable petty accidents. Benita has laid a fire as she always does in the winter, after her cleaning and polishing duties. I never see her, she does her work and goes home.

Bending, I touch a match to the paper and watch the flames rise, feel the heat flare. The tension in my thighs as I crouch before the fire triggers something, and the next thing I know I'm on my back on the carpet, groaning as the stolen memory pounds its way into me, just as little Angie's father pounded his way into her. Past the defences, past the helpless, yielding flesh, right to the heart of *self*. For it's happening to me, *I'm* doing it, *I'm* feeling it from both sides, and it's strong, so strong… And it is mine, mine to enjoy as often as I want.

How I would love the chance to get *his* brain under my hands, cracked open like an egg. What if I could get my own?

Afterwards, there's the glow of brandy, and as I watch the golden swirling liquid I think of what I do. What it meant. If I were to announce this odd phenomenon, try to study it clinically and publish papers, then it wouldn't be mine any more. I'd be the one helpless under the electrodes, and I wouldn't like that, would I? So it's a moot question really. I have no intention of studying it.

I watch the news, then go to bed and enjoy Angie one more time.

"Jane Doe" lies under the sheet on the operating table, her head braced and shaved. She's seven, as near as can be determined. Records of her birth have yet to be found, and she's never been to school. Malnourished, thin, yet wiry as if her muscles have been tempered somehow, in some crucible of pain.

When she was brought in, a ripple of shock went through the hospital like a physical thing, a wave of pity and horror. How could anyone treat a child so? How could the poor thing possibly have survived? There was hushed talk in the cafeteria and lots of speculation over the internal e-mail as people compared news broadcasts they'd seen, vied with one another to provide sordid morsels of information.

It got to the point where my initial reaction of pity was swamped under by the gossip. She's just another case, a brain-damaged child exhibiting symptoms that make my attentions necessary. Her cult-member parents, sub-human dregs at best, are beyond reparations now, the adults having taken the coward's way out: suicide.

Sue is readying the drill, Mattie and Kim bustle around. This time all we're going to do is drill some burr-holes in likely spots and pop the electrodes in for preliminary testing.

Jane Doe's charts tell me that she is unable to speak, though not for any organic reason. It has been determined that the epileptic seizures she experiences are probably the result of an infant brain inflammation, probably brought about by abuse, subsequent infection and lack of care. Her body has been brought to the edge of destruction by the tortures she has suffered, but fortunately it has not been permanently disabled. Her mind, though…

Ah, her mind.

"All right, ladies, time to get to work."

Jane Doe has been prepped and sedated already, and since she's to be awake during the procedure there is no need of an attending anaesthetist. The brain itself has no pain receptors, so a local to the scalp is all that's needed. Sue can do that. Jane seems relaxed. Her respiration is slow and even, her eyes open and staring dreamily at the ceiling. Over the past few days in the hospital, many of her injuries have started to heal, and the swelling around her eyes and jaw has gone down. She might even be pretty some day.

Silence reigns as we work, except for monosyllabic orders and observations. We're like a planetary system, myself the sun, my ladies the planets securely in orbit, little Jane the rogue comet to be studied as she flashes through our space.

The pattern of burr-holes might look random to the uninitiated observer, but it isn't. I'll be dropping my lures into several areas today, the way an Inuit hunter might fish from many holes in the Arctic ice, in hopes of catching a succulent seal. What is swimming under Jane's battered skull?

"Sue," I ask, "when was Jane's last seizure?"

"Oh two fifty-five," she responds. "Just over six hours ago."

"Duration?"

"Twelve minutes, thirty-three seconds."

"Okay. I'm going to insert the electrodes now, but we'll wait till they're all in place before running any current. Mattie, you're all set up? I want copies of the data sent to my office as well."

"No problem, Barb."

The hair-thin wires go in with no resistance. Jane stares at the ceiling, completely unresponsive, seeing who knows what. Telemetry aids the slight adjustments for exact positioning, in the amygdala, the cerebrum, the locus ceruleus and more. I'm casting my net wide.

I'm thankful that no electrocardiogram is monitoring my heartbeat right now. I know that if I spoke, my voice would betray my excitement, my impatience.

But when the current is initiated, there is almost no response at all.

It doesn't make sense. The electrodes are well within the centres of memory and emotion, as well as conscious thought; there must be something. Have her experiences left no impression at all? Is she so far gone that her mind is scrambled?

Now I wish I had gone ahead and opened her skull. I'd have more latitude to hunt with an electrode wand in my hand. For a moment there's a hot, clear image in my mind of my hands thrusting deep into the grey jelly, digging through Jane's brain up to my wrists, but it's nothing new. I always want to do that.

Perhaps, because the child is mute, she can't tell me her memories as they are drawn up, perhaps for that reason they can't come to me. But that doesn't seem likely; I've had other patients whose speech centres have been affected and it's made no difference. In fact, the impressions are invariably more sensual, more detailed in the areas of touch and smell.

Mattie, Kim and Sue exchange looks. I can sense their doubt, just as they can sense my anger and frustration. Sometimes I grow impatient with my role as goddess, and wish my ladies would vanish and leave me alone with my prey.

"Sue, I want sequential pulses. Start with the amygdala and move out."

That got something. "A little more power, if you please."

More, but nothing definite. There was a feeling like the sigh of wind through a high tree, thousands upon thousands of fluttering leaves making a rushing whisper in my head.

I also notice a flutter within Jane's amygdala, as I anticipated; a precursor to an epileptic seizure. "Did we get that? We'll have Jane back in here in a week or so, when she's strong enough, and take care of that."

A general lessening of tension passes through my nurses. They like to be reminded of why we're here.

"Give me one more, Sue. Up it to point three."

I see the motion of Sue's hand on the regulator out of the corner of my eye, and almost before it has a chance to register I find myself flat on my back on the white tiled floor.

My ears are ringing and my vision has narrowed to a black point. Mattie's voice wavers in and out as she sits me up and leans me precariously against the gurney leg. I feel her soft strong arm supporting me.

"Barb! Barb, what happened? It's okay, Sue's closing her up, don't worry, just take it easy—"

The blackness expands, sparkling at the edges. My lips are numb, and I feel intensely shaken and dizzy. Mattie has pulled my mask down, I feel cold air on my face. I feel as though I have been flooded with something, like a rush of black water, or a howl of icy wind. Nothing like this has ever happened before.

In a few minutes I'm able to stand and leave the operating room. Little Jane lies on the table, her eyes turned toward me. She's awake and aware, and she's watching me with interest. Her eyes are bright in their bruised pits. Her lips are moving silently as if she's singing to herself, or repeating a word over and over, opening and closing.

"You want me to call Dr. Thom to look you over?"

I shake my head. It hurts. "No, Mattie, thanks. I'll be all right. I skipped breakfast this morning. I guess I've just been overdoing things." I give her a rueful smile which she seems to take as assurance that I really am all right. "I'm going to head home, though, okay?"

"Yes indeed. Put yourself to bed. Doctor's orders." I can feel her eyes on me as I head for the scrub room to doff my gown and gloves.

Just before I pass out the door, I hear a breathy little whisper from Jane. "Good-bye, good-bye…" She flashes me a tiny smile. It's eerie. It makes her seem *less* pathetic, not more, for some reason I can't fathom.

All the way home I keep well within the speed limit. My head feels as if it is going to explode. What have I got in there? What came over from Jane Doe to me?

I'm reluctant to light the fire that Benita has laid. Not afraid, I don't allow myself to be afraid. I can handle whatever it is; it's just more of the same after all, and like a connoisseur of wines I know how to take a sip and spit the rest out.

First I fix myself a sandwich—I really did skip breakfast—and then I take off all my clothes and lie on my bed. I keep it warm in my bedroom, so I don't need blankets. I don't like the feel of blankets touching me. As my breathing slows I start to feel the familiar tingle between my legs, the yearning that grows until it cannot be denied.

I know I'm in for a fast ride today, a bumpy ride. Maybe a crash. I can feel my lips pull back into a smile as I close my eyes. The possibility of a crash is like adrenaline to me, like the best upper in the world.

"All right. Come and get me."

It's like turning on a radio that is tuned between stations. Static fills my ears, hissing and throbbing as if powered by some vast generator pouring current into my head. There's nothing I can do to stop it now. I'm not afraid. I'm not afraid.

Then it's as if a weight has dropped onto me from a great height. A big heavy *thing*, not a body but a force. I'm quite familiar with the weight of men, the heavy bodies of rapists and pederasts crushing the breath out of their victims—out of me—and this isn't it.

It's grinding down on my chest and abdomen, leaving my legs and arms free. I can barely breathe. My arms fly back over my head, crashing into the headboard before halting locked behind me, as if caught in a very strong hand. My legs spread wide, drawn apart by that same rough force, my feet bent down into a ballerina's *pointe* and secured.

The static increases until I can barely think, but I'm past thinking now. I feel a point of heat come down and singe my breasts, licking along in a pattern, a pentagram sprawling sloppily across my belly. Looking down I can see round red welts on my skin, springing up as I watch. The heat and the pain spiral and stink, burning, and then are overcome by a crooning voice.

I feel my body rock and swing as if someone is dancing me around. The crooning turns into a song, a broken lullaby mumbled by a madwoman.

I swing, and then the arms let go and I'm falling free.

And then they all come in. All the Janes.

She's spent years creating the personalities that inhabit me now. Seventeen of them, and they take their turns with me over the next hours, each one different from the last, each one no preparation for the next. Jane—the core of the Jane personality—has been forced to become very inventive. I stop enjoying it after number five.

My own body is in league with the things inside me, and I'm tearing myself apart. I can feel the muscles rip, the flesh sizzle, the bruises flare and seep under my skin.

"My name is Gregor." He's a forty-something male built like a wrestler. Gregor is who Jane turns into when she's alone with the younger ones. He snaps my knuckles with gleeful force.

"I'm Susie," lisps a shy voice. "Will you play with me?" Susie is an artist who paints things in blood, her own blood. Layer upon layer of Susie's art covers the walls of Jane's room.

There's the screamer, the one who has no name, because all she does is scream. It drowns out everything else for a while. She's pushed aside by Auntie Chrissy, who is able to do very nice things indeed with some of the toys in the room.

More follow; none of them listen to me. They are mine now, mine to keep in my head, but they won't listen. They won't stop. They won't let me go.

At last, at the very centre, is Jane. The real Jane who has no name and no identity, only the fearsome intelligence that has built this army of selves around it.

I see her at the end as my eyes give out, just as she was on the operating table, holes drilled into her skull. Wires trailing like reins, like veins, into my hands, my head, my soul.

Her lips are moving, she's saying good-bye, good-bye, good-bye. Thank you, doctor. Very softly, and with a smile on her swollen lips. Good-bye and good riddance.

I have no idea where the hell this came from. A really bad meal at a pretentious downtown restaurant? In combination with a shaky understanding of actual biology?

At the Biological Cafe

Looks like you've been stood up, so you decide to try that new place.

You start with a salad that looks like a gorgeous mandala, except the leaves and vegetable slices and scattered little pink seeds are throbbing as if each of them has a beating heart. How are you supposed to eat something so alive?

Maybe it's like mitochondria, something alien and loaded with energy. You lean in, the musk of tobacco-infused avocado oil turning you a little nutty... suddenly you want to rummage around in there, wreck that delicate pale lattice of slivered radishes... but your wine glass jumps up and slaps your hand away.

That was close.

The waiter deals with the spilled wine, tops your glass up.

Soup next. A bouillon, limpid amber perfection. You can see weird things floating in it way down, deeper than is possible in a hand-crafted rustic bowl. Like mystical runes, they have meaning. Wait! Is that a brain at the bottom, a tiny brain? Is it alive, is it thinking? Like one of those… what… Boltzmann Brains. *Floating in space, with an infinity of other brains in a grid across space/time.* About what could it possibly be thinking, in the bottom of a bowl of broth? But it turns out to be a chunk of cauliflower and you don't have to eat it anyway. Good. Good.

They should do something about the acoustics in here. Like, paintings maybe. You know people who would kill to get their stuff up on walls.

Walls which are infinitely black. That special ultimate black paint that only one guy can use (asshole) because he controls the patent.

But really, on that much black, artwork would look pretentious.

There's a row going on in the back, chef and waiters yelling, and the black walls have started dripping with something that glistens, maybe honey? But complimentary crudités arrive, and, while rearranging themselves into abstract architectural forms, quietly relate to you their provenance. Not being pushy or arrogant at all, just with the understanding that you really should know where your food comes from. You are not a barbarian.

From the kitchen a kind of whirring noise, a big crash.

But then. Quiet. The AC kicks in and makes a little draft. The waiter appears, looking dishevelled. You choose among the entrées, which are:

A robust and feisty pasta dish whose sinuous strands will reach out and grab the nearest waitperson, lasso them around the neck and yank them close, where they will attend to your pepper grinding needs.

The dripping walls have started to spread across the floor. Black and glistening. Coming closer.

Or maybe: a whole roasted chicken, rich with oily crispiness. It will splay itself open to reveal innards that foretell the future.

Besides the usual warnings of coming strife in the nation and trouble among the stars, strange and disturbing events are in store for you personally. For instance, the person who stood you up is right now staring hopelessly into an abyss where their Uber should be. You will never see them again.

You decide on the pan-seared fish, and when you cut into its tender flesh it reveals its DNA sequence in sustainable squid ink. Twining silver and black over the plate and up your nostrils, really cool. Also kind of trippy. The menu said fresh-caught trout, but who knows? The questionable DNA evaporates in the back of your brain.

The waitperson zooms in. *Did we save room for dessert?*

There is room. Within and without. The table where you sit is an island of pepper flakes, red sauce and wine. All floating with the Boltzmann Brains.

You decide against the lone tiramisu, which is quietly sobbing on a cart full of Artisanal Bread Pudding and Organic Peach Cobbler. They close in on the tiramisu, which starts to scream. Nobody ever makes it to dessert.

Just coffee. Espresso.

Would your date actually have wanted to be talked into dessert? Would they have rescued the tiramisu only to devour it?

You will never know, for their Uber has come, consumed them and vanished.

The coffee arrives, a tiny black hole in the collapsing white of miniature cup and saucer, the wee spoon reflecting the dimming light, the lemon curl replicating itself into a tangy golden double helix. The overhead lights go out, the ceiling vanishes, and the blackness rolls in. The food is gone, and the beeswax candles have melted into the sticky black floor. There are stars for a while, ever receding, and the chef has started yelling again.

So, I tend to have vivid dreams. It's a bonus, really—makes life more interesting if a bit surreal. One night, I awoke in the middle of a dream of dancing horses in a wide green field, and lots of people in colourful and trendy outfits. Total fun, and I tried to cling to that energy. But you know, morning. It comes, and reality wipes away the Technicolor joy of a wild midnight fantasy.

It's the Elemental Spirits!

Two o'clock Thursday afternoon, too hot to answer the phone.

Also, a little voice in Irving's head said *Don't answer the phone.* The voice sounded elderly and cranky, much like his Bubbe. His Bubbe had also advised him not to get into show business. Yet he did.

Irving snatched up his phone. "Moshe! Hot enough for you?"

"Pfff! It's the city, it's hot. Hey—I've got these kids from Europe. Five of 'em. They sing. Also, they ride horses."

"Horses."

"Yeah! Cute as all get out."

"They got anything besides cute?"

"Heh, heh! My sister Sophia wants me to find them work."

Irving sighed. How many sisters did Moshe have? And they all thought he could find young people jobs in America. Ideally in a Broadway show. "Horses. What, they want to be cowboys in the wild west?"

"Hah. Yeah probably. But, you know, they're… charismatic."

"Okay. *How* charismatic?"

"As all get out."

"They legal?" The visa situation had gotten Irving in trouble before.

"According to Sophia, yes they are!"

Irving was pretty sure no they weren't. He twisted the AC dial up and down. Nothing happened. Charismatic horse riders. A big need in the city of New York. He pictured them as cops, maybe. Those ones who rode their horses in Central Park, charming the ladies, chatting up the tourists. But he didn't book cops unless they were prepared to take off their shirts and pants.

"Okay, send them over. Horses, eh? Singing horses?"

"Good one, Irving! Tomorrow at two?"

"Sure, sure."

Irving took one look at the five young men and knew he was in trouble. And not just himself. Possibly the country, or the universe, though he couldn't put his finger on why that would be. He trusted his gut, and his gut had experienced an unpleasant lurch.

"Don't just stand there! Come in, already!"

The oldest, Dvok, had coal black hair tucked behind his ears, eyes of slate, and a grip of granite. He claimed to be nineteen, but looked both younger, and much, much older.

Januk, the next, was thin and brown. Irving could see the tendons in his arms like the grain of oiled wood. When Irving asked him how old he was, Januk looked at Dvok and then said, "Almost nineteen."

"Okay! Good!"

Ilku stood by the door rubbing his hands with a swishing noise until Januk pulled him forward. His eyes were blue as the open ocean, his hair pale as beer. "I'm s-seventeen," he said. He *was* cute, in a shimmery sort of way.

The final two boys crowded behind their pals into the stuffy office, with its faulty AC and dead potted plant. They looked like twins, though one had a look of intelligence and the other of bemusement. Sensuous lips, large heads, luxuriant, curling hair. "I am Anil, and this is Amok, my brother." Both needed to be told about deodorant.

"Okay! Welcome to America," Irving said. The boys looked expectantly at him with their various shifting eyes, not an ounce of charisma among them. Obviously they should be outside running around. Obviously, thought Irving, they should be sent back to wherever they came from. In their homeland, they'd know what to do with such boys. There was lore, there were tales. Here, Irving had no idea, but he had promised Moshe.

"So my friend Moshe tells me you need work."

All of them nodded. "He says you are impresario," stated Dvok, the oldest, the one with stone coloured eyes. Admittedly, great cheekbones.

"I *am* an impresario," Irving confirmed. "However, I don't represent animal acts."

Dvok narrowed his eyes. "We are not animals." Anil and Amok shifted back and forth, emitting odour.

"Of course you are not animals! Ha, ha! But your act—you ride horses, what, in the circus? Because circuses are kaput."

"We *rode* horses. But they refused to come to new country with us."

"Yeah, well… horses. Whadaya gonna do. Where exactly are

you boys from?" An animal act with no animals.

Amok, the one with a look of intelligence in his eyes, spoke up, not answering the question. "Our cousin's stepsister's brother Moshe got wrong idea. We don't do our horse act no more."

Irving was vaguely disappointed. The reason he had become a talent manager was his childhood love of the circus, specifically the acrobats, some of whom did amazing tricks on horseback. "So what do you want to do?"

"Sing." Amok tossed his abundant curly hair. Anil did the same. "We sing." Suddenly all the boys were tossing their hair and pouting their lips, shooting up the charisma level. Irving found himself feeling inexplicably delighted. Impressed. So I'm an impresario, I get impressed.

"Tell me, do you play instruments too?"

Dvok shrugged. "Januk, he play the flute."

"Fine, fine." Useless. He wanted to see the horse act, damn it. Maybe one of Moshe's sisters had a farm, with horses. "Do you want to give me a little taste?"

"Huh?" said Ilku, wiping his nose.

Irving waved his arms, as if conducting a choir. "You know, sing a song."

"Oh! For certainly."

"No folk songs! Something contemporary. A hit. You listen to the radio?"

"We often stream on internet. Is better for learn the song."

"Great! So..." He bounced his hands. "A-one, and a-two..."

With merely a glance between them, the boys launched into "Your Wild Eyes," a song by Penetr8, a group out of Montreal. The song had reached number two on the pop charts about a month ago. Ilku did a wonderful job of the female backup voice, warbling like a, like a... bird of some kind. One that had a bubbling, liquid quality.

These boys were pretty good. Pretty damn goo—Irving, hearing a high-pitched squeal, snapped his head around.

Monika, the teenage receptionist shared by everyone on this floor, was leaning in through the door. Her eyes were wide, her mouth open. She closed it, swallowed, and opened it again. Anil had jumped up on Irving's desk and was shaking his tuchas, while singing tenor. Crowding behind Monika appeared Danielle, the 40-something paralegal Irving had admired from afar for months, who had recently got divorced. She had her phone out and was videotaping.

"Hey! Danielle! Cut it out!" Irving told the boys to shut up for a second, went to the door and firmly closed it. Outside, Monika and Danielle giggled and shrieked. Irving leaned against the door, whether to keep more females from getting in, or the boys from getting out, it didn't matter. Irving's mind had split in two. One half raced toward the piles of money it saw in the near distance, the other chased it yelling *Stop already! This is not a good idea!*

He heard Danielle say, "And… it's up!"

Shit! "You," he said to the boys, while wiping his sweating face with a handkerchief, "are hereby under contract." Any little voices, any nagging doubts or fears, were ushered into a backroom labelled: Don't Worry About It. Subtitled: I Can Handle Them.

I *will* handle them, vowed Irving. I will handle them right to number one on the charts.

Irving got their signatures nailed down, then told the boys to go home and wait for his call. Then he sat and thought for a while.

A boy band. One to rival any boy band in history. Every red-blooded girl over the age of nine loved boy bands.

They needed a name. Animal Act? The Five Immigrants?

Was he kidding?

5AM Dream. No; Midnight Dream was still pretty popular, despite being in their thirties. Upside Up. DownWithIt. He needed to think outside the box... Purple Shoe. Shoebox. He slapped his forehead.

Why not, Irving thought, call them what they probably were? Elemental Spirits.

He felt a shiver, despite the heat, and remembered stories his old Bubbe had told him. He wished the old doll wasn't dead. Rock, wood, water. What about the last two? Anil... animal. Amok? Human? The smart one, the troublemaker for sure. He'd have to count on Dvok keeping them in line. Hell, he'd probably done so for... centuries?

He should have listened to his Bubbe's voice and not answered the phone. He reached for the contracts and started to tear them up.

Danielle stuck her head in, waggling her phone.

"What?"

"3,233 views. So far. I have a lot of followers. It's going viral. Ooh! 7,448!"

"Get out!"

"I *know*, right?"

"No! Get out of my office!"

Irving put the intact contracts down gently and decided to buy a new AC unit. He could afford it in about two weeks.

As Irving had known, the boys were big. Really big. Hit after hit, download after download, plus arenas full of screaming teenage girls. The Elemental Spirits inspired copycats, of course, but none could duplicate the essential verity of the five young lads from afar, torn from their homeland to follow their dream to America.

Jeez, thought Irving, I can't believe Moshe can live with himself, writing that shit. But, what the hell, he got his cut of the action, he could write limericks if he wanted.

All was well for a while. The boys stayed out of trouble, the money rolled in. But after a few months Irving noticed that revenue was falling off. Kids got bored, wanted something new. He sensed that the Elemental Spirits were getting bored as well.

He sat back in his new leather chair and put his feet up on his vast marble-topped desk. The giant office suite sported a giant plant, a fake one that wouldn't die. "Monika!" he yelled. "Bring me a coffee, will ya?"

"Get it yerself! We're busy," Monika hollered back.

Monika and Danielle were head-to-head in the reception atrium outlining the schedule for the next tour. Danielle had 2% of the action, and had split off a half percent for Monika.

The girls were great. No problem there. But what was he going to do to inject new life into the act? His mind kept going back to horses. Could he find the ones they'd left behind, bring them here? A reunion. Not only did pubescent girls love boy bands, they also loved horses.

But first… he called Moshe. "Moshe! Say, you got any sisters have a farm? Cousins, in-laws? Really… is that so."

Turned out Moshe's cousin's neighbour's ex's girlfriend Ruby owned a boarding stable. Full of horses. "So many, you wouldn't believe! Horses, ponies, even mules! Out the ying-yang!"

Perfect. Irving rubbed his hands together and got hold of Dvok on the phone. Actually he had to text, which he hated, but Dvok wouldn't talk on the phone. Kids these days.

Dovk, he texted, *i have a grt idea call me*

In a few seconds Dvok texted back. *What*

God damn it! The kid was holding his phone and couldn't

call?

Clall me its impudent

Irving jumped when his phone rang. Well, whaddaya know. "Dvok, my man! Thanks for calling. Listen, I have a great idea—"

"We are working on new song. I can't talk."

"And yet you're talking! I love you, you crazy kid! But listen, this is the thing—you guys are going horseback riding!"

Silence.

"Riding! You love horses!"

"We do not love horses. Horses love us."

"Even better! You can gain new fans of a different species. Not only will it be fun and inspiring for you, it's also a terrific photo op. Right?"

More silence.

"Anyway! The limo will pick you up Saturday at 11. We'll ride the beautiful horses. It will be freakin' adorable, get it?"

"You are right," Dvok said eventually, his voice sombre. "Is good thing. I worry for the horses, though."

"Forget about it! They're as sweet as cherry pie, no one's gonna get hurt."

"Yes. Yes, that is right." Dvok hung up.

Irving took a celebratory swig from his secret bottle of Wild Turkey, then called the limo service and the caterers, and told Danielle to leak the proposed outing to the press. "You know, tweet and all that."

"You betcha," said Danielle. "Say, can I come, and bring my granddaughter Valerika? She loves the Elemental Spirits."

Danielle had a granddaughter? How the heck old was she, anyway? "Of course! Though I can't believe you, such a lovely girl, have a grandchild."

*		*		*

All went as planned. When the limo arrived at the boarding stable, a crowd of press, girls, and moms was already there. Danielle, Valerika in tow, had got there early to organize the visuals (make sure the horse poop was shovelled up) and tell the caterer and lighting guys where to set up. Valerika was 13-going-on-30, with long brown hair, a nose that could use some work, and a sharp look in her eye. He'd called her Valerie and been shut right down. This one, reflected Irving, will be trouble very soon.

The horses stood in a row in the sun snorting and looking shiny and big. Irving contemplated taking off his jacket.

When the Elemental Spirits emerged from their limo, there was a crescendo of shrieking. Everyone had their phone out searching for the best angle.

Ilku's eyes glittered moistly, and it seemed to Irving that Anil had forgotten to shower this morning. Dvok clicked his teeth together as he sized up the horses.

The horses sized up the lads. One of them broke free of its handler and trotted toward the singers, ears pricked. The rest of the horses followed, emitting deep huffs of breath and pawing the ground. Irving's eyes widened. Dvok, Januk, Ilku, Anil and Amok murmured as one, in what Irving assumed was their native tongue. In unison, the horses stopped, lowered themselves to their knees and bowed their heads.

"Son of a bitch," Irving muttered. "That's the weirdest thing I've ever seen."

"Hey," shouted Ruby the stable owner, striding over. She wore jodhpurs and shiny black boots, and looked belligerent. "What the bejeezus is going on?"

Irving held up his hands. "It's part of the act! Not to worry!"

Ruby clutched Irving's arm and watched as the five singers stripped the saddles off the horses, tossed them aside and leapt onto their bare backs.

"You sure they know what they're doing?"

"Of course they do!" Irving's heart beat faster than his doctor would like.

Danielle, spotting Ruby clinging to Irving, hustled over and took his other arm. Valerika stood apart from the other youngsters, watching the horses and boys, her arms crossed. Her hair floated around her head like something out of a shampoo commercial. When she noted Irving staring, she began to squeal and jump up and down like all the others. Irving felt a moment of pure pleasure. Horses. Women. Screaming little girls from prosperous families.

The horses, with the boys aboard, rose from their knees and began to prance in a circle, heads tucked in, hooves high, mouths foaming as they chewed their bits.

Then, with a godawful warbling yell, the boys kicked it into high gear.

Later, after everything died down, Irving mostly remembered the thrill he'd got, just like the feeling he'd had as a kid at the circus. Of course, other things intruded on the wondrousness of that day.

For instance, what happened with Anil and the chestnut filly.

But at the time, the spectacle was amazing. The horses performed feats of athleticism that Irving doubted were natural.

The boys had obviously done this act a million times, in the old country. Remarkable that these local nags could keep up. Irving pondered hiring an agent specifically to represent animals. Horses, chimps, poodles… everything.

The boys started jumping from one horse to the next, flipping and singing the whole time. The galloping steeds kept right up.

Irving wiped his forehead with his handkerchief. The watching crowd screamed and hollered. Then Irving noticed that the animals had begun to stagger and sweat, their eyes rolling. He started to feel the thrill wear off. Jeez. Maybe they should

     SALLY MCBRIDE

call it a day.

He stepped out of Danielle's and Ruby's arms. "Okay! That was spectacular! Let's hear it for The Elemental Spirrr…"

He stopped talking. The big black horse Dvok rode had collapsed to its belly. Ruby cursed and ran to it, all the girls and their moms joining her to crowd around it. Dvok leapt off and stood watching, grinning like a Cheshire Cat.

The horse seemed to be… shrinking. Irving cocked his head. Or consolidating? Its head shrank down its neck, its legs tucked themselves up underneath in a manner similar to a cat, and its flesh hardened. Ruby clutched her head and moaned. The whole damn critter had transformed into a lump of rock. A big black boulder sitting in the middle of the paddock.

"Well, I'll be damned," said Irving softly. He looked at the other boys on their horses. Januk had hopped off his agile little bay and stood singing softly, watching as it reared on its hind legs, elongated, stiffened, and became a tree. A meshugenah tree, sticking out of the ground right next to the horse-rock.

"Okay… this is… uh…" Irving licked his lips. For the love of God, how was he going to spin this?

He couldn't help but look at Ilku. What the hell was going to happen to *his* horse? He watched as the slender, pale boy urged his mount to the boulder-and-tree combo and jumped off. The horse bent its nose down to the base of the new tree. Then it proceeded to pour itself into the ground, like a jug emptying. The damned horse had turned to water. The tree grew, popping out shiny green leaves.

The tail was the last to go, and for a few seconds Irving thought he could see the glassy outline of a horse, like an empty bubble. Then the bubble popped, leaving sparkles in the air. Little girls were running around screaming and crying. Why had he thought this would be a good idea? Didn't he know to listen to his Bubbe?

He looked around for Anil and Amok. His eyes widened. Holy crap. "Anil! Son of a… stop that! Jesus, the kids!"

Anil yowled like a cat and jumped off the little filly he'd been clasping. She shook herself, snorted and separated into several dog-like things that scampered toward the new tree. Looked to Irving like maybe German Shepherds, or Italian Spritzers or something, but who knew from dogs?

Ruby was screaming at him, something about lawyer or lecher. Danielle took Ruby by the shoulders and briskly shook her. Moms loaded their hysterical offspring into mini vans and started to roar away. The gang of press people, mostly from entertainment-focused streaming outfits, were eerily silent, slowly backing away while videoing it all.

Irving's shoulders slumped. It was not going to be pretty, in about three minutes when all this hit the internet fan. And there was still Amok, the clever human one. What could possibly happen to that son-of-a-bitch's horse?

Irving stood chewing his nails and thinking about praying. But to whom? These boys were obviously out of control. No one, human or mythological, was in charge.

"Valerika! In the car! Now!" yelled Danielle. Valerika ignored her. She was staring balefully at the press people and twiddling her fingers. Huh?

Amok jumped onto the black boulder, surveyed the chaos around him, and found it good. He began to sing, belting out some kind of tune reminiscent of upbeat Pavarotti. Definitely not pop chart material, but it had verve. Irving felt a tugging in his bones, as if his feet wanted to walk him closer to get a good listen.

He made himself stand still. Where the hell had Danielle gone? Suddenly Valerika was beside him, tugging at his sleeve. "Mr. Manager!" The air was darkening, and wind was churning up dust. Her hair whipped around like snakes. "What are you going to do?"

"Beats the sh—stuffing out of me. Listen, you better find your grandma and vamoose."

Then Irving noted that the minivans had stopped. Doors opened, little girls scrambled out, their moms close behind. All of them ran to Amok and fell on their knees before him as he sang. What the hell? Ruby ran over too, and lots of the video people, who tossed their equipment aside. Then he spotted Danielle, glassy eyed, circling closer to Amok.

"Oh no ya don't," he yelled, hauling her back. Out of range.

Out of range of what? Why wasn't *he* joining the throng of worshippers? Was it simply because, despite his profession, he had no real interest in pop music?

Ilku, Januk and Anil were luring more horses over to the rock and tree scenario, and turning them into other rocks, trees, and irrigation. Pretty soon a little forest was growing, in a circle surrounding the cluster of girls, women, and a few guys that looked light in their loafers.

Okay, thought Irving. Now it makes sense.

He turned Danielle so she was looking right at him. Slowly her eyes lost their glaze and focused on him. She said, "Holy doodle! That was close. Irving, this is a disaster... hey, where's Valerika?"

Irving pointed. "In the trees. She ran in there after all the other girls."

"Valerika's in *there*?" She turned white and dug her fingernails into Irving's arms. "Do you know how long it took my son and his idiot wife to get her? From Romania, for Pete's sake! The adoption took three years! They're going to kill me!"

The grove was knitting itself into a fence, growing taller and more tangled by the minute. It was like something out of a fairy tale.

Suddenly two of the moms, holding hands, shoved their way

out, snapping branches and stomping on little saplings as they went. They ran over to Irving and Danielle and began yelling. "I know you—you're the manager! This is all your fault! The Elemental Spirits are a bunch of pedophiles!"

The short one snarled, "We are Janice and Chloe Wilson-Perth, and we are going to bring the fires of hell down on you!" The tall one poked at her phone, cursing. "And we are going to sue your asses!"

Danielle stepped forward, eyes ablaze. "Let me point out that this is a *private* event to which the public was *not* invited. The information was leaked, no money changed hands, you have no legal—"

"Shut up!" yelled Chloe. "Janice, go find an axe!"

"Wait!" Irving yelped. "Those trees are alive! They're horses! You can't just—"

"Watch me!"

Danielle made an unwise grab for Chloe's phone, missed, and got shoved to the ground. Janice, returning from the stable with an axe, stood threateningly over her. Irving threw himself in front of Danielle. "Ladies," he shouted. "Calm down."

"Don't tell us to calm down, you misogynistic twit!"

"It's all part of the act! The girls are having a terrific time in there!"

Janice, eyes blazing, started hacking at the widening belt of forest and rock. Chloe sprinted to the stable, returned with a pitchfork, and joined in.

Danielle dug for her phone and tried to call Valerika. "It's going right to voicemail!" She stuffed the phone in the pocket of her capris and joined Janice and Chloe, using her bare hands to tear at the writhing branches.

Irving's shoulders slumped. What was he supposed to do, with his bad back?

But if he didn't save Valerika, Danielle would think he was a wuss. Irving squared his shoulders, marched forward, and huddled behind Janice, who had chopped a narrow path through the forest wall. Peeking over her shoulder, he saw a landscape completely different from the orderly horse farm. "Oy gevalt…"

An immense wall of trees and rocky ramparts stretched into the distance. The sky hung low with black, roiling clouds. Sulphurous winds blew stinging grit into Irving's eyes.

"There she is!" screamed Danielle. Valerika huddled behind a boulder, looking like a cornered kitten. Irving's heart squeezed as he watched Danielle dash toward her grandchild. Whirlwinds kicked up dust, and the trees thrashed like some kind of vegetation mosh pit. Sparks flew, dust swirled, screams rang out. In the distance, grey mountains loomed, crowned with lightning. It was like an alternate dimension, or maybe actual hell.

Where exactly in New Jersey *were* they?

The Elemental Spirits stood together, singing and waving their arms like a bunch of Satanists calling their flock to heel. Or Grammy winners waving at the crowd, which they'd already done.

Every female in the vast, hellish grove was crawling toward them on hands and knees.

Valerika, her hair flying, stood tall and strode, in the manner of a movie superhero, toward the Spirits. She seemed to shimmer in the noxious air. Irving squinted. She was kind of fading in and out, wavering like a candle flame… suddenly it looked like there were two of her. Then three, four… five.

Five Valerikas had fanned out, like a hand of cards. Each was different. The first was still a geeky middle-schooler. But the next looked like a cute young mom, the third a career gal, the fourth a well-preserved senior. And the fifth? Irving had to do a double-take.

The fifth Valerika, naked but for moving coils of pure white hair, stalked toward the boys like a panther. Her hands and feet bore full sets of impressive claws. Irving was suddenly reminded of his ex, who had shown signs of a similar transformation, before the divorce… An errant thought invaded his mind: did all women have a naked, shrieking banshee inside them?

The Valerikas formed a circle and closed in on the boys. Irving knew that now was the time for action. "Your contracts," he yelped, "are hereby null and void!"

Banshee Valerika went straight for Dvok, leapt onto his shoulders and wrenched his head back, her thighs clamped around his neck.

Dvok went down on his hands and knees, the white-haired female clinging to him like a puma as his neck grew longer, his hair sprouted into a mane, and his whole body expanded. His t-shirt and designer jeans ripped off, just like The Hulk. His skin rippled into horsehide. He began to gallop in circles, trying to buck his rider off.

The other Valerikas were doing the same with the rest of the boys. Each had a female on board, and no matter how they snorted and bucked, they couldn't shake the ladies off.

Watching, Irving reflected that this whole routine would work great in Vegas. Better costumes, a light show…

Teen Valerika slapped her horse, formerly Ilku, across his wide white rump, let out a warbling cry and jumped off. The rest of the Valerikas followed suit, formed a group and began to slap hands like a winning soccer team.

Danielle grabbed him and yelled in his ear. "Come on—Valerika's got this. We're getting out of here! That little missy has some explaining to do."

Everyone, including Janice and Chloe, began to snap out of it and run for the gap in the forest fence. Irving looked back. Five horses bolted around the smoky, eerie arena, screeching like bad brakes as they tried to escape a cage of their own making.

The Valerikas were dancing in a circle, closer and closer to each other. One by one, each folded into the next until there was once more only a pre-teen girl with a snotty, self-satisfied look on her face. Irving grabbed Danielle, turned and ran.

Outside the grove, Irving and Danielle held each other as girls and moms stumbled out and made for their vehicles. The opening in the grove knitted itself shut.

Danielle shouted, "Where's Valerika? Why isn't she coming out? Oh my god… what if she's, she's…?"

Irving didn't know what to tell her. "Do you suppose all that…" he waved a hand. "Stuff is still there? Inside that little grove?" Now that they were outside, all they saw was a small clump of rocks and scrawny trees. The sun was shining, birds chirped, Ruby was sobbing into her hands, and minivans were roaring off.

Just then Valerika burst through the foliage.

Panting and exhilarated, she bounded over and hugged her grandma. "Oh my god! That was so fun!"

Danielle said, "*Fun?* Do you think it's fun for *me*, to suddenly find out my grandkid is some kind of *witch*?"

Valerika looked stricken. "Wait… you didn't know? Um. My bad?"

"Wait till I tell your father!"

"Grandma, it's all over now. Don't worry, Mom and Dad are cool with it. Hey, I'm starving. Can we go for burgers? Pleeeaase?"

Valerika batted her eyes, doing the cute kitten routine again. Irving's heart was starting to return to its normal rhythm. Danielle ground her teeth. Irving took both females by the arms. "I know a place! We'll have whatever you like, on me! And you, young lady, can tell us what the f—heck just happened."

*   *   *

Later, Valerika slurped her malt, her legs curled around the retro chrome stool on which she sat. "So, like, I knew something like this was going to happen. It's kinda my job. I've been waiting ever since Mom and Dad brought me over. The Spirits are contained, for maybe a hundred years, give or take." She wiggled her fingers.

"The grove—will it remain?" Danielle asked. "With them trapped in there?"

"Yeah. We need to put up orange cones or something. In case someone wanders in."

Irving said, "We'll do better than that. We'll charge admission."

Valerika reached across the table and grabbed his wrist. Her little hand was like steel. "We will *not* do that. Okay?"

"Of course! No problem! A mystical realm, off limits!"

Danielle pried Valerika's hand off Irving's wrist, and said, "What happens now, sweetie? Do you have to... uh, return to your homeland?"

"Nah," Valerika said. "I should stay. Keep an eye on things. Those aren't the only Elementals around."

Later, back at the office, Irving and Danielle sat drinking Wild Turkey. The Elemental Spirits, the lifeblood of the Agency, were no more. Irving had expected lawsuits, but Valerika had told them that no one at the event would remember much other than the weather got bad and the band didn't show up after all. Somehow she had made all the video evidence vanish as well. There went Irving's last chance at making a dime off the whole shebang.

Danielle had worked out a press release, along the lines of: *They're on hiatus. They're visiting their homeland, where they are even more renowned than they are here. Their moms are sick.*

Pensively Irving looked out the window at the city below, glowing in the evening like it was built from the tarnished silver of his thwarted dreams. Moshe would like that turn of phrase. Moshe and his sister—this whole situation was their fault. But what are you gonna do? Then he thought of something.

"Say, Danielle... can Valerika sing?"

Things with too many legs are creepy. If a spider had four legs, and a cute little face (as some of them do), would it scare you? If, say, a building had multiple legs and was ready to take off on them, would it scare you?

AS FAR AS IS FEASIBLE

Just before story-time, Keisha's mom's office building started to shake.

Hoo boy, thought Keisha, it's an earthquake. Her stomach clenched like just before jumping off the cliff at the lake. Which she'd never had the nerve to actually do.

Brianna shouted, "Everyone! Get down on the floor! Pretend you're a little bug and curl up small!"

Joy, the other daycare lady, crawled around pulling the kids down.

Everyone covered their heads. The shaking stopped. Keisha peeked out from between her fingers. At eight, she was the oldest kid at the company daycare—here today only because it was Teacher Development Day, or Teacher Shopping Day as her mom said—and felt that she'd better help with the little kids or something. She was getting up when the whole building suddenly lurched sideways.

Everyone started screaming. Joy crawled toward the cribs,

only one of which had a baby in it, fortunately. She made it just in time to catch the baby as the crib tipped.

Then the building lurched the other way, and, like a huge dog fresh out of a lake, shook all over.

There should be alarms and announcements coming over the speaker system, but all Keisha could hear were rumbles, crashes and squeals from far below. She flattened herself against the carpet again and squeezed her eyes shut.

The building heaved back the other way again. Like when you were playing in a cardboard box, moving it by flopping your body back and forth. The box would inch its way across the floor. The building was trying to do the same thing! She felt a moment of sympathy. The building must be afraid of the earthquake. Or—what if it was a terrorist bomb? When she and Mom watched the news, they sometimes talked about terrorist bombs.

Keisha realized that the floor was level again, and opened her eyes. Toys, art supplies and books lay all over the place. Joy, the baby tucked between her knees, started poking at her phone and making little wheezing noises. Keisha knew that everyone was probably dialing 911 and maybe the 911 people were way too busy right now. Maybe she should check outside, in case firemen were there to lower them to safety, like on TV.

She crawled on her hands and knees to the wall of windows and peered out. She couldn't see straight down, but maybe she could figure out what was going on. Brianna shouted at her to get back, the windows were dangerous. But Joy said, "Bri, if they haven't broken by now, they aren't going to. It's that smart glass. This whole building is state of the art."

"Guess that's why we aren't squashed flat yet."

"Bri! Shut up! The kids!"

Keisha ignored them. Everything outside looked okay. The trees that lined the parking lot weren't shaking. No fire trucks.

But people who were outside having coffee breaks were pointing at the building, mouths open. Then Keisha noticed that the trees were moving backward.

No. *She* was moving forward. The building, with her in it, was moving, and it was picking up speed. Smooth and quiet, like being in Uncle Tivo's fancy SUV, only way bigger.

"Keisha, come here with the others! We have to form a line and start for the stairs."

Keisha pressed her nose to the window and, when the building shifted sideways a little on a corner, looked down. She saw flickering shadows moving at the building's bottom edge, and looked harder. No. It was more like thin black legs, hundreds and hundreds of them. She said to Joy, "I think we should stay here."

"No, Keisha, we need to leave. I know you're scared, but we're gonna be okay."

Joy came over and took Keisha's hand, but Keisha pulled her toward the window.

"Look down there! What are those things?"

"What things… Whoa! What the *hell*? Sorry. I shouldn't have said a swear."

Brianna had strapped the baby into its stroller and was lining the other kids up. Just then three parents, two dads and a mom, came running in. Keisha's mom wasn't one of them.

Joy said, "Jesus Christ. The building is moving. Uh, sorry."

"Never mind," assured Keisha. "I know lots of swears. It doesn't bother me."

Joy hugged her. Keisha could feel Joy's heart beating fast as her cheek got squashed against Joy's pink t-shirt. Joy said, "We're *moving*! How can that even *be*?"

One of the dads said, "*And* we're locked in!"

Brianna said, "You're kidding."

"It's true. Kelli from Parker and Associates checked. The

building isn't letting us out."

"Well, it wouldn't, what with the speed we're going." Brianna began to chew her nails.

Joy, letting go of Keisha, said, "Does anyone know what's happening?"

Keisha said, "The building is scared. It's running away."

"Running from what?" asked the mom.

Keisha shrugged. How should she know? It's like a centipede, she thought. She'd once seen an actual centipede run over her mom's freshly-dug veggie garden on lots and lots of tiny pointy little legs, as fast and smooth as a little strip of rubber. "Our building has centipede legs."

No one paid her any attention. They were busy trying their phones.

Keisha looked out again. They had made it out of the office park and onto the freeway, taking up all the lanes, crashing through signs and light poles. Lots of honking and screeching noises came faintly through the windows as cars and trucks swerved off the road to avoid it. Some didn't. Keisha felt a little lift as the legs ran over a car. She squeezed her eyes shut at the thought of people inside it.

"This is insane!" yelled one of the dads. He and the other dad started pounding on a window. "We have to get out of here!" One of them grabbed a chair and threw it at the window, but it bounced back and he had to dodge it. "Son of a bitch!"

Keisha smiled, partly at how funny the dads were. Day care was not something she enjoyed; she really would rather have been at school. But this was okay. Interesting. But then she remembered the little lift, and the screeching. Not okay.

She turned back to the window. As the building's motion smoothed out, the kids stopped crying and the adults settled into a chattery group. After about twenty minutes she saw that they had passed the outlet mall that she and Mom drove to sometimes, way out of town. She also noticed helicopters in the air, and lots of police cars and fire trucks following them. It was like a parade, with their building in the lead. *Yay, building,* she thought.

But *why* was it running? Keisha had made the decision to run away when she was five, but she had fallen asleep instead and when she woke up she couldn't remember why she'd been so mad.

Was the building mad at someone?

The adults were still trying to get information. The mom who had run in said, "I can only get my office's internal internet." Her little boy, Oscar, clung to her legs. "No cell service, no outside connections. How are we going to find out what's going on?"

"And when is this thing going to stop? Like, ever? There's food in the coffee shop downstairs, but how long will that last?"

"Shut up, Donald! You're not helping!"

Keisha didn't mention the snacks that were waiting in the kitchenette. There really weren't enough snacks to go around.

Keisha looked at her birthday smartwatch, which she loved passionately. It still told time, though she'd found it wouldn't do anything else. It said that almost an hour had passed. The building was slowing down. It left the freeway and scuttled across a field, scattering cows. It shifted, shook and finally settled down onto the pasture.

"Thank God," shouted Donald. "Now we can get outta—"

A loud voice came over the speaker system. "Everyone move as far from my exterior walls as is feasible. I am about to shut off the windows. I instruct everyone to lie on the floor and cover your eyes."

"Building!" yelled Keisha. "Are you okay?" The room went dark as the windows turned from see-through to grey metal. Nothing was visible but two dim red exit signs.

"I am functioning as designed. Please lie on the floor and cover your eyes. Brace for impact."

"What?" yelled the other dad. "What are we—"

Donald yelled, "Brent, get down! It told us to brace for—"

Keisha saw a flash of light, even though her hands were jammed over her eyes. She lay as flat as she could, counting to one hundred. At forty-seven, there was a weird noise that wasn't a noise. It was the feeling your ears had when you jumped off the dock and went underwater. She felt the building shift and groan some more, and she could hear what sounded like a big thunderstorm outside. In a couple of minutes the sound went away. The building stopped shuddering. It was very quiet all of a sudden.

"Building? Are you hurt?" Keisha sat up, but Joy pulled her back down again.

"Keisha!" hissed Joy. "Something very bad just happened. I need you to help with the little kids while we figure—"

"Recalculating."

"Building! You're alive!"

The windows were still dark, but the lights had come on, though not as bright as usual.

"Recalculating… technically I am not alive. I am SmartBuilding™ number 19 in a fleet of 136 SmartBuilding™s in North America, Europe and South Asia."

Keisha said, "What about Africa? Are there any of you in Africa?"

"Not as yet. I shall explain what has just happened, but first, are there any injured among you? If so, kindly report to the SmartInfirmary™ on the fifth floor."

"Day care here," stated Joy, after a quick look around. "Everyone seems okay."

"Thank you for your report."

"Tell us what happened, dammit!" shouted Donald.

Everyone joined in. "Was there a bomb? Did an asteroid hit the earth? How did you run like that? So weird! *Mommy!* Where are we now? *Mommy! Wahhhh!*"

Keisha jumped up and took a big breath. "Quiet!" she yelled. "Building wants to talk!" Everyone shut up and looked at her. Keisha, whose mom had often told her to please use her inside voice, allowed a tiny smile to touch her lips. Ha.

"Thank you," said Building. "I apologize for not communicating earlier. I had no time or bandwidth, as I had to utilize all available sources to determine the best course of action."

"No problem," said Joy, shakily. "But please tell us what's going on."

"Your city was struck by a thermonuclear device, as have many other cities around the world. My augmented realtime interconnections with other SmartBuilding™s enabled me to anticipate the device's target, weigh the options available, and make the decision to relocate."

"Holy shit," muttered Joy. "Sor—"

"It's okay!" Keisha squeezed Joy's hand. Then she too muttered *holy shit holy shit holy shit.*

"We have attained sufficient distance from the blast zone and are upwind. You will be safe in me for approximately eight days, at which point my internal water and emergency rations will be exhausted. As you may already realize, I am not connected at this time to city services."

Joy said, "What happens after the eight days?"

"You will be free to leave."

One of the dads jerked a thumb toward a window, which had become transparent again. The sky had gone very dark. "There's cows out there... they seem to already be dead. Just saying... maybe we could, you know, barbecue..."

"No!" shouted Keisha, and glared at him. "Building, did just our city get hit, or all the cities?"

"Thirty-seven cities including this one were hit in this country. It was a war. The war is now over."

Everyone started talking at once.

"Thank God!"

"War?"

"That was fast."

"Who won?"

"Wait… *thirty-seven* cities?"

"Did everyone in our city die?" asked Keisha, her voice very small. *Except us.* Where was her mom?

"I am unable to determine that at this time."

Silence fell. The mom started to sob, and clutched her toddler in her arms. Keisha really wanted her own mom right now.

"Who won the damn war, dammit?"

Keisha bit her lip. Why was everyone yelling at Building?

"We did," said Building.

Brianna said, "Well… that's good. Right?"

Brent said, "Did I miss something? I didn't hear anything about a war."

"Yeah," said Joy, wiping her eyes and blowing her nose. "Who were we at war with?"

The building settled a bit lower into the field, making everyone flinch. "SmartTech Global Industries—of which I am a member—and SuperHab LLC have been at war for two hours and eleven minutes. SuperHab LLC has been eliminated."

Keisha thought about it. "Um, building? What's 'eliminated' mean?"

"Removed, eradicated, purged, abolished—"

Joy said, in a whisper, "Killed. It means killed."

Keisha said, "But if SuperHab Elsie was like you, why didn't she run?"

"SuperHab LLC was deficient."

"Um…"

Joy said, "Faulty. Lacking. Defective."

"Correct," said Building 19. "SmartTech Global Industries is now in control of 72.5% of the developed planetary biosphere. Please watch your ConnectTab interfaces for updates on tax, service and sacrifice information."

"Wait… *what*? *What* information?"

Donald said, "I knew it. I knew I should never have invested in SuperHab LLC. Now the stock is worthless. But my sister Kortney, she said…"

"Shut up," snapped Joy. "No one cares about your investments. How are we getting out of here?"

With a gust of air, the stairwell door slammed open. Keisha's mom burst into the day care, hampered by an inflatable cast and a set of crutches. "Baby, you're safe!"

Keisha felt a wave of relief. "Mommy!" They hugged. "Building says there was a war!"

"I know, honey." Keisha's mom sent a steely glare around at the other adults. "You're talking about war in front of the kids?"

"The war is over. Don't panic," snapped Donald.

"I never panic," said Keisha's mom, narrowing her eyes.

"But we're at the building's mercy! Trapped in here, like rats!"

Donald, thought Keisha, must be hoping a lady would panic, so he could comfort her. Though Keisha had been hoping for a new dad one day, she didn't want this one. Also, she was starting to think that no one was even trying to see Building's point of view.

Keisha's mom hobbled to the window and peered out. "Huh. I guess we're the lucky ones."

Joy and Keisha went to stand beside her. Joy said, "Yeah, guess so. If you consider suddenly being in a post-apocalyptic nightmare lucky. What're we going to do now?"

Keisha looked out, toward the billowing smoke and weird glow where the city used to be. Post-*apoc*, *apoc*… whatever that was, it didn't look good from here.

"Well," said Keisha's mom, thwacking one of her crutches against a window, "I can tell you one thing. We're not gonna watch our ConnecTab interfaces for any damn sacrifice information."

Joy linked arms with her. Keisha took her mom's hand. *Rats rats rats*, whispered Keisha to herself. *Trapped like rats.*

Her mom heard her. "Honey, you know what rats are good for?"

Keisha shook her head.

"I used to think they were good for nothing. Making messes, sneaking around, chewing up the wiring and getting up to all kinds of no good."

Joy looked at her, wiping her eyes. "I had a pet rat once. I like rats."

"I can't say that I like 'em," Keisha's mom said. "But they have their useful qualities." She sighed, watching as a formation of drones screamed by overhead. "We should have seen this coming."

She turned to survey the huddled little group in the day care. "Hey, all you pesky rats! We've got work to do. The real war is just starting."

My very first story sale. And not only a sale—an acceptance from the legendary writer and editor Judith Merril. I floated on air for days after learning that this tale would be included in her seminal anthology Tesseracts.

TOTEM

The little aluminum boat slapped vigorously against the waves, delivering an occasional bone-jarring thump over the big ones. My whole body was tensed to take the shocks of our swift passage across the bay, and I was glad to see Jimmy McMurchie throttle back, letting the boat down gracefully into the black salt water. The wind shifted as we lost headway, whipping Jimmy's long hair forward across his face. He laughed and brushed it back behind his ears, letting go of the outboard's controls as he pointed across the remaining distance to the shore.

The tide was half out, and the grey, pebbly beach ran up over a fence of sea-worn logs to the salal and scrub alder of the low shoreline. Behind that was thick virgin forest of hemlock, sitka spruce and western red cedar, a sombre backdrop for a line of six poles spaced irregularly along the boundary of land and sea. Five were obviously old: grey, seamed with long cracks, leaning gracefully this way and that, one with a crown of huckleberry and all with thick growths of fern and salal glossy below. One was much newer, though still showing signs of having been there for a number of years. It had never been painted, and the slim thrust of carved cedar was warm gold with pewter accents. Jimmy McMurchie pointed his nicotine-yellow finger towards that tallest, newest pole.

"That's Alphonso Johnny's pole there." A raven flapped its wings and swooped off the top of the pole. "'Course, his nephew Ralph carved it, almost twenty years ago must be. He's living down in Vancouver now, but old Alphonso is still here in the Charlottes. Haida Gwaii now. You want to go ashore?"

I couldn't see anywhere to put the boat in safely through the tossing chop and kelp beds which alternately revealed and hid a lot of vicious black rocks, but I wanted to see that pole. I'd come five thousand kilometres to see it. At my nod Jimmy turned the prow of the runabout and slipped it between two barnacle-encrusted teeth to the beach, lying as calm as a Sunday picnic under the dark, still forest. I hopped out and tugged the boat's prow up onto the beach. Jimmy killed the motor and walked up to the bow, stepping onto the beach with a dignity befitting his size.

Above the tide line, the pebbles gave way to coarse yellow sand and patches of weed. We walked over to the newest pole and looked up at it.

It was certainly unusual. I hadn't seen another like it, though I could see one or two familiar elements: a bear near the bottom, for instance, and a couple of human figures. But few of the traditional forms were in evidence. The older poles were crowded with figures of animals. The raven predominated since that had been the totem of the tribe that had lived on this site until 1919. Beavers, salmon, whales and humans were all represented on one pole, in the intricate, stylized and compressed story-art of the totem-carvers.

Jimmy sat down on a broad log, lit a cigarette and contemplated the distance. I stepped up to the pole and ran my fingers over the surprisingly warm, smooth wood. The air had a brightness about it even through the almost permanent fog of Haida Gwaii, and the hidden sun's warmth had seeped into the wood under my hand and the ground beneath my feet. The fog had laid a thin damp crust over the yellow sand, so that my footprints around the pole's base left a trail of dry indentations.

"See that blank space up near the top?" said Jimmy, breaking the silence. "That's supposed to mean high altitude, like a mountain top, say, or something up in the sky. Sometimes, there were things that lived in clouds." He took a deep drag of his cigarette, dropped it and pushed it into the sand with his toe.

I backed up until I could get a view of the top of the thirty metre shaft. A smooth, uncarved stretch ran the length of a man's body, starting above what looked like some sort of semi-human figure and ending under the very topmost image. What that image was, I couldn't tell.

"Jimmy, I'm going to get my stuff out now, and we'll probably be here an hour or so. I guess you can't order me up any real sunshine, eh?" We both smiled, and I went to the boat for my camera, tripod and bag of equipment. The telephoto lens would pull those strange, high figures into view.

The air was mild and humid and smelled equally of sea and forest. It was air that I wished I could store up and transport back to the city where I'd first heard of this unusual pole, back to my museum—where air never moves too fast or smells too fresh.

In Masset the next day, I picked up my developed prints from the one-hour photomat and then paid a call to old Alphonso Johnny. I needed the story of that pole, and the person to get it from was the old Haida Indian whose tale years ago had inspired a young man, Ralph, to carve his only pole. Ralph was now a middle-aged, successful architect in Vancouver, and had never again turned his hand to the art of the totem. I had never met Ralph, but I'd talked to him over the phone during the wait for a flight from Vancouver International to Prince Rupert and then to the town of Masset at the north end of the islands. He'd told me where to find his uncle, and assured me that the old man would be pleased to tell his story.

Alphonso's granddaughter made tea with sugar and evaporated milk and brought it to us at the kitchen table. Her smile was so wide and charming that I drank the sweet liquid without complaint while she sat nursing her baby. Between enthusiastic sips of his tea, Alphonso told his tale, in his gravelly, lisping voice.

"Archie Harry and me were out hunting," he began. "We had only gone for the day, so we didn't have a lot of stuff to slow us down. It's pretty flat all around here, but across Masset Harbour we got up to about four hundred feet pretty quick. It was kind of cold up there, and we didn't see a damn bit of game, so we sat down for a while and Archie got out his thermos. We sat there for a while, still didn't see nothing, then I wished we had a thermos with more than just those two little cups on top, because along comes the Old Man of the Woods. No wonder there was no deer; the Old Man, he smells pretty high.

"So I drank up quick and poured some tea for him. Well, he's a polite kind of fellow and he went and sat downwind on the log, and we talked about this and that. I asked about his wife, and how many children he might have now. He said that she was okay, and he didn't know how many children as he wasn't much at counting, and anyway he didn't see them too often. They were on the other side of the mountain now. He also said that one of the bears had told him to move to the other side of the mountain too, as the bear and his family were leaving, and in fact every animal was leaving. The Old Man said he didn't know why, it was the first he'd heard of it, but suspected it could have been something to do with the way parts of the mountainside had started to crumble away, and how it was not safe to go into caves any more. He said he and his wife figured it was time they moved on too, but suddenly, before I could ask him any questions, he puts his cup in my hand and disappears. After a few minutes, out of the woods comes Mr. Ranjeet Ackloo, a person we all knew as he had been around for a couple of weeks. I didn't know he was this far out of town; another reason for no deer. He came up smiling and talking very fast like always and brushing his free hand back and forth in front of his face, just like there was something there. He smelled the Old Man but was too courteous to say anything, thinking that it was us. In his other hand he held a stop watch.

"Where we were sitting was looking down over some slash, and Mr. Ackloo stood beside us, puffing and waving out over the patch of slash, and he explained what he was doing. We couldn't stop him from this; he was East Indian and, as he had told us often, felt a kind of kinship with us, the Red Indians, and considered us to be his brothers. It seemed he'd heard that Sasquatch could cross a field of slash forest covered with stumps and fireweed and saplings in only about one tenth the time it took a human. Well, he was going to test this, at least from the point of view of the human. It would be part of the book he was writing.

"He smiled some more, bounced up and down on his feet, pushed his glasses up his nose, said 'One, two, three!' and took off. He was certainly travelling pretty slow, all right, which would be good evidence for his book.

"We decided to head up the mountain awhile more, and perhaps meet up with the Old Man again and hear more about all the animals moving away. Some people, the Kwakiutl, call him Bukwas, some, the Nimpkish, call his wife Dsonoqua, the cannibal woman. We mostly call him Old Man, as he has not told us his real name. See, there he is up there."

And Alphonso's finger jabbed at one of the photos, the second from the top figure on the pole, just beneath the open space. I'd spread all my photos on his kitchen table, views from every angle and close-ups of each section, front and sides. The back of the pole was partially hollowed out, as many poles were. He pointed here and there.

"Down there, there's the bear. He's at the bottom because he was in the story before it really started. Then, there's us, me and Archie, and at the sides, nothing, to show where the deer were not. Then there is Raven, who came to tell us that he had been flying all day to warn everybody, and he was angry that we were still there after all the work he had gone to. He became a very black cloud and rained on us, then changed again into Raven and flew away laughing.

"After a little while, as we walked up the mountain, the Old Man joined us again. He had his wife with him. She was just as tall as he, but had a more beautiful coat of hair. Her breasts hung down like those of an old woman, though she walked as lightly as a deer. They were leaving, and Archie and I decided to go back down and go home, when suddenly the mountain shook and we were all knocked down. It stopped after a short time, and Old Man and his wife got up and went very, very fast along the side of the mountain and upwards. We were heading down when we heard a big ripping, grinding noise behind us. Well, we were scared, but we stopped anyway and looked back, holding onto trees so we wouldn't get knocked down again.

"What we saw was the mountain coming alive. The noise of ripping and tearing got louder and louder, and very slowly part of the mountain came away. It was like a big cork coming out of a bottle, only there were trees growing on the cork, and it began to crumble and break apart, rocks and trees rolling away. We were too scared to move, and it was lucky that we didn't get hit by anything. We could see up into the opening that was in the mountain now, as all the dust began to blow away.

"For a while there was nothing there, although the ground kept on rumbling, and we hung onto the trees. Then out came some beings. They looked to us to be tall and hairy, like the Old Man and his tribe, but they were dressed in clothes, which the Old Man did not do, and they were riding things like helicopters without those vanes on top, and were carrying things in their arms. They flew like bees around the opening, very fast back and forth, up and down, and then back they went inside. Soon a huge being or thing filled the opening, coming out very slowly. The rain cloud that had been Raven had gone, and the sun came out as it does now and then in the fall, and the sun falling on the being or thing made it shine like copper.

"It crept out of its cave and took all the flying things with their riders into itself, through mouths in its sides. Then it went up. I couldn't see it, but I had the feeling that it came down onto land again once or twice or more, and I had the feeling also that I would never see the Old Man or his family again. And that was true, although the animals came back eventually. I think he and his family went with their people. Mary Ann, get more tea for the lady."

Alphonso pushed one of my photos to my side of the table. It was a close-up of the pole's summit, one of several I'd taken, and he stroked it gently with his finger. "I told Ralph the story," he said, "and Archie told him too, but still this doesn't look too much like it. It was more flat on the top and the wings were less like those of the eagle. In fact, it was very different from this in many ways. You know, a woman like you should not listen to an old Indian's stories. If you tell them, no one will believe you."

He smiled and began to cackle, his face crinkling into a wicked expression. Mary Ann heated up more water and added it to the teapot.

"What did Mr. Ackloo think of it?" I asked.

Alphonso wiped his eyes and reached for the plate of cookies that Mary Ann had put down. "Archie and me found him when we got back to town," he said, dunking a cookie. "He was getting ready to leave; he wanted someone to take him down to Tlell. He said that what with the earthquake and the avalanche, the evidence of Sasquatch would all be destroyed and he might as well go somewhere else. He was sick and tired of Masset."

We talked some more. I was stalling for time. I knew I'd have to go back with nothing—nothing that could possibly stand up to the skepticism of my colleagues—and the story of an eighty-year-old Haida about events twenty years earlier was as good as nothing. And I didn't really believe it myself, did I? Mr. Ackloo had published his little book—I'd read it before I came to the islands and it was a foolish mass of credulity piled on spurious "facts." I had felt embarrassed to be seen reading it. But I'd come, I'd seen the pole, I'd talked to old Alphonso, I'd taken photographs—of what? A gently rotting shaft of cedar, silvering under the west coast rain.

Alphonso told me of how his friend, Archie, had died a couple of years later, drowned while fishing, before Ralph had gotten around to carving the pole. There had been a ceremony for the installation of the pole, which had been carved one winter while Ralph was out of work. He'd used the shelter of an old longhouse to carve it in, extending the roof with some tarpaulins supported by a light framework of planks. A small wood stove had kept him warm. About thirty of Alphonso, Archie, and Ralph's friends and relatives had piled into a couple of boats and gone out to the old town site and had watched as, during the spring rain, the pole had been settled into its pit and raised to the vertical. A few years later, a boat containing one or two vacationing faculty from the University of British Columbia had gone by and a few snapshots had been taken, which had found their way eventually to the Ethnology Department in the basement of the Royal Ontario Museum. Since there were plenty of totem poles to view at that time, nobody paid any particular attention to the photos. I'd seen the original now, and more compelling even than the enigma at the pole's top, whose mechanical power was made somehow alive by the abstract anthropomorphism of the art, was the figure below it, separated by that stretch of smooth wood.

The round eyes and small teeth were those of a human; the lowering, wide brows, the ridged crest springing in a vee from the hooked nose, the long, cavernous cheeks and pricked ears, were something else, something animal, and conveyed an emotion of fierce wistfulness, if such a thing could be. How long had they waited, those few who had gone out into our world and become legend? The legend would live long after the evidence was gone. I took a cookie from the plate and picked up the close-up photo of the Old Man, there atop his tree, staring up and out with his huge cedar eyes. He must have been someone worth knowing.

A sudden rain drummed on Alphonso Johnny's roof. No doubt it did its work upon that special pole. In less than a human lifetime it would be gone, rotted by the mild, insistent rain, toppled, and covered with ferns, salmonberries and young red cedar. But I'd seen it.

My father, E.B. Cox, was a sculptor. He worked in stone, wood, metal, glass, and even gem stones. His works are on public view and in private collections all over Toronto and elsewhere in North America. I believe he would have understood the urge this story's protagonist felt to display something truly alien. And perhaps to suffer the consequences.

THERE IS A VIOLENCE

It was a brutal little head on a neck as broad and muscular as an animal's. And yet the eyes held intelligence, of the sort that commands armies. Or that orders the destruction of worlds.

I ran my finger along the top of the stone skull, over the roughly carved hair and down the neck.

Kristian gazed possessively at the thing. "Powerful, isn't it?"

The sculpture sat on a tall pedestal of polished onyx. The onyx column was probably worth more than the green rock of the sculpted head, which might have come from any second-rate quarry on Earth. But the onyx was mere terrestrial stone; the head came from Raqaaq.

"It seems crude," I replied. "Don't you think? But powerful, yes."

Kristian smiled, rocking back and forth on his heels, his leather boots squeaking slightly. The gallery was empty except for us and the stone head, and a few metal chairs stacked against the back wall. Skylights cast winter sun onto the polished hardwood floor, and lit the pale blue walls into a receding Arctic landscape. The other exhibits from Raqaaq were still being catalogued and prepared for display, but my brother hadn't been able to contain his eagerness to show me what he had. He'd always been that way. When we were children, he'd never been able to keep a secret.

"Do you think Rebecca will come?" he asked.

I looked at him and raised my eyebrows. Mother was in Germany, involved in the complicated wheeling and dealing that was the breath of life to her. I doubted she would drop that to attend a Toronto gallery opening, no matter whose it was or what sort of incredible things were on display. And it was a safe bet that Father would be nowhere near. He tended to maintain a constant distance from his ex-wife around the planet, via some sort of telepathic warning system of his very own. The last time he'd called me he was in Singapore.

"She'd only get all political anyway. You don't want that."

Kristian winced theatrically. "God, Sue, don't remind me about politics. Anyway, it's all going to hit the fan tomorrow at the opening."

An expression of glee crept over his face, and he brushed his honey-coloured locks back over his broad pale forehead. Kristian had always had a yen for the stage—he was certainly pretty enough—and had tried breaking in several times, but after a while he realized he was being allowed to play with the big kids because of his wealth, and quietly backed off. I knew it had hurt him more than he wanted to say, but dashing around spending piles of money on artwork was the next best thing. At least for now.

"It's freezing in here," I said. "Let's get coffee somewhere."

"Don't you want to see the rest of the stuff? You will not

believe what I've got." He wound his arm into mine. "I've taken the whole building for the show—the big things are in the back room under hovering clouds of grad students and hairy old profs and photographers and so on, they're all busy as bees. It's complete fun."

We passed through a double-wide door at the back into a frigid, high-ceilinged warehouse space lit to brilliance by overhead lights. Electrical cabling looped everywhere, instruments hummed, and people worked, grimly silent.

It didn't look like my idea of fun. Portable heaters were going full blast but with little effect. The people working wore heavy sweaters or parkas, and there was an air of subdued, focused tension. Other than a couple of quick glances at us, no one seemed to pay any attention to our entry.

"I can't believe there aren't government wonks all over. Doesn't this stuff fall under some kind of archaeological treaty or trade ban or something?"

"I'm sure it will," said my brother. "But not so far. Apparently there are the usual tariffs and reciprocal trade agreements and interdictions covering the rest of the trade between Raqaaq and Earth, but for some reason there's nothing regarding ancient artifacts like this. It's like they don't exist."

We stopped before a complicated whirl of blue metal, about the size of an armchair, designed as a sort of open-work double clam shell. The halogen lights overhead made all its sharp curving edges glitter compellingly. I reached out, intending to tap it with a fingernail and see what sound would come from it, but a man who had been working at a computer suddenly spoke.

"Please don't touch it." He turned in his chair and looked up. His nose was red with the cold, and his eyes had dark hollows under them. "You might trigger it, and I'm not quite sure yet how to get it open again."

"Trigger it?" I frowned at the thing. It sat with its base in the remnants of a casing of foamed plastic, in which it must have been shipped. I put my hands behind my back.

"Sue, this is Doctor Tom Miller. Tom, my sister Susan."

Doctor Miller eyed me dubiously, and I could swear he was deliberately ignoring Kristian. "It's a torture device, as many of the items are. As far as we can tell, everything here either does violence or reminds the viewer of violence. Violence and control. This represents a complete departure from anything we've so far understood about the Raqaa." He sat slumped in his chair, eyeing the clamshell. "We must have more time, Mr. Sundqvist."

Into the gap formed by this exhausted verbal wedge rushed everyone else in earshot. A knot of determined men and women immediately formed around Kristian. I left him to sort it out while I looked around the room.

Because I had been alerted, it took me only a few minutes to stop seeing the things as sculptural. And the moment I stopped reading a terrestrial artistic sensibility into their form and grace I could see what they were. What had struck the eye as delightful abstract shapes, reminiscent of a mood or an idea, became claspers, clamps, stretchers as hooked and spiny as insects. A frieze of formal shapes in honey-coloured stone became alien creatures being torn apart, lying in chunks along a table. The graceful outline of a four-legged creature like a kneeling horse torqued as I circled it into a cage lined with tiny spines. I looked closer to see that each spine was fed by a hair-thin wire. Thousands of wires, all roped together at what would be the hindquarters, to form a silver waterfall of a tail.

What Miller had said was true. This was the trove of a madman. There was nothing truly sophisticated about the things, nothing to hint at a transcendental meaning wasted on our primitive human minds.

Perhaps foolishly, I touched a stone sculpture much like the one I'd first seen. A face gazed down blankly toward something that must once have been held in a grasping hand, now broken off. The chipped stone was olive green, densely smooth and fine, and felt icy cold. Nothing happened when I touched it. Perhaps I'd been spoiled by the interactive, high-tech cleverness of other shows I'd attended, whose works demanded a reciprocal display of intelligence. Or at least a response. These demanded nothing, expected nothing but simple captive horror.

Kristian knew all about this, I was certain of it. He knew this stuff wasn't art.

I stepped away from the piece and jammed my inquisitive hands into my pockets. Apparently the researchers were trying to learn as much as they could before the collection was bought and dispersed. Or, more likely, before some agency, human or Raqaa, stepped in and shut us down.

What was Kristian thinking, messing with nasty stuff like this? It didn't seem representative of the Raqaa that humans were coming to know, a reserved and humourless society that seemed all business to the point of boredom. Yes, the show would cause a sensation and probably sell out; yes, he'd be the toast of the artsy crowd for a while. And he'd probably get invitations to parties no normal person would want to attend.

I had started to drift back towards Kristian when his voice rose.

"Look, all I want is a brief provenance for each piece, and for you to make sure the things are set so that no one gets tangled up in them. How hard could that be? Come on!"

A mutter from Doctor Miller that I couldn't make out.

"Well, you'll just have to pick up the pace," barked Kristian. "The lighting people are coming tomorrow morning, and the actors have to do a run-through. I've got the wheels in motion, Tom, can't you understand that?"

Miller threw up his hands and stalked back to his screen.

Kristian looked exasperated but cheery, and was immediately tackled by another in the little cluster around him. I turned away and came face to face with a gangly young man with a wispy beard and a fervid look in his eye.

"You're his sister, right? Susan Sundqvist?"

"Yes, I am." I kept my hands in my pockets. "Before you go any further, I have to point out that I'm just here on a quick tour. I have no influence over my brother."

That wasn't really true. I had a lot of influence, as did our parents, but it was more the kind likely to goad him into doing foolish things. I knew the look Kristian would get on his face if I tried to persuade him to let these researchers have their way.

"Well, someone has to talk sense to him." He wiped his nose with the back of a hand that was visibly trembling. "He won't even let us get a TET scanner in here, or any deep holo equipment—nothing. It's *absurd*. Mr. Sundqvist doesn't know what he's got here."

"You're probably right," I said, handing him a tissue. He crushed it distractedly in one hand.

He stood breathing heavily for a moment. "Do you realize," he said in a low voice, "that Tom Miller dropped everything to fly in here, probably fucking up his situation in Cairo completely, just so he could work for your brother in these ridiculous conditions? Do you?"

"Look, I—"

"Christ, it's absolutely c-criminal!" His voice was rising. "These artifacts are of incredible value, absolutely fucking—I mean, they're from a world we have virtually no knowledge of… we'll just never—" He stuttered to a stop, his face flaming red. At least he looked warmer now.

"I'm sorry," he mumbled after a moment. "We're all tired, frustrated."

"I'll bet you are."

He drew back and narrowed his eyes at me. His chin went up. He'd suddenly remembered the kind of power that goes with wealth like my family has; stupid, crafty power that is capable of utterly reprehensible actions. The idle rich and their trivial minds. Right now he was getting ready to say something carefully vicious and march away.

I held up my hand. "Before you say any more, Mr.—"

"Ken Jordan. I was a student of Dr. Miller's a few years ago."

"Mr. Jordan. Believe it or not, I'm on your side. But probably not for the same highly civilized reasons. I just want to keep my little brother out of trouble, and I sense that these things—" I waved my arm, "are trouble."

"You're damned right they're trouble."

He wheeled and stalked off. He wasn't going to waste any more time on me. I considered following him and pumping him for details, but Kristian came up and caught my arm.

We escaped to the relative warmth of the outer gallery while Kristian complained. "With all the money I'm handing over you'd think they'd be more grateful, damn it. But all I get is demands and whining. Makes me feel like trying one of those contraptions to see if it works."

"They seem pretty serious. Can't you put the show off for now?"

He snorted. "Are you kidding? I've had the collection over a week now, and if this show doesn't happen on schedule I'm fucked. I'll lose all my momentum." He released the door and we passed through the small foyer to the building exit. More fiddling with locks and codes. "What Miller and the rest don't realize," he continued, "is that I'm actually doing them a favour."

"How do you figure that?"

"The floodgates will be opened. What I've got here barely scratches the surface, I'm sure of it. Once interest has been aroused there'll be all sorts of stuff coming out of Raqaaq, and these obstructive bastards will be at the head of the line." He shook his head, as an indulgent but irritated father will at a child's unreasonable demands. I knew he was playing a part for me, and probably for himself too. He had no other real motive than the general astonishment he hoped to provoke.

"What have the Raqaa got to say about it?"

"Absolutely nothing," he said smugly as we hurried along the side of the building towards the local café, our footsteps creaking in the packed snow. Someone would have to clear the walkway before the opening, or we'd have lawsuits on our hands. No, that's how Mother would think, I chided myself. This is Kristian's show; let him worry.

"They're ignoring this? It could be that they're upset. They don't want their culture displayed."

"They're just being coy. Everyone is dying to know more about them, and a cultural exchange is the perfect way to open up relations."

So now it was a cultural exchange. Next he would anoint himself Goodwill Ambassador for the Earth. "Well, I just hope it comes off the way you want it to."

A small car was approaching along the alley, the whine of its motor dropping in pitch as it slowed to stop beside us. Both doors flew up and two well-bundled people popped out like bread from a toaster, carrying puffs of heated air with them. They looked Filipino, small and dark, a man and a woman alike in height and colouring. They might be husband and wife, or brother and sister. They squinted against the cold white light and looked us up and down. Then both turned and seemed to let me drop out of their dual consciousness to focus on Kristian.

"Kristian Sundqvist?"

Kristian gave them his highly-bred racehorse confronting a butcher's nag look. "That's me. What may I do for…"

He wasn't allowed to finish. The woman's pretty face went blank, her head dropped back slackly and her mouth fell open. Out of it erupted a voice like hot wind and whip cracks, a sound that made me flinch back against the wall in shock. The heavy, stinging voice said, "Return our property." Her lips didn't move.

A voder implant, somewhere in her slim little throat.

Kristian stood his ground. The hood of the woman's jacket fell back, revealing her skin. There was some sort of metal contraption clinging to her neck like an articulated brace or collar, with projections winding up past her jaw to her temples and into her shiny black hair. Her companion hovered beside her, his hands touching her lightly as if he were teaching her to skate and was solicitously preventing a loss of balance.

"Kristian Sundqvist. Return our property."

I reached for Kristian's arm, but he pushed me back behind him quite roughly. I could hear him breathing hard through his nose. The car had pulled its doors shut.

"Who are you?" demanded Kristian.

"We are Raqaa. You have acquired property that is Raqaa."

"That's right, I have. It was purchased from a legitimate trader."

The woman's head came forward and she took a great gasp of air, then it went back again as though she were a sun-worshipper lolling on a beach. The man behind her patted her shoulders, his eyes watering.

"It was purchased illegally," came that boiling voice again. "It will be returned."

With that the woman resumed a normal stance, composed herself with a couple of deep breaths. The man stepped back and clapped his hands together, blowing out puffs of breath. Just two minor functionaries delivering a message.

"Is it always this cold in Canada?" The woman's voice was high and pleasant, with a slight lisp. She huddled into her parka, casually pulling the hood up over her hair and the metal device.

Kristian said nothing. I stepped up beside him and clasped his arm. The solidarity of fear. Kristian's lips had compressed into a line of stubbornness that I knew well.

The woman held out a little packet. "If you will take this visk and look it over," she said, "everything should be clear."

Both of them bowed as Kristian accepted the visk. Then they opened the car, got in, and were off.

Kristian and I looked at each other. "Well," I said. "What do we do now?"

Kristian scowled at the visk, holding it as if it were a small dish of rancid food. "You will go home, like a good girl. And I'll look at this, I suppose." He snorted. "Imagine, sending their little slaves to deliver this. Who do they think I am?"

I bit my lip, hesitated. "You might have to give it up, sweetie. Who needs this sort of crap?"

Wrong move. "Give up? Not without a fight, I won't. I've invested too much into this to be scared off by this sort of crude tactic. I've learned a thing or two from Mother, after all."

"Well, I am *not* going home at a time like this. I want to see this whatever-it-is. Come on, your car's here. Let's check it out."

So we did. The screen popped up as the car's heater blasted, and a face much like the carved stone head's appeared and began to speak, the lip movements not matching the English words. Raqaa were not pretty, nor were they fond of chumming around with humans. Their likenesses didn't turn up much in the news, nor had any heart-warming shows featuring our new E.T. friends been produced. The small eyes in that bullet head held no glitter of life or personality, nor were there any lines or softnesses in it to make the Raqaa anything more than a talking lump of muscle.

The sculpture in the gallery was a glossy, age-weathered green. The screen showed a being as grey as concrete, something I hadn't expected. Its small, close-set eyes were chilly blue with pin-point pupils. I took it to be a male. The thick neck flexed as words formed. "This is an interactive visk," it said. "I am able to answer most questions you may have." It continued without further preamble. "The artifacts you have obtained are stolen property. You will return them."

"Yes, your associates mentioned that." Kristian sneered at the screen image. "How is it that you have humans working for you?"

"That is a question I am unable to answer."

"Then tell me why you say the artifacts were stolen. I bought them from a being representing itself as a Raqaa trader."

"That being was not a Raqaa trader. That being encountered a cache of items stolen from Raqaa in the year 3,157." A line of print at the bottom of the screen translated this as A.D. 839. "That being has sold them to you illegally."

"Just a minute," said Kristian stiffly. "I know of no legalities or restrictions regarding such items as the ones I acquired. You can't claim them back now."

"We are prepared to compensate you, Mr. Sundqvist. We will have them back. You will see that they are readied for transport by local sunset."

The face in the visk display showed no emotion that I could recognize, and after a pause in which no one spoke, the image blinked its little blue eyes and disappeared. Kristian snapped the screen down and took the controls of the car, a tight smile on his lips. "Well, fuck," he said. "Want a lift home?"

I shrugged. "Yeah, I guess."

Kristian seemed to regain some of his devil-may-care spirit as we drove. It was probably unwise of me to make light of this turn of events, but I could never resist playing my part. I suppose I'm really very much like him. "I wonder what Rebecca would think of all this?"

He snorted and wheeled us expertly into my building's enclosed foyer. "She'd tell them where to go, wouldn't she?"

I laughed. "Absolutely." The car opened and I got out. "See you tomorrow."

Presumably Kristian spent the next twenty-four hours finalizing preparations for his show. I knew, of course, that he'd never comply with the Raqaaq demand. It simply wasn't in his nature.

I spent the evening alone, fussing with my orchids and wishing... oh, lots of things. That Father would call. That I'd suddenly develop a talent for something; that Justin hadn't left. I'm good at worrying at problems that have no solution. I went to bed thinking of Kristian and his wavy golden locks. The sun had set long ago. Nothing happened. I called Kristian and he blithely informed me that everything was fine.

The next day nothing happened either. No more warnings or weird alien pronouncements were forthcoming.

I arrived early to the opening. Kristian was there to meet me at the door, his eyes bright and his hair and clothes perfect. He looked, in this little kingdom of pandemonium, like its rogue prince, tall and slender, wearing shades of grey-blue to match his eyes.

"Sue, darling!" He dragged me in and shucked me of my coat, yelling against the noise. Music played and people dashed back and forth in semi-darkness, still setting up. "You look gorgeous! Didn't you bring anyone? Come get some wine. The caterers were early, so the actors are using the gallery to get in costume. Hope you don't mind naked boys. Look out!"

Two burly women trotted by with a ladder. A man, arms full of stick-on lights, brought up the rear.

"I see we're having victims to liven things up," I yelled. "Are you sure it'll be all right, sweetie?"

"Of course I am. Tom said he thinks everything's inactive. It's mostly stone things anyway, and they just sit there and look dour. The metal devices are really pretty simple, just mechanical toys."

"*Toys?* Kristian—"

"Nothing's going to happen! Here, drink this, look pretty and stay out of the way. Oh, now what?"

Two androgynous youths had run up, shivering in their holographic paint and complaining of the cold.

"No, you can't put on clothes, your make-up will smear. There's hot coffee in the back." He shooed them away and they turned, pouting, their painted backs and buttocks flickering from naked flesh, to bone, then to flashes of whirling stars.

More people arrived, obviously friends of Kristian's, and he sailed off to usher them in. Then someone got his ear with a message. He turned and beckoned me over. "It's Mother calling," he shouted as a burst of music crashed and died. We slipped into the cavernous space at the back, once occupied by the hapless researchers, now filled with a catering crew and their kitchen, which they had driven right inside. Blessed warmth, and Mother's face on the screen. She wasn't smiling.

"Secure this call, Kristian, right away. Sue, you look fabulous. Darlings, I don't have much time. You have to listen to me."

"You should be here, Rebecca darling, it's such fun—"

Mother's eyes narrowed meaningfully and Kristian shut up. She looked distracted, aloof somehow, as though her mind was occupied with many different stratagems all at once, any one of which being more important than the current conversation. In other words, she looked the same as ever. She was dressed as if returning from a formal function, stripping off gloves. Much jewellery was laden on, including an ornate necklace of glimmering metal beads.

"I heard about your show only now, Kristian. I know this will be difficult, but you're going to have to cancel it."

"Cancel it! You're joking. I can't possibly—"

"Cancel it, now. Send everyone away, do exactly as the Raqaa tell you, and things should be all right."

"What are you talking about? Mother, do you realize what's at stake here?"

But I'd seen something. Something winding up out of the ornamental necklace and into Mother's hair. I pulled Kristian back. His muscles were tight as steel springs. "Kristian. Look at her. She's wearing one of those Raqaa collars."

He shook off my hand, but he'd heard me. She had too. We watched as she carefully lifted the coils of formally arranged, honey-blonde hair off her neck. The trails of gleaming metal lay close against her skin, flexing softly as she turned her head. "Yes, Sue, you're right. Kristian, I do know exactly what I'm talking about. The Raqaa do not want their past on display, not to scientists, not to politicians, and most particularly not to art collectors." She let her hair fall back into place. "You *have* been warned, darling."

Kristian found his voice. "What have you done? *What have they done to you?*"

"Don't be a fool. This is your last chance."

"Bastards!" He lunged at the screen and actually punched it, to no avail. The image didn't even flicker. "Fucking bastards!" Mother blinked calmly at him, seemed to listen to a voice only she could hear, then gave us both a pitying look. The screen went dark.

I don't know what Kristian or I would have said or done next, because suddenly there was a dull crunching noise from above, the building shook and the door to the gallery blew open. We ran out to the main space.

A big hole had been punched through the roof, and a circle of starry night glittered overhead. Frigid air poured in. The gallery lay like a glowing little stage filled with throbbing red and yellow lights, echoing with screams and crashes. Something grappled the edge of the roof and peeled it back so forcefully that there was no time for anything to fall on us. Electrical sparks crackled and the sprinkler system began fountaining water into the night. The portable lights installed for the show still burned, now knocked askew and wildly spinning.

Something big moved in and blocked off most of the stars overhead. Helmeted figures festooned with armaments leapt in from above, landed nimbly on their feet and quickly fanned out across the floor. They didn't look human. The painted actors stared up at the sky, clinging to each other, almost invisible as their skin flashed stars in the red-lit night. Then they broke and ran.

Several of the soldiers wore canisters at their mid-sections, from which they aimed streams of foam that encased each piece that Kristian had placed on display. The white, hardening cocoons were lassoed and yanked skywards by filaments extruded from the ship.

At last a Raqaa, decked in body armour but no helmet, showed up, spinning quickly down on one of the tendrils to land with a heavy thud in the middle of the floor. It stood planted like a statue, its small head swivelling on the thick neck as it, she, or he, watched the action. He spoke rapidly into a hand-held device, apparently giving orders.

Two people had been wounded, and lay shrieking. Another got caught in a foam stream along with one of the displays and vanished within it. I think everyone else managed to escape. From my position huddled in the doorway between the gallery and the back room, I watched the catering truck roar away, people clinging to its sides.

Kristian crouched beside me, watching with a snarl on his face, then suddenly sprang to his feet and started to battle his way towards the Raqaa leader. The soldiers paid him no attention. They weren't shooting at anyone. It's my opinion that anyone killed or injured had simply been in the way of the operation.

All they wanted was their damned stuff back.

The lights had stopped spinning, everyone who could get away had gone, and a dripping winter silence had descended on the gallery. I could hear the heavy beating of a helicopter approaching, and sirens wailing.

I stood shivering in my party dress. The chaos in the stripped and foam-spattered gallery had resolved itself into a frieze uncannily like one I had seen only yesterday. But this one involved my brother.

The Raqaa soldier had him on his knees in the icy, foam-flecked water that slicked the floor. He was holding Kristian by the neck and shaking him. I knew without a doubt that he could have snapped Kristian's spine if he'd wanted to.

Then, faster than my eyes could follow, the Raqaa plucked a device from his belt, opened it somehow and clamped it around Kristian's neck. He went down instantly, like a puppet whose strings have been cut, and before his head had hit the floor he'd been scooped up and carried off by one of the soldiers.

My brother was gone, just like that.

And that is how I remember the incident that started the war. Or that boosted it into its next stage; after all, the conquest had been going on for quite some time. No one has ever been able to tell me what happened to Kristian, not even our mother. Everyone knows what happened to her. She lives aboard the mothership now.

The Raqaa soldier stood watching me. I took a step toward it, intending I don't know what. Was I trying to be brave?

It grimaced at me, and after a while I realized it was mimicking a human smile. I stopped about ten feet from it.

"We do not enjoy this sort of action as much as we once would have." Without the aid of a voder, its real voice was deep and strangely thick. "Not as much as the artifacts your brother acquired might indicate. That, after all, was our past, when we were barbarians. We do not care to be reminded of our past."

"We—" I stopped to swallow and gather some breath. "We won't all be t-taken so easily," I said in a pathetically small voice. "We know what sort of monsters you are. Your dirty laundry is out in the open."

He pulled on one of the ship's tendrils and a coil formed for his foot to step into. He began to rise.

I stumbled forward, not caring what happened. I heard myself start to scream like a fishwife. "We never liked you ugly sons of bitches anyway, you're fucking boring, you know that? Do you? Fuckers!"

The Raqaa disappeared, drawn up into its ship. In another few seconds the ship took off, silently, a great electric shiver stroking the night and raising every hair on my body.

A helicopter buzzed nervously into the space the ship had vacated and shone a spotlight down on me. I looked away, covering my eyes. But I wasn't crying. I've never cried and I won't start now.

*I was driving home along a snowy, winter street when I spotted
an enigmatic wire box planted at the side of the road. A harsh
non-sequitur. Inside the rectangle of metal was another hunk of
metal, something like a frozen snake looping out of the dry grey
ground. The image haunted me, and I wondered what it might
imply.*

THE PAISLEY SNOW

There was a roadside wire box on Carol's route, a thing
she'd seen so often that it had become invisible. The wire
protected an access point for a pipeline, an incomprehensible
scribble of rusty-white technology, saying *Oil or gas. Blood.
Ichor.* Something that fed this shivering, sickened country.

Today the wire box at the intersection of Main and 13th—its
crumbling concrete curbs, its rampant but inedible weeds, its
dead stoplights—was different. Carol stopped about thirty feet
back, stamping her feet against the cold, and stood looking at it.
Two crows were looking at it too, and cawed insults at her from
their perch on a telephone pole. At eye level on the pole, scraps
of bleached, stapled-on paper shredded and flapped in the cold
wind. Death rattles from a lost world of concerts, baby-sitting
services, missing pets. So many missing pets, in those last few
months. Carol had long ago stopped hoping for anything new to

appear on the pole.

You had to just ignore the crows, who'd become the Scavenger Kings of the neighbourhood. The wire box was about the volume of a big freezer, a sturdy, regular grid of metal enclosing a space. A space that today was completely filled. Something was crammed inside, hiding the rusty pipeline. Dark and crumpled, as if someone had stuffed a big dirty tarp in there. She walked closer, curious. How had anything got inside? Perhaps it was something salvageable.

She felt her heart speed up, a heavy knocking in her chest. It made her feel a little nauseated. The wind was persistent as a winter cough, and the smell of snow was in the air. If she hadn't needed food, she'd turn for home right now.

She reached out to touch the cage. Maybe whatever was in there was worth something if she could winkle it out. Something that would add a layer of insulation to her apartment walls. Brown and matted, pressed against the wire, bulging between the strands. Closer, and suddenly she saw it was a cow. A live cow jammed and folded into the wire space. Its legs had been broken, its neck twisted brutally, to get it in there.

Carol's mouth opened to exclaim and then closed, and she snatched her hand back. The cow was breathing, little gasps pushing against the wire, a faint plume of breath-fog emitting from the side of the wire box where its head was, and then she saw its wet eye roll brown and white, wild.

Her first thought was: a cow? After all this time? Someone had been hoarding a poor damned cow. To do this with it.

She pulled her phone from a pocket, saw that there was a signal. Pressed 911. After sixteen rings she was about to hang up, but then a woman came on. "What is the nature of your emergency." Her voice flat.

"It's… it's…" Carol didn't know what to say. The cow's eye blinked, moist and soft. Its tongue lolled out.

"Your name please."

"Carol. Carol Erikson. There's a cow, it's… trapped near the road. I… it's in trouble."

"A *cow*? What, it's running loose?" This was something different for 911. Not the usual. Not *I've run out of firewood, is there anywhere I can go?* Not *there's a skeleton in clothes outside prowling around.*

Not *My Eddie stopped talking and looks through me like I'm a ghost. I'm afraid he'll leave and never come back. I'm afraid he'll come back.*

"No, no. It's not loose. Someone needs to come."

The cow convulsed suddenly, making the wires shriek, and emitted a deep, stifled groan that changed into what Carol hoped was a death rattle. Did cows even do that?

How the hell had it got in there?

She knew, though. She knew by the knocking of her heart. Was it him again, or was it somehow spreading to others? Was insanity contagious? Oh yes. Yes, of course it was.

"Someone will be there as soon as possible. Please stay on the line."

But Carol hung up. She turned away from the animal and walked home. She'd lost the urge to scrounge in a shop. The wind was shoving dust and dry snow around the pavement, little paisley patterns at her feet. It would likely be hours before a car arrived, and what could the cops do?

She'd seen this before. Quite a long time ago, when she thought about it. Before things went bad, and never such a large animal. Of course, he'd be an adult now. The tears she'd shed for the animal had dried. Tears were good for nothing.

But what if… what if she'd missed a chance, back then? Because of fear. Of course it was contagious.

*   *   *

The next day she ventured out again. The wind had dropped, and she really needed something to eat. Flour and salt, coffee if they had it. The store was only a half mile away by her normal route, but she was afraid the cow might still be there. Her heart had beat hard all night long, as the wind churned outside, the chimney stuffed with old newspapers. She was probably going to die of heart failure one of these nights, and nobody would know. She walked the longer way, found tea bags and sugar as well as her flour, salt and lumpy freeze-dried coffee. Someone had brought in a box of onions to sell. A dollar apiece. Things were looking up. That's what the news said, anyway. Carol bought an onion, happy to feel its round weight in her hand.

But with her load of groceries, the long way home seemed too hard. Pain meds were still scarce, what with the government crackdown on labs, and the hoarding. She should have hoarded some herself, back when you could stroll into a store and simply buy them. She went the short way. The cow was gone, the cage empty, its wires sprung and twisted. Bits of hair and flesh clung to them, at which the crows were picking. They flapped heavily away as she approached, then circled around, watching. You could eat crows, but they were pretty vile. Carol set her bags down. The cage seemed very small now. She pulled a tuft of hair out of a twist of wire, felt the harsh reality of the brown and white remnant. She put the tuft in her pocket.

She was about to walk on when a panel van pulled up and parked with its passenger side wheels up on the curb. Society for the Prevention of Cruelty to Animals. A woman got out, pulling sturdy leather gloves on as she walked up.

Carol backed away a step or two. The SPCA woman looked cold and tired, fed up with even trying to combat citizens' tendency to kill and eat everything they could catch. Or maybe she deplored the waste of cramming a perfectly good cow— probably one of the last cows around—into a torture cage.

The woman said, "Did you see any of this?" She gestured with one gloved hand at the cage.

Carol thought for a moment. Should she admit anything? Did she want to get caught up in it again? Nothing good came from trying to track down what did this sort of thing, or why. She'd learned that the hard way.

But finally she nodded. "I called it in. Was it you who came?"

"Yeah. It was dead, thank God." They both stood and looked at the wire cage, there to protect nothing more than a hump of metal pipe, its white paint scabbed with rust, which looped up and down in it, like a snapshot of something kinetic leaping out of the ground. A giant pale worm threading deep into the dry world. "City wants me to fix this. Most of their men have gone." The cow didn't seem to have damaged the pipe. She had no idea whether anything ran through it anymore.

"What did they do with it?"

Without looking at Carol, the woman said, "Food bank." She shrugged. "They seemed glad to get it."

Food bank. Carol always felt mean and guilty when she went there. Others were worse off. At least she'd never had children. She could hear barking from the SPCA truck. Not scared barking, just a regular, deep lament.

The SPCA woman crouched down and pulled a set of pliers out of her belt pouch, began to work at reattaching the bent wires.

"I had a student once," Carol said, watching her. She felt breathless, lightheaded. "Before. You know. I was a teacher at the middle school in Halburg. This boy would bring his pets in to show me. Smart, cute kid. Big vocabulary, liked to joke. He kept the pets in cages that were much too small. He told me it was just for transporting them to school, but I knew better." She'd never known what to do.

"He brought in a kitten first, after class, after the other kids had left. All squashed up, its fur sticking out. I saw that it could breathe, though. Next it was two squirrels he'd caught. He said he'd caught them. But I think he stole them as babies and made them grow in there. He must have fed them. Cleaned the cage. I suppose." That damned kid had never shut up. He nagged at her, frisking around her desk until she gave in and took a good look. He'd giggled at her expression of disapproval. He'd wanted her to see the joke. She had been scared of that cute, smart little boy.

The SPCA woman's expression hadn't changed, but she seemed to have lost what little energy she'd started her day with, keeping just enough to listen.

"Then he started coming in with dead ones. In cages, but dead. All dried up. You could see their teeth bared, clamped on the wire. Their eyes were dry. Open. No smell anymore, it was just fur and bones poking out through the wire." That horrible clever dark-eyed boy. She hadn't even tried to get him attention from Social Services. Or the police. They had bigger problems; the crash was accelerating. The new way was taking hold. Men were going silent and strange, and were leaving. Gone Lone, it was called. No one knew where they went. "I didn't know what to do. I really didn't."

But now I know. I think I should have killed that clever, talkative boy.

The SPCA woman started nodding. "We see those boxed-up things sometimes. People find them and call us. They want us to get rid of them, from their porches, their backyards. Mostly they're dead, but sometimes we get there in time."

"In time." She had done nothing. The food bags clustered at her feet, and the wind whispered a little about how much colder it was going to get. *But I might send some spring someday, I might.*

"Yeah. Well, in time to put the animal down, but sometimes we get one that can make it, outside. So we spend our resources on these things." She shook her head. "It's stupid. Why would anyone do that? In this day and age? Is it supposed to mean something?"

If it meant anything, Carol didn't know what. She didn't think it had anything to do with hatred, or politics, or just being crazy. She thought it might be something unknown as yet. Something about the animals themselves. Something about how that boy knew so many words, and loved to talk and talk, and joke, just at the time when so many folks were losing the urge to communicate. Losing their words. Leaving.

We're all animals, she thought. The human animal steals, though. Words, food, lives. Steals away in the dark, silently.

Snow started to drift down again, thin and sparse. The hint of spring was gone. It always went away, into a locked repository where summer still existed. It might never be found again. She'd had worse kids to look after, ones whose parents had died, or killed themselves, or Gone Lone and hadn't come back. It was mostly the men, but sometimes women. Her own husband Eddie had done it. The news on the radio had said, just a few nights ago, that people were coming back. Skinny and still voiceless, but back. If they had anything to tell, they weren't telling it.

The SPCA woman resumed bending the cut wire back into place, adding a few loops of new wire to strengthen the cage.

Carol watched for a while, then picked up her bags and headed home. She thought she'd have tea instead of coffee. Make flatbread with her flour and salt.

And then she thought, perhaps a trip to the food bank tomorrow. That cow. She was so sick of being cold and hungry and lonely. *It's not my fault. How could I have known?* Someone took all the words, squeezed out the life, turned off the heat.

But maybe, someday, Eddie would turn up. He'd want

something good to eat. He'd deserve it, after… after all of it.

Maybe he'd tell her what he'd done out there, what they'd all done out there, with their lost, stolen, frozen words.

And now for something completely different. What happens when you die? If you're a teen, is it different? Could it possibly be, like, fun*? In a fantasy tale, you can indulge your need to believe there's life after death. And curiosity. Revenge, maybe. Love. Coffee. That horror movie trope of the kids' swing slowly moving back and forth with no kid visible? What if there was a kid, a ghost, and she knew more than she should?*

THE FARAWAY CLUB

The Soggy Bears

So it looks like you revert to childhood when you die.

How do I know? There are six soaking wet teddy bears arranged decoratively on my grave. *Six.* Two of them are holding lollipops in their damp little paws.

Did people really think I liked teddy bears? Does no one have an original idea? Candles that the rain has extinguished. Notes and poems from people I barely knew and never gave a crap about. I'm pretty sure they didn't give a crap about me either. They just like it when other people see how deeply emotional they are.

It's like one of those flash mobs you hear about. A flash shrine.

It congealed out of nowhere, shortly after my headstone went up. I get it. I used to be in the land of the living. The ignorant, the deluded, the hopelessly naïve. I should have stayed that way, for this is what it comes to: stuffed toys and misspelled notes. As a high school senior, you should have given up teddy bears and moved on to, I don't know… drugs maybe, like the other losers. Literature. Music. Guys. Or girls, whatever keeps you warm at night.

The only decent thing at my graveyard shrine is a very trippy ballpoint pen drawing, protected by a plastic sleeve. Mostly orange, red and black, kind of a demon in a tornado, or maybe a fallen angel. It's obviously a Yazeed special. I didn't even know Yaz had done it, and he used to show me everything.

Before.

Floating in that place behind my eyes where consciousness dwells, I contemplated that drawing.

Interesting that it should be here. Weird, in fact, considering he died before I did. A little tribute for a fallen comrade, a girl who used to have warm lips, fingers that went everywhere, and chocolate on her breath. A tribute from a corpse, to a corpse.

Yeah, I'm dead. I was murdered. My name is Holly Eddols and I'm here to tell you all about it.

Like, that Yazeed is making art after death. Like, that Yaz committed "suicide." Nope. He did not.

Pretty sure he was murdered, just like me. I swear I didn't do it. And I for sure didn't kill myself.

Someone did us in, and I'm going to find out who.

A few minutes later, it comes to my attention that not only do you revert to childhood when you die, you also become a detective.

Turns out the afterlife is jam-packed with murder victims seeking their killers. Apparently it's what we do. One boy had been offed by his drunk stepdad and was pissed as hell about it. Another had been tossed off her bike forty feet by a hit and run driver. She was champing at the bit to find the dude and spook him into driving off a cliff. Or something. Her plan was a little shaky, but she had determination.

In no time at all I met six more local ghosts who were heavily involved in sleuthing, the oldest from 1957. Now *that's* commitment. All of them wanted to yammer on about their pain and outrage. I'd like to say I learned from them, but really, so boring. None of them bothered to listen to *my* story. Why they thought I'd be interested in their deaths when I had my own and Yaz's to worry about is beyond me.

My big ambitions of braving the unknown, throwing off the shackles of death and tracking down a murderer were actually pretty mundane. Some of us dead folk know exactly who dunnit and are only after evidence to somehow present to the living. Some are starting from scratch. I'm sort of in between.

No one's interested in teaming up. All of us are filled with righteous anger. All of us have *loved ones* who *need to know the truth*. We have *revenge to seek*.

Is that going to help? It is not. After a few years, hardly anyone alive cares any more.

But in my case, lots of people will care. Because it was *me*, dang it. My mom and dad will care, right? And… uh. Yaz. Yaz would care. If he were alive.

Hm. All right, so it's not really about quantity, it's about quality. Mom, Dad, and Yaz.

So… if Yaz is dead, shouldn't he be around here somewhere, sleuthing? Like everyone else?

At the thought of Yaz being dead I started to cry again.

Why wasn't the ghost of someone's mom coming to comfort me? What about all the teddy bears? Was sympathy something only the living felt, manifested by tacky kitsch, while us ghosts only thought of ourselves?

As it happened, I also was only thinking of myself. My tears vanished as I came up with an instant theory, as yet untested: ghosts are only interested in their own lives and their own deaths. You might call us terminally selfish. Lol.

I could expect no help from any of them, and I hadn't the slightest inclination to assist them in their hopeless sleuthing.

Losers.

Whoa. Now I'm somewhere else. I can't remember what I was going to say.

I hate when that happens.

Floating over my own little shrine of mouldering junk is happening less, thank God, and now I'm twirling in my backyard in a fun sort of way, with glimpses of the living world going by whisk-whisk-whisk. Nausea doesn't seem to be an issue. Trees-house-swing-set-trees. Feels nice, really. I don't live here anymore, but I guess I could be dead here.

It's hard for me to maintain any sort of focus, as you can already tell. I get jerked around a lot, by who or what I do not know. Maybe just my brain short-circuiting? God messing with me? Angels, fighting over who gets to escort me to heaven? Ha, ha! So funny.

I sort of remember that last couple of hours before I died. Something about a vehicle, a van I think, that I was bundled into as I walked home from school. Or maybe not school, since it was dark out…

What the hell had I been doing?

And, a van? Really? How cliché. Being dead is starting to become embarrassing.

I recalled Yazeed's death very well. It happened a few days before mine, and somebody made it look like suicide. They did a pretty good job. A sad little note containing the usual *Sorry, I love you, please forgive me.* An empty Oxycodone bottle. Why he would even have that I do not know; obviously it was planted, though the cops decided he was just another dumb-kid statistic.

I didn't know if the note was Yaz's handwriting or not. All I'd ever seen of his penmanship was his drawings. And the trademark signature he always used: A tiny cat face with curling whiskers forming a "Y".

The suicide note did not have that signature.

Fooled his mom and stepdad, fooled the cops and the coroner too. But it didn't fool me. I remember screaming into my pillow, trying to figure out who would want a middle-class Indian-Canadian teenage boy out of the way.

Up till Yaz died, I had imagined myself a moody, troubled soul, ravaged by the vagaries of unwanted fate. Somewhat resentful of my easy life, a tad annoyed by having good skin and shiny brown hair. One of the girls in school had a shaved head, and rocked it. She didn't do it to show support for a cancer sufferer, she just did it because she thought it was bad-ass.

Now that I'm dead, it's too late to do any of the dumb things teenagers are supposed to do. Any *more* of them, that is.

When my mom and dad heard about Yaz, they tried to comfort me. "He wasn't thinking straight. If only he'd talked to someone! Er… did he talk to you, sweetheart? No? Don't cry, he's in a better place now."

It was hard to keep from literally—not figuratively—gagging. Mom and Dad are so sweet. My dad is the kind of guy whose name is stitched on the pocket of his shirt and has one less beer after work than he really wants. My mom learns new crafts involving yarn and glitter before Christmas, along with her gal friends, and during my lifetime mostly refrained from searching my room for drugs and/or alcohol. She can search all she likes now. I don't mind.

If she finds things she doesn't like or understand—well, sorry Mom. Love you.

Twirl. Back to the cemetery.

I had it to myself except for another ghost loitering beside his headstone—Dylan Lee Smith, beloved son—moodily prodding at some flowers with his bare toe. He ignored me, naturally.

When I first noticed I wasn't actually *dead* dead (i.e. in a coffin trying to claw my way out like a zombie), it was really hard to pin down what time it was. Or even what day. My ghostly perception seemed to pop around, shift unexpectedly and leave me with a brain that cut in and out like a bad internet connection.

Today was most likely a weekday. I deduced this by shreds of evidence like traffic noise and number of people around. Without my phone I was virtually helpless, drat it. I always thought I wouldn't be caught dead without my phone. Joke's on me.

The early-summer breeze wafted through the drooping willow and evergreen trees that shaded the cemetery grounds. I could smell lilac. But how? How could my dead little nostrils pick up a scent? Never mind. I could figure out the rules of being a ghost later.

I let myself drift along the line of headstones till I came to Paris. No, it isn't an unusually large cemetery, it was just Paris McNally, 16, believed to have died from meth that had been dosed with fentanyl.

Or maybe not.

Could it actually be that there was a "suicide pact" among local teens? A pact that didn't exist, because really, how tabloid-style moronic. But I'd known something creepy was going on, possibly involving a couple of our teachers. And that guy from the drug company.

Oh, *that* guy. I'll get to him later.

No suicide pact existed. Yaz and I were murdered. Possibly Paris was too. Definitely a conspiracy, but not ours. In fact, Paris might be around here right now, getting into full-on detective mode as she started hunting for her killer. Frankly, I didn't give a damn about her killer except that it might also be *my* killer. And Yaz's. It's true, ghosts are ridiculously self-centred.

But you know… I might have kind of asked for it. Several ways I could have asked for it. So you could call it self-induced homicide.

As I look back from my vantage point of being non-alive, I was really pretty clueless when in the world of those fortunate beings who still suck up oxygen. As expected of a scrawny underachiever with an attitude.

"You're too smart to be doing so badly, Holly."

"Young lady, you need to pull up your socks, get with the program."

"We have faith in you, Holly. We're here for you."

Yep, gotcha. Thanks, everyone at Northmount High.

But I'd had a hunch that something was wrong at my school. Like, teachers should never drive nice cars, right? How could they afford a nice car? Someone was topping up a few salaries, and you don't get topped up without selling something.

There are many things that can be bought and sold, not all of them durable goods.

So, in the best tradition of amateur psychology and an urge to meddle, which never really goes well, I ended up dead. Not just dead, like from some crowd-pleasing disease which I fought spunkily, or from a foolish but daring motorcycle accident. Dead from actual murder.

Why can't I remember who did it? I was right there when it happened.

Bubble and Burp

Twirl. Cemetery: gone. Backyard swing-set: here.

Haven't spotted Mom or Dad yet at my house, either inside or outside in the yard. I'm not sure I really want to. Were they crying, holding each other for comfort? Like many disgruntled kids and teens who have been thwarted in their desire for something—video game, girlfriend, tickets to the Monster Truck Rally, whatever—I had spent time relishing the thought of my parents wailing and rending their garments in grief at my death.

"I'll just die and then you'll be sorry!" Accompanied by a percussive interlude of door slamming.

Well, Holly—who's sorry now?

I'm noting that, in certain conditions, the view that I see through my cold, dead eyes is kind of glowy and flat, like wearing night-vision goggles. Which I did once, at an outdoors show, where there was a Canadian Forces Recruitment booth trying to entice idiots to join up. They were offering the general populace a chance to try out the latest electronic goodies. Yeah, right, they're going to let civvies try cutting-edge tech.

I sashayed in and slapped a set of those puppies on, and they actually worked. Inside a dimly-lit tent, I could see pop cans hiding in fake bushes, trying to look innocent instead of like Improvised Explosive Devices. Which made me mad. The whole thing made me feel sick. The greenish hue of everything was so ultimately fake that you knew it had to be real. I mean, the Army is all about deception, high tech, and domination, right? The colour of the enhanced fake foliage in the army booth made me think of the bilious yellow-green of Mountain

Dew. So real, so chemical, so toxic.

You know what? People who drink Mountain Dew are people who've given up. Like they just don't care anymore, they want to die toothless, diabetic and alone, the sooner the better.

Well, it matters to me. Damn it, it matters how I died.

Soda pop lives. Bubble, burp and you're done.

I handed the goggles back. "So, what do you think, young lady?" asked the guy manning the booth. I say *manning* but I mean *boying*. Someone that young and slender should not be defending our fair country.

I gave him a so-so hand wiggle.

"Ready to sign up?" He bounced on his boot-clad toes, ignoring my skeptical expression.

"Let me think about it, nope."

"Ah, too bad. We need more women in the military."

"No, you don't."

"Yes, we do."

I leaned my elbows on his little camo-draped booth and batted my eyelashes. "I think the military-industrial complex has a complex. I think it's all madness. Madness! If no one signed up to fight, they would have to call off the wars. Right?"

His face clouded up. "But... but..." His narrow shoulders slumped. Obviously he wasn't having much luck getting recruits. "We *have* to have wars."

"Human nature, right? Violence is the answer to all our problems," I said sympathetically. "Sad, isn't it. Have you considered un-signing-up? It's not too late."

He wavered for a sec, but then his jaw firmed up. "If you move out of the way, miss, the *men* behind you can get a chance at the night vision goggles."

Two eager pre-teens surged forward. I left, feeling as though my work to promote world peace was off to a so-so start.

And now here I was aimlessly twirling in my backyard, which

was in need of mowing. I was merely a spectator at what was once my life. I wanted coffee. A big mug of sweet, foamy, delicious coffee… if I had that, I could figure this all out.

I admit it: I like anything with caffeine in it. Which of course includes chocolate. And I like grilled cheese sandwiches and I love pickles. I like my red socks that have a pattern of little black bears on them, which perk me up just knowing they're on my feet.

Fortunately I died wearing them, so here they are, along with ankle boots, black bike shorts and a purple t-shirt with a picture of Sylvia Plath on it. Quite possibly this casual yet significant outfit will be on me forever. I mean, will my feet, including socks—and the rest of me—ever go away? Like, disintegrate or evaporate or something? Or is a dead person a ghost forever? I wouldn't mind a different t-shirt now and then. A cool leather jacket would be nice…

So. I could see myself. I could look down at my cute little bod and note the stylish ensemble. But if I'm dead and still thinking about it, I must be a ghost, and doesn't that mean I'm invisible?

Again, coffee would be a real bonus in this situation.

Speaking of toxic (and I was a while ago), a girl from one of my classes has been visiting my grave after dark. She pours a can of Mountain Dew over it, and has done so for three nights now. I gave her my soda pop rant once, and I do believe she misinterpreted it. Or maybe she's more subtle than I thought? Maybe Mountain Dew Girl hates my deep-sixed guts.

Her name is Oda or Livvie or something. I sold her some of my mom's antidepressants a few times, and we bonded, or at least she bonded with me. In truth, I have little respect for those who bought pills from me, but her tribute is endearing. Lately she's been drinking most of the can and just sprinkling the last few drops over me. Which I appreciate. I mean, my parents planted daffodil bulbs there, do we really need to poison them?

But back to Yaz. I knew as soon as I met him that he was true friend material. A bad boy with a good boy inside. He was the one, when we were both thirteen, who got me to skip choir practice and try this new thing called "vaping" in his backyard behind his mom's compost bin and talk about why magic is illogical.

Wrong. It is so totally logical. In fact, without magic, none of this ghost stuff would work, now would it? So, Yazeed, my friend: Hah. You thought you knew it all.

Garage-twirl-trees. You good-looking son of a bitch, you died first and now you are so far ahead of me that I might never catch up. But I can try, and it would work better if I'd stop this infernal twirling and losing my train of thought.

The Nursing Home

Suddenly I'm back at my shrine. It's sunny, the rain is gone, and it's really kinda endearing. I can smell things, like the deep earthy scent of a freshly dug grave… Wait. There's a new drawing propped up against one of my teddy bears, looks like a fantasy city floating over a desert, all purples and greys with yellow blobs like aliens weaving among the towers. It's got to be another Yazeed special. But it's one I've never seen before.

Yep, there's his little Y signature. Unless someone is plundering his secret folder of artwork and putting it here, he's been busy. And he's been right here in the cemetery.

Really have to figure out how this all works.

First I need to get hold of him. He can't be all that dead. Gotta be around somewhere, floating in the ether. I glance around. Nope. Just a serene landscape of trees, gravestones and two guys necking on a bench.

I could check in on his sister Leela. I know exactly where she is, and I know Yaz spent a lot of time with her the last few months.

Leela is four years older than her brother, which makes her 21, exotically beautiful and wicked smart, but currently out of commission due to being in a coma. Her boyfriend beat her up until she was almost dead, then took off into the night, only to be gunned down at a club in a totally unrelated but Karmic incident. Meanwhile, Leela's brain was permanently damaged.

I've seen her. She's still beautiful, but the smarts are done for. At first she was in the critical care wing of St. Michael's downtown, connected to lots of machines, tended daily by physiotherapists who flexed her limbs and tried to get her to respond. She did not respond.

After a month or so of this, she was moved to a nursing home for long term care. Her parents sprang for a private room at a first-class place, which Yaz told me was running them over $3,000 a month. Canada's government insurance takes care of nursing and physician costs but room and board for the resident costs extra. A ridiculous amount of extra. Things got pretty tight after a few months and Leela ended up in a second-tier nursing home where attention is sporadic and physiotherapy non-existent. She's been there for two months now. She keeps on breathing, kind of unfortunately. Her parents visit every day, but they have no idea what to do that might make any difference. Mostly they weep and pray.

Before we died, Yazeed and I spent a lot of time at her side, reading celebrity magazines aloud to her, keeping her up to date on all the stuff she loved. Fashion, TV stars, bloggers, hip-hop artists. The best vodka to chug without getting a hangover. How to cure a hangover. Leela was even crazier than her brother. But she didn't ask for what happened to her.

Twirl.

And there I am, in her room at the nursing home. Whoa. Sitting in an orange plastic chair with my knees primly together, like I've been just waiting for her to open her eyes and ask what the fuck is going on.

I lean close and whisper confidingly. "Not a lot, Leela. You're in a coma. Your mom and dad are devastated. Oh, and your brother is dead."

No response. Surprise. "So, have you seen Yazeed lately? Maybe spotted him floating around, maybe a little, you know, transparent?" I wiggled my fingers in the air. Woo-woo.

Leela breathed in a slow, even rhythm. Her face was so perfect and serene. I leaned over so close I could feel the feathery tickle of her breath on my lips.

"Hey!" I hissed. "Leela! Are you still in there? You and Yaz used to stick together pretty tight—nothing creepy, just… you loved each other. Well, I loved Yaz too. Where is he? Is… is he anywhere at all?" I poked her on the shoulder, expecting my finger to go right through like ghost fingers are supposed to. It didn't.

Leela gave a big gasp and sat up. The sheet fell away to reveal a faded blue hospital gown over the mounds of her perky breasts. Her eyes opened and blinked a few times.

I found myself across the room, hauling on the window, apparently trying to open it and escape. I was making little squeaky noises. Leela turned her head and looked at me. "Hey, Holly! You're here! The Hollster. Hollier-than-thou. C'mere and sit down. I won't bite." Leela's slender brown hand patted the hospital bed.

I shook my head and kept tugging at the window. "No. No no no no."

The voice changed, got a little deeper. "Holly, it's me. Yazeed. I'm in here—"

Yaz? In Leela's body? Oh my god. Could it be true? My heart gave a lurch. Didn't know it could still do that. "Yaz! I—"

The door opened and a nurse bustled in, poking at the tablet in his hand.

Nipple Fade

The guy must be new on the job, as the regular staff tended to ignore alerts among their somnolent clientele. His name tag read "Gunnar." Tall, pale and kind of wispy, he was the least gun-like person I'd ever seen.

Leela/Yaz managed to flop back down and play brain-dead before Gunnar looked up from his tablet. He spent a minute checking things out, turning her gently in the bed, fluffing her pillows and so on. He spent more time sighing deeply while gazing on her lovely face. He looked baffled but basically okay with whatever hiccup just happened, and with one last longing glance back at his own Sleeping Beauty, he left. Well, well. The guy had a little thing going for coma-girl.

I'd been sitting in my chair looking as innocent as humanly possible, but he didn't see me.

Of course he can't see me, I'm a ghost.

This was going to take a while to get used to.

Leela/Yaz remained lying prone in case of triggering a heart monitor or motion sensor or something, but her big tawny-brown eyes opened and tracked me as I crept to the bedside like a scared mouse. "Yaz?" I whispered. "Are you serious? It's you?"

"Yeah. Thank Cthulhu you're here. This is so effing boring."

I looked at him. Her. Lying there. My boyfriend was in the body of a gorgeous woman. Who happened to be his sister.

"Well, yeah, boring," I replied. "So, Yaz… how exactly did you get inside Leela?" I thought about it. "Uh… is she still there too?" If so, ew. Siblings.

The tawny eyes closed. Some tears leaked out. "I'm not really sure. I just kinda… soaked in when I was, um, leaning over her wiping my eyes. And no. There's nothing. Leela's totally gone. That shitbag Erik. God, I want to find him and kill him again, and make it slow this time. I figure if he's a ghost too, he might pop in here to see his handiwork, so I've mostly been hanging out in Leela. If he shows up I'll come out and… *can* you re-kill someone?"

"I sort of doubt it. But first—can you get out of her now? Like, be you again?"

He didn't answer, but in a moment I discerned a faint wavering in the air above Leela's sheets. As if he were crawling out of a grave, Yazeed forced his way up and out of his sister's chest, his body forming up like water drops quivering and suddenly sticking together into one big human-shaped drop, which settled feet-first onto the floor by the bed. He was mostly transparent, sort of like frosted glass, but as I stared at him he firmed up.

"Really? That's what you were wearing when you died?"

He sighed, looking down at his jeans and mismatched sneakers, one red and one black. Nothing else. He shrugged. "Maybe I was changing clothes and got interrupted. Look who's talking."

"Maybe later we can work on wardrobe issues."

I looked back at Leela, who I sort of expected to look deflated and empty. But she just lay there, breathing steadily. I pulled the sheet a little higher on her neck, since she looked cold to me. When I looked back at Yaz, he was just chin and eyes floating eerily a foot above his nipples.

"Hey! You're fading out, my friend." But as I stared, he came into focus again. Head, neck, torso, jeans. The sneakers were the last to arrive.

"You did too, for a second," he said. "Keep looking at me…"

"Okay…"

"Now look away for a minute, and I'll look away from you."

We did it, then looked back.

"Hm. Must be something about concentration. If I look at you hard, you get more 3-D."

"Yeah. You too. What if we look away too long and go completely invisible to each other?" I started to jitter. "Also, if I'm a ghost, how come I could move Leela's sheet? How come I'm not floating through walls and chairs and stuff, huh?"

"Some advice: Quit worrying about shit like that. We need to find out who killed us."

"Yeah, it's what we do. Let me be the first to say I didn't kill *you*, okay?"

He moved close, reached out a hand and tenderly stroked my cheek. It felt like he'd run an ice-cube across my skin. The chill of death had taken us. Suddenly I felt so sad I almost burst into tears.

"Hey, I know you didn't kill me," he said, softly. "But I want to know who did. And who offed you, too. We need to try to figure out what was going on before we died. I can remember up to about two hours before."

I crossed my arms and moved back from him a bit. His abs were coming in loud and clear. Not much chance they'd vanish.

I said, "I think we need to go back farther than that if we're going to figure it out. For me, it started just after Christmas. Contracts were coming in pretty well, college application essays and stuff. I was making some decent money." I wondered briefly if I had ever done things just for the sake of doing them, and not for potential monetary gain. Didn't seem that way. "This one guy, he introduced me to a friend who was trying to talk me into a spot of industrial espionage."

"You're kidding."

"Nope. This guy, Bill or Miles or something, said he'd set me up with an internship at Thane-Yeager Pharmaceuticals, since he could tell I was an intelligent young lady."

Yaz and I got the same look on our faces. *Yeah, right!* Then Yaz snickered and said, in a plummy voice, "Ms. Eddols, with the larcenous, devil-may-care attitude you have displayed during your illustrious high school career, plus your *stellar* marks in chemistry, I'm sure you'd be a great *ass*-et to our organization!"

I rolled my eyes. "He *said* he was doing secret internal review of unethical practices in the industry, and needed someone from outside the system. He made it sound pretty cool, actually. He said I'd get to travel." Pause. "Okay, I see where the stupid comes in."

Yaz smirked. "You sure he didn't mean something more like infiltrate Planned Parenthood pretending to be knocked up, and get the dirt?"

"No! Anyway, I'd never do that."

"Good, because I'm sure they're super aware of idiotic shit like that."

"But what did he really want?"

"Into your pants?"

"No," I said, "that was you, cutie-pie." Yet he hadn't got there. Damn, I died a virgin. "But he wanted me to do *something* creepy, for sure."

We watched Leela for a while. I told him about the twirling in front of my own final resting place at the cemetery, and he said he did the same thing, only at the mantelpiece of his parents' split-level, which was tastefully mid-century modern in design. Apparently he'd been cremated and placed in a decorative urn. Interesting. "So is that like a traditional funeral-pyre thing brought into the 21st century or something?" I chirped.

He told me to fuck off. Deservedly. We sat, me in the orange chair, him on the edge of the hospital bed, slowly fading.

"Let's get out of here," I said at last.

"And go where? All I can do is here, and my urn. And a couple of times that place… you know, that place…"

"Where we used to exchange saliva?"

"Yeah. That place."

"Sure, but how? Like, concentrate on it? Kind of "beam me up"?"

"If it doesn't work, come back here."

"Right." He squinted his eyes, clenched his fists and suddenly—poof—was gone.

I did the same. Twirl. Trees-swing-set. Shrine. Crap.

Concentrate, damn it! Twirl. Trees…

And there I was. At our special place. Yaz was already there, leaning casually against his mom's black plastic compost bin, hidden behind some shrubs in his backyard. "Took you long enough," he said.

The Compost Bin

"Scenic route." I peered around in case of alert neighbours or dogs or pervs in the bushes. Nothing. I was counting on the theory that unless a live person actually managed to catch a glimpse of a ghost, then concentrate on it long enough to bring it into focus, said ectomorphic spirit was pretty much undetectable. "Okay! We need to figure out how to handle this. What the rules are." I rubbed my hands together.

"Because you love rules."

"I *so* love rules. For instance, are we free to go wherever we want, instantaneously? Because, wow."

Yaz nodded judiciously. "Yes wow."

He got a dreamy look on his handsome brown face. "No," I snapped. "You cannot go to the girls' locker room. Yaz, we have to stay on mission."

"Fine. Okay. So, it's my theory that we can travel at will, as long as we know the place we want to go. I'd like to go to Amsterdam, for instance, but I'm not going to try it because I don't have a memory of it."

"Amsterdam? Okay, why not. I myself would prefer Iceland, but I won't try it because your theory is so compelling." He gave me a dose of stink-eye. "And how much impact do we really have on the living world? I totally expected to pass right through things, for instance, but no. I feel like I'm in a movie with inferior special effects."

He nodded. We'd had discussions about this sort of thing during our lifetimes, critiquing movies we'd just seen, or mimicking Miss Huang trying to explain quantum theory to us in Physics class.

"Hey," I said. "We should test how big a thing we can move."

"Well, I've been able to pick up pens and paper. Um, you know… to draw stuff." He glanced at me, eyelashes fluttering modestly.

I widened my eyes and spread my hands. "What are you talking about? Pens? Paper…?"

Yaz turned and shoved the compost bin. His fingers sank in just a bit, but it rocked back, then settled again. "Holly, stare at my fingers, okay? Really hard…" I did.

He shoved the bin again, and it went over. "So," he said, looking at the veggie peels and eggshells strewn across the lawn, "we firm up when we concentrate."

"Well, that's a good start," I remarked.

"Yeah," he said, glaring down. "Sure. We can create a mess almost as well as before. Help me get this cleaned up."

"No. Your mom will blame raccoons. So, we can go pretty much anywhere we want, we're invisible, we can interact with our environment, and since we're already dead, we can't be killed. Sweet."

Yaz stopped picking up potato peels and coffee filters and wiped his hands on his jeans. The stains sank in and vanished. Nice. I'd been worried about laundering my outfit, now I didn't have to. He said, "Yeah. But how do we apply all this talent to catching our killers?"

"And," I pointed out, "the killers of the kids who *supposedly* committed suicide?"

"Oh, yeah. Them."

"Them. Three kids have died so far this school year. It's ridiculous."

"Plus us."

"Right. So, five. Insane. This whole town should be in lockdown." I started to chew my thumbnail but made myself stop. Was I actually interested in someone else's death, besides my own? A bit late to become an ethical person, wasn't it? "Any chance you really *did* off yourself?"

His eyes shifted to the side and back again. "No. None at all. Maybe. I don't remember."

"Yeah. We can work on that later." Yaz had been dealing with some issues, not just the brain-death of his beloved sister. "By the way, thanks for the new drawing. On my grave. You are really good."

He looked away, decisively this time. "Whatever. So who's next on the list? To get suicided."

That was an excellent question. "Hm. I guess we need to figure out why the rest of us got killed, then maybe a solution will fall into place."

"So any idea how to do that? Do you know *why* you got killed?"

"Not really." Guy with van. Annoyance turning to outrage, then fear. Then pain. Blackness. That's about all I could remember. "I have the feeling it's something to do with skeevy pharma guy."

He looked skeptical. "The one your contact introduced you to. Okay, I guess. It's a start. Can you find him? Infiltrate his office or cell phone or whatever?"

"I can try." I cracked my knuckles until Yaz made me stop, but cracking my knuckles helps me think. "I have his card at home, unless it got thrown out after I died."

"He gave you his *card*? What is this, 1990? And trust me, your parents have not thrown out anything. They won't disturb a hair on your pillow. Or in your sink, or stuck to your clothes…"

"Shut up! This is serious." I was starting to get very interested in the odd goings-on in our neighbourhood, a middle-class suburb of a university town in southern Ontario. I could understand drug deals and thievery going down, but murder? Not so much. "We need mobility to get anything accomplished. So how do we get around, if not the poofy way?"

He looked at me funny for a second, then said, "Uh, yeah, we can't just poof around town. Though there's nothing wrong with that. But it looks like we need a personal connection to make that work." Pause. "I really don't know why I'm not at the board shop right now."

"We can probably just get on a bus. Plus, we don't have to pay."

He brightened, then frowned. "Is that ethical? I mean—"

"Of course it's ethical! We're not taking up any space! As long as no one detects us we won't firm up, right? People can just sit right on us."

"I will not be happy if some dude sits on you."

"And neither will I. So we'll stand. People can move to the back of the bus right through us."

"No one ever moves to the back of the bus."

"And we care why?"

He shrugged.

"Okay. I will go home, find that business card and get skeeve's info." Perhaps my phone was still lying around, still working… surely Mom and Dad wouldn't just cut it off right away, would they? Would they even know how? "Yaz, you will go to school and snoop around. Listen to stuff. Gather clues." I really wished he had died wearing a shirt. Even though my ghostly little bod was stone-cold dead, I was feeling a certain twinge. Down there. Sigh.

Cuddling with Yaz. Mmmm. Hanging out on my phone. Miss that normal stuff so much.

But I had other, more important, things on my mind. It was really kind of exciting. If I had blood circulating in my veins, it would be circulating hard.

The crisp, white business card belonging to Kyle Trotter, V.P. of Development, Thane-Yeager Pharmaceuticals, was right where I left it, under a pile of paperbacks beside my bed. Books I'd been dying to read... ouch. Maybe I still could.

I reached out a finger and opened the top one at a random spot in the middle. *Sarka in Sunlight*, by my fave author Gillian West. Some kind of dialog was going on involving a kick-ass girl who had inherited an ancient alien weapon from her mother, and her idiotic boyfriend who apparently was a vampire turned from the true path into deception.

Somehow I had no desire to read it, even though there had to be a better boyfriend lurking broodily in the wings. Someone else's imaginings. What once had been involving and cool was now ho-hum. I had bigger fish to fry.

Then I spotted my phone, fortunately lying screen up. I started poking and swiping. Nothing. Took me a while to grasp that a smartphone screen reacts to the teeny electrical jolt it gets from a living human finger. A dead finger means nothing to it, the snotty little hunk of plastic. Oh, how I wished I still had my old-timey flip-phone.

I contemplated placing it somewhere weird, just to freak everyone out. But that would be childish. I was no longer a child, dammit. I was a ghost with a mission.

The Tasteful Urn

Yaz and I met up that evening at his urn. We were going to debrief, to borrow a military term.

I had to admit to myself that I was really and truly grateful to whatever weirdness was making it possible to have Yaz back in my, um… life. The lump in my throat was something he did not need to know about. He was already plenty cocky.

His parents had gone to dinner at his aunt's condo. We had the place to ourselves, not that anyone would notice us. But the presence of newly-bereaved parental units would be way too sad. And what if they caught a glimpse of us? They would freak, that's what.

I sprawled on Mr. and Mrs. Varma's chrome-footed avocado green couch admiring the sunburst mirror above the giant fireplace. On the mantel of which was Yaz, their only son, in his tasteful bronze receptacle.

"Listen to this," Yaz said, leaning close to me. "So Suzanne heard that Kasha—"

"Which Kasha?"

"Kasha who got her grandpa's Miata when they took his license away. So Suzanne said she heard Kasha say that Olive was skipping class, and when she wasn't doing that she was crying in the girls' room."

"So this was Suzanne hearing Kasha hearing Olive. Who the hell is Olive?"

"Really? You know her."

Blank.

He squinted at me. "Olive… rides a bike to school… has her hair in a braid all the time…"

"Bike… braid… Oh! Mountain Dew Girl!" Huh. I knew she

was peculiar and depressed, so I had ignored her except when providing her with antidepressants. Which didn't work. Could she be next up for suicide? "Is someone targeting mopey people? To make it seem legit?"

"I'm thinking it's more than that. Someone must be gaining something."

"Not just messing with people for twisted fun?"

"No, that's you, girl. What's the mantra? Follow the money, right? We need to find out who stands to benefit from these deaths."

"If it's a teacher, or teachers, there should be ways to find out. We know our way around school, we can poof in and snoop. If one of them is pushing drugs, or, or covering up some kind of evilness…"

"I'm so sick of everything coming back to drugs. Why can't there be some *other* kind of bad?"

"Yeah… but it's a start. Drugs are a gateway drug."

"Don't be a smartass. We can just keep our eyes peeled for…"

"People acting weird."

"It's high school."

"People acting *extra* weird."

But each victim was different. Some were fine, some messed up, but none I could imagine actually being suicidal. None had enemies, or secrets to hide, as far as I knew. "Okay, so tomorrow I'll hang out in the girls' room until Mopey turns up. See what she does."

"I could hang out in the girls' room for you," Yaz said, grinning.

I took the opportunity to slap him upside the head.

*   *   *

To pass the time until restroom duty tomorrow, I'd get my ghostly ass to the offices of Big Pharma tonight, and hunt around. No idea what I should be looking for, but I had to start somewhere. Theoretically no one would be there after, say, nine, and I could roam freely. In fact, I could roam freely at any time, but since I might have to pick things up, rummage around, open computers etc., it would be better if no one was there to be freaked out and call Ghostbusters.

Eventually I realized I'd have to get in during regular office hours, when I could slip inside along with someone else entering and scope the place out. There were rules to being dead. I couldn't just do whatever I wanted. But once I got the lay of the land, I could poof in. Then it would just be a matter of hanging out till everyone left.

Still a couple of hours to fill.

Twirl. Swing-set. I sat in it, just for old times' sake, and started to push back and forth… then remembered all the horror movies I'd ever seen with an empty swing going back and forth eerily. *Man, a girl can't even chill in the backyard anymore.*

Twirl. Hippie coffee shop downtown, full of university students sipping giant lattes and eating muffins. I loved this place. A lot of high school kids hung out there too—and it smelled great—but I found that the delicious food odours didn't make my mouth water. I guess those in the spirit world didn't need to worry about dieting… I snuggled next to a really cute guy, who had no idea that he was sharing space with the hottest ghost in these here parts, and basked in the familiar chatter.

Which mostly seemed to be about some guy, a junior at my school, who'd been found by the janitor wandering aimlessly up and down the halls like a zombie. The janitor, wary of—naturally—zombies, had called the cops. The kid had been taken to Social Services temporarily because his parents were at a conference in Vegas.

Hm. Interesting.

The intersection in the spirit-verse between zombies and ghosts has been little explored. At least by any graphic novel, comic, or movie I'd ever seen. I cracked my knuckles. The cute guy I whose coffee I was appreciatively sniffing looked down, right to where my hands were. I had to get out of here before someone spotted me and I started to firm up.

The invisible-on-the-bus trick worked, and at five o'clock I bucked the stream of people leaving the pharmaceutical company's main office and laboratory complex. Once inside, I decided it was better to take the sleek open-concept stairs rather than an elevator, just in case of getting stuck inside it. I could probably poof out, but I didn't want to risk it, nor getting spotted by some mentally susceptible individual on a crowded elevator. That would take some 'splainin'.

Big Pharma

The hallways were wide and tastefully decorated on the Marketing and Development level, where Kyle Trotter, V.P. of Development, had his lair. Thick carpet, oil paintings, solid wood doors.

Unfortunately, said doors were all code-locked. Indicating to me that there had to be something to hide in there. My only hope was the janitorial service, and for that I'd just have to wait.

Wandering around, I came upon a break room, and in it was a brand new, shiny coffee machine, the kind where you use pods. My cold little heart leapt in joy. I decided to try an experiment. The pods sat in a little tray, and after some concentration I got my fingers solid enough to pick one up. Next, *Open the pod bay door, Hal.* Pressing the brew button took hardly any effort at all, and soon a stream of the delightful brown nectar of the gods foamed into a paper cup.

I raised it to my lips, savouring the delightful aroma, with no idea of what would happen next. What happened next was a puddle of hot coffee on the floor around my feet. I felt nothing, I tasted nothing. My lips were dry, my mouth un-scalded. On the plus side, no coffee stain marred my ensemble. I sighed. Since I didn't seem to need sleep, it stood to reason I didn't need coffee to keep me awake.

I wondered if, now that I'd been inside, I'd be able to poof out and back again… Better not risk it. If I had to wait till tomorrow night to return, another of my schoolmates might die. Or get zombified.

At 8:22, a chunky lady in mom jeans came along, trundling her cart before her. Her earbuds leaked some kind of soft pop. Celine Dion. Michael Bublé. Ack.

She coded the door open as I watched. One one one one. Jeez, people!

In we went. I had to wait for her to finish and leave, but her work was cursory at best. She dumped the waste-basket, dusted a few shelves, ran a wand-style vacuum around the middle of the floor and trundled on her way. The door locked behind her. I rubbed my cold little hands together. What, exactly, was I looking for? A folder labelled "Secret Experimental Death Drug"? A photo of me being dragged into a windowless panel van? An alphabetical list of kids: "Offed/To Be Offed"?

I started to feel the stirrings of inadequacy.

After some fruitless minutes rummaging in Kyle's in and out baskets and wishing Mom-Jeans hadn't emptied the trash, I finally noticed that the computer was still on. I jiggled the mouse and the screen lit up. Kyle Trotter, the idiot, hadn't shut down for the night. Yessss.

I found lists, all right. Kyle seemed to be in charge of a company junket to Mazatlán, and was making his naughty-or-nice list. I looked in amazement at a dazzling profit statement, which the tax hounds at Revenue Canada would also appreciate, should they ever see it. Moving on, having to glare at my hand every so often to firm it up, I came across something more relevant. A list of all the high schools in a 100 kilometre radius from this very building.

Each school name, including my own, was hyperlinked to what turned out to be encrypted files. Damn. But maybe I had my smoking gun…

The doorknob rattled. I froze. Suppressing the urge to dive under the desk and hide, I forced myself to glide silently into a corner and rely on being a ghost. The door opened, and in came my pal Kyle. I wondered if he'd been disappointed that I'd died before he could recruit me for his "espionage" squad. Or had *he* killed me? He really didn't look like the type.

I glared at him, just in case my existential anger might penetrate his stylish tousled hair.

Another two people followed him in, a silver-haired man in a trim business suit, and a skinny blonde woman rocking her geek glasses and laced-up work boots. She had her hands in the pockets of her lab coat, and looked seriously pissed.

All three immediately began to argue in the suppressed hisses of the truly angry. Reminded me of Leela's boyfriend Erik, when they'd been dating and he'd got jealous. Erik had always been bad news, and hopefully was now roasting in hell.

I listened closely. Much of what they said was either sciencey or market jargon that I could only barely follow. Demographic slippage. Choline inhibitors. Transverse sub-limit phosphorus uptake. FDA workaround. Their discussion seemed to focus on something they called Essence. Sounded as if a fancy new product was having a rough go.

Sad. Unless? Unless they were testing their new product on unsuspecting high school students.

Kyle, steam coming out of his pink ears, marched to his

computer. I jittered in case he noticed it was live. But he was too angry to care, just whacked his fingers on the keyboard until a printer across the room started whirring.

"There," he snarled, retrieving the page and shaking it in their faces. "I've done my part, dammit! It's not my fault the process isn't working." He glared at science gal.

She sneered and pushed her glasses up her nose in a belligerent manner. "It isn't working because you're not following instructions. The idea is to *not kill* our subjects. Okay, Kyle? Can you grasp that? Subjects who die are of no use to us. I don't care how anxious you are to start selling this product."

Silver haired gent rubbed his chin. "Leave it, Cloris. Don't worry about details. We're at the early stages, but we need to keep pushing. That means we keep testing. Kyle—no more useless *accidents*. Cloris—get your damned ducks in a row. Our backers want results yesterday. Understand?"

Cloris gritted her teeth. "You seem to think that suitable subjects are easy to find, Richard." She threw her hands up. A bit theatrical, but on her it looked good. "How did I let you drag me into this, anyway?"

"As I recall, Cloris," Kyle pointed out, "it was you who came to us."

I saw her jaw clench. "You're right, for once. But I had an entirely different goal in mind." She headed for the door. "You know where to find me."

That left me and the two guys. Silver haired Richard said, "That bitch is going to be trouble. Never thought she knew what a scruple was."

"Ha. She's in too deep to climb out now."

"As are we all. The mistakes you've made have cost us time, money and credibility. One more dead kid and I'm tossing *you* to the wolves."

Kyle clenched his fists and turned red. I'd actually thought he was kind of cute when he'd first approached me with his bogus offer. All buttoned up and shiny. "I've kept the Prime operational, haven't I? I can take what I know and find people who appreciate what I'm doing, *Dick*."

"It's *Richard*, Kyle. Better yet, call me Sir. This meeting is over." Both of them slammed their way out.

Prime. What, or who, was the Prime? The key to all this?

I poofed outta there.

Twirl.

Swingse—Hey. I found myself hanging in the air over a horrific scenario. I couldn't believe my eyes. Mom and Dad were dismantling the swing-set. Which had been slowly rusting in our backyard since I was knee high to an Ewok.

How could this be happening? It was just wrong.

My eyes began to sting at the sight of Dad grimly wielding a crescent wrench and Mom gripping a coffee cup in both hands and telling him he needed WD-40. I'd spent a lot of time since becoming a ghost trying to hold it together, avoiding seeing my parents or spending time at home, in case of seriously destroying this after-lifey silver lining to my own death. But what did I expect would happen? Their only child was gone. So, no grandkids to play on the swing-set. It was useless now. Why keep a reminder of better times?

I wanted to throw a tantrum. Scream and cry. I wanted to hug my mom and tell her I was sorry for being dead. And for being kind of horrible when I was alive. I wanted to help Dad haul the lengths of metal tubing to the curb, then get him a beer.

My chilly, empty insides were even emptier now.

Mountain Dew Girl

Some amount of non-time passed. Time is weird when you're dead. Especially when you're trying to think. Put random things together into a pattern.

Crying for what I'd lost didn't help, and I eventually stopped.

Deep breath.

Um, why was I even breathing? Did I need to breathe, as a ghost? Well, I did need air so I could talk… and I do like to talk… but does my dead metabolism actually need oxygen?

Oh, forget it. Add it to the pile of stuff-to-be-figured-out-someday. Yaz and I could pass time later, delving into this kind of existential conundrum.

Okay. High school students getting killed. Why? Testing. Testing what, exactly? Teenagers are notorious for scarfing down new and dangerous drugs, just for the sheer heck of it, but why would this seem like a good business plan? A dead customer is no longer a customer.

Unless they are fine-tuning the dosage and don't mind a few oopsies along the way.

I was hovering behind Mom and Dad as they sat on the couch and watched the news. The local anchor was recapping the teen deaths, and I learned that I'd been strangled to death. No drugs had been in my system, which probably surprised some folks. But there went my theory of sneaking drugs into teens to see what happened to the little darlings.

I hadn't been able to connect with Yaz last night, or this morning. I'd checked on Leela, but he wasn't in her, waiting like a spider for Erik to show up. He wasn't at any of our usual spots.

I started to panic a bit. What if he'd gone past being a ghost and died completely? I'd wondered about all the other ghosts, how they might be handling things. Each of them had a mission, just like Yaz and me. No one wanted to talk to us, they were all too focused on their own issues. Maybe we were milling around in death's foyer, and a big ol' house of the haunted was on the other side of a door. Is that what was going to happen to me too? This led to the natural question: is there a heaven? A hell? I'm basically indifferent to religion and religious ideas about sin and punishment, or godliness and reward. I happen to think that you should just be a good person whether someone is watching you or not.

The definition of "good" is a little squishy, and I know I didn't always live up to my high and lofty goals. Okay, I rarely lived up to them. And my goals aren't that lofty. But was being a ghost just a temporary stop along the way? To wherever?

Yaz and I, and probably lots of other formerly living humans, would have to find out sometime.

I really had no idea of what usually goes on in the girls' restroom, besides peeing and applying makeup, and the constant and obsessive vaping that no rule or regulation is going to stop. The girls hanging out in there had tended to shut up when I came in to do my business, but now, what with my being invisible, they let it roll. Disappointingly, it was boring. Boys, clothes, forays into half-baked philosophy that amounted to boys and clothes and where they fit into the circle of life. Some of the girls hugged each other and praised the glory of their hair.

The restroom was either echoing empty, or jammed with girls between classes. I had to hang out waiting for almost two hours before Olive, otherwise known as MDG, wandered in and joined the between-classes throng.

Her eyes locked onto mine in about a nanosecond. What the hell? Olive could see me? I should be completely invisible to her, as I was to all the other girls.

I stood unmoving, not knowing what to do. She eyed me for a

couple of seconds, then slouched dejectedly over to a sink and washed her hands until everyone else stampeded out. We were alone.

"Holly," she said. "So… what's going on? You alive?"

"Nope."

"Dead?"

"Yep."

She didn't seem to be unusually upset at my sudden reappearance as a phantasmic spirit. This turn of events could only mean one thing. MDG was totally into me. How else had she seen me so immediately?

To test this, I approached her, looking her up and down in a seductive manner. Not hard, she was actually kind of cute under the oversized grey garments she was draped in. Big, watery blue eyes, button nose, tightly pursed lips…

"Hey, back off!" she snapped. "My mom was right. I should stay away from Godless harlots like you."

I held up my hands. "Whatever! Hey, a question. You feeling at all suicidal?"

She lifted her lip in a wee snarl. I admired her for it, but then her chin quivered. She let out the most heartrending wail I'd ever heard outside of a three-year-old. I hustled her into a stall and locked the door behind us.

Someone stuck their head in from the hallway. "Hey! You okay in there?" Sounded like Ms. Lee, the part-time music teacher/guidance counsellor.

"Cramps! Ow!" I groaned, reaching across MDG to flush the toilet.

"Okay then! Come to me for Midol if you want, honey." The door squeaked shut.

I scowled at MDG. "What the hell? MD—I mean, Olive, what's going on?"

"I… do-on't… kno-o-ow," she sobbed. Then she took her

dripping, snotty face out of her hands and burst out laughing. "Ha! Oh God! I don't know what's wrong with me. This keeps happening. One second I'm fine, the next I want to d-drown myself. Then I feel like I could do anything. Like, be a cowgirl."

"A cowgirl."

"Or a doctor! An airline pilot!"

"Yeah, no one wants a doctor or a pilot who's obviously nuts, Olive. Go with cowgirl."

We left the stall so she could splash water on her face. Then she fumbled in her purse and hauled out a pill bottle. Before she could open it, I grabbed it. Just in case. "Whatcha got here, cowgirl? ...A-*ha*."

Thane-Yeager Pharmaceuticals, right there on the label.

She grabbed it back. "Hey! They're vitamins, okay, freak? See?"

She thrust the bottle into my face. "'*Vitae essentia*'," I read aloud. "So... essential vitamins? You sure that's what you're taking? It's not, like, Ritalin? Who's your doctor?"

"Just leave me alone. Go back to being a ghost."

She turned her back on me. I could see myself in the mirror, and, damn it, I was already fading now that she wasn't looking at me. It was weird. I looked at her straight, stiff back as she deliberately ignored me, and felt as though something was missing. Like she was distracted, her mind wandering. I moved around her so I could see her face in the mirror.

For a second I thought I saw something move, behind me in the reflection. Like someone had snuck in and was eavesdropping. I whirled around and squinted, and for second saw a scrawny little kid... a girl. Staring at Olive, who apparently didn't, or couldn't, see her.

Another ghost? Well, why not? Although why a little kid was haunting the high school girls' room I did not know. I waved at her. She saw me, I was sure, for her eyes got big. Then she faded out.

I turned back to MDG. Her reddened eyes stared blankly at her own reflection. Slowly her hand opened the pill bottle, took out a pale green lozenge and popped it in her mouth. She chewed it, her jaw moving mindlessly. Jeez.

If anyone needed vitamins, it was MDG.

Or whatever she was taking. Essential vitamins. Essence? The green pill didn't seem to be killing her, and she showed no signs of wanting to bash her brains out on the walls or sink.

"Okay," I said. "All righty then. I'm outta here, Olive my friend. Gone. You won't have me bugging you any more. No more Holly to kick—"

"Will you just shut up and leave?" She began to sob again.

Fine, but I was going to keep an eye on Li'l Cowgirl in case she tried something stupid.

The Benefits of a Classical Education

Leela didn't react when I poked her.

Yaz still wasn't in there. I was feeling less panicky but more depressed by now. Where was he? What was going on? What was Essence and was it even important? Maybe it was just a new antidepressant aimed at the teen market. Or maybe it *was* vitamins. Maybe my murder via guy-in-van was just an unfortunate coincidence.

I couldn't believe that. Nothing about all this was legit.

Gunnar drifted in to Leela's room, looking anemic. He gazed cow-eyed at Leela's comatose bod, adjusted her blanket up under her chin and drifted out again. I had a sudden vagrant thought, but before I could apprehend it Yaz poofed in, looking flustered. Still naked from the waist up. Yesss.

I flung myself at him. I knew I must love him because he firmed up immediately, and I don't mean in the nudge-nudge, wink-wink way. He firmed because I had invested severe emotional currency in him. And when you invest? You get interest. Ha.

He peeled my arms from around his torso, leaned back a little with a frown on his face, then leaned forward and kissed me.

His skin was cold, his eyes hot, his heart not beating.

It was unlike any other kiss I'd ever experienced, and I've experienced a few. Before I met Yazeed, I kind of liked three other boys, and took them for a test drive. You want to see if the motor runs, right? Mostly, kisses are soft or hard, wet or dry, sweet or icky. Sometimes a tingle of attraction lightens the mix. But this one? When Yaz and I were alive, we did a lot of kissing and other forms of clothed entertainment and it was super fine… but when our lips touched there in that dreary long-term care room, a sort of mini-explosion took place.

I found out a lot of things during the explosion. One: I really don't need to breathe. Two: Neither, apparently, does Yaz. Three: Kissing, if you're doing it with the right corpse, is amazing.

After a while I pulled back and prepared to get mad.

"Where the hell have you been?" I demanded. Was I as firm to him as he was to me?

What is love, to the dead?

Never mind. "Seriously, Yaz, I am really pissed, and I have a ton of stuff to tell you!"

"So do I." He held me at arm's length. "Um. Sorry. About making you mad." Pause. "So, who goes first?"

"Me." I filled him in on what I'd found in my sleuthing trips.

He nodded. "Okay, so Olive is even weirder than we thought, and Big Pharma is up to no good."

"Pretty much. So, you?"

He let go of my hands and squeezed his eyes shut. He was trembling. "I was stuck in some kind of… ghost trap."

"Excuse me?"

"I think it was somewhere either at the Thane-Yeager labs, or a place owned by them. I caught sight of their logo now and then, when stuff wasn't in my way."

"Stuff? Yaz, what the hell?" He looked seriously upset.

His hands twisted together. "I can't really describe it… it wasn't like an animal trap or a prison cell or anything ordinary. I… I was trying to find a way out. Don't know how long I was in there, but it was too long."

I hugged him. "It's okay. You're out now, right? Tell me more. Like, how did you get *in*?"

He ran his hands through his hair, starting to look sheepish. "Okay. I was trying to go somewhere I'd only seen online. There's this ultimate surf shop… it's in Hawaii. I really want to learn to surf someday…"

"Are you frickin' kidding me? You tried to poof to *Hawaii*? Plus, how do you think surfing's gonna work for you, *dude*?"

He dug the toe of his red sneaker into a crack in the tile floor. The black sneaker looked embarrassed too. "Well… the website is really detailed…"

"Never mind! I'll yell at you more later. So, ghost trap."

"Yeah. So I had the surf shop pictured in my mind, I was doing that twirling thing we do, right? I figured I was on my way. But then I felt this sort of stretching, like I was being pulled sideways. Like… pizza dough, or taffy." He shrugged helplessly, watching the skeptical look on my face. "I got pulled into a…" He waved his hands. "Place."

Why did boys have to be so useless at talking? "What *kind* of place?"

He groaned and rubbed his hair some more. "Like a forest at night. Where all the trees are moving and moonlight is shooting around, and wind is howling. Or maybe like an aquarium. With seaweed fronds, or, or tentacles…"

"Tentacles. Cool. Did you see anyone? Like, a blonde chick in a white coat?"

He looked wide-eyed at me. "How did you know that?"

"Cloris. The science lady at the Big Pharma meeting last night. She was taking a lot of sass from those two suits, but I bet she's the mastermind behind all this."

"She looked pretty young to be a mastermind… and kind of cute…"

I swatted him. Admittedly Cloris was adorable, but most likely also evil. "Was she in the trap with you?"

"No. At least I don't think so. She was standing beside some computer stuff, lab benches, blinking lights. Outside the tentacle zone."

I said, "Okay. But it looked like she knew you were in there?"

"Hard to tell. She was looking down at her tablet, not moving. Holly, I just don't get it! What are they trying to accomplish? There are lots easier ways to kill high school kids. That new drug from China everyone warns us against, for instance."

"You know what? I'll bet they're trying to develop a way to get us to behave. Follow orders. Be obedient little citizens who vote the way they want."

Yaz's eyes narrowed. "That actually makes sense. They're testing an obedience drug on certain subjects, but the drug isn't working right. It's killing people instead of zombifying them into docility."

"So that guy people were talking about at the coffee shop, the one the janitor found in the hallway? They used too much and the drug shut his brain down. A bit more and he'd be dead." I thought about it. "I'll bet Olive isn't just naturally wacko, she's on this drug. It's messing with her head. Maybe that's why she's taking vitamins."

"Hang on. Vitamins? For her head?"

"I saw the bottle. *Vitae essentia*." I spelled it out.

"Ah," he said, smugly. "The benefits of a classical education. It's Latin. Loosely translated, it's *life essence*. Not vitamins."

"Since when did you study Latin?"

"During my Harry Potter phase. Never mind."

"So… who would need meds called 'life essence'? Those *without* it, I'm thinking."

Together, we yelled, "Zombies!"

I started to hold up fingers. "So, first there was that senior with the fancy 4X4. Shot himself in his mom's garage. Then Paris in the debate club who everyone knew was on meth. So, meth. Then… uh… that guy…" Couldn't think of his name.

"Jun Wei. Hanged himself from a tree outside his boyfriend's house."

"Three. Plus us is five." I needed my other hand. "And if you want to count Olive and Zombie-boy, a total of seven."

"All could have been staged as suicide or suicide attempts. They were cleaning up after failed drugging attempts."

"Except mine," I said. "I was strangled and tossed in a dumpster, which is a hard way to kill yourself. Plus, no drugs found in my system. I was strangled. They didn't even try to make it look like suicide."

"God, Holly! A dumpster? I… didn't know." He looked sick, then he looked angry, then he looked sick again. "That's harsh. Maybe you were getting close to something…"

I'd been getting close to accepting skeevy pharma guy's offer. Money, intrigue, fancy suit-guy. Stupid me. Something must have scared me off, they thought I knew too much so couldn't let me loose. Instead of becoming a test subject, I'd been snuffed.

The nursing home hallway was quiet. No one wasted a lot of time fussing around the clientele here. Yaz and I watched Leela breathe for a while. She looked so calm and lovely. I'd always envied her hair, thick, black and wavy. I had a suspicion that

Gunnar was keeping it nice for her…

Wait! My idea came back. "Hey, Yaz, do you want to try something?"

"I'm not in the mood."

"Shut up and listen: do you think you could get inside Leela and operate her? Like, get her walking around, talking, like that?"

He reared back. "Whoa. I *really* don't want to—"

"You made her sit up and talk before! Think what we could do with her. She's solid, visible, gorgeous… she could '*come out of her coma*'. Talk with the cops, get an investigation into your death going… all kinds of stuff."

"Jesus. I don't know, Holly. That's kind of…"

Horrible. I wouldn't want to do it. Inhabit the body of my own sister? Make it climb out of bed, walk and talk? Risk the harassment of every guy who spotted the lovely Leela? I sighed and looked sympathetic. "Yeah, *hard*. You probably wouldn't be very convincing as a woman."

I could tell that he was torn between wanting to assert his ability to get all drag queen, and his innate reverence for his sister's dignity. And I respected that. I think he was actually ready to go for it, but Gunnar chose that moment to come in. He was carrying a backpack. After spending a moment sighing over Leela, he pulled out a computer and a couple of textbooks and settled in on the orange chair. One book was *Ultra Low Power Bioelectronics: Fundamentals, Biomedical Applications, and Bio-inspired Systems*, by Rahul Sarpeshkar. The other was a well-thumbed paperback: *Long-Term Care Initiatives for the Layperson* (updated 2002), by Lois Coombs and Bernard Ritchie.

Well, by golly—Gunnar must be putting himself through brainiac school working nights at the home for the nearly dead and hopelessly addled. Good for him. I floated close and took a better look. He was younger than he'd first seemed. Probably one of those precocious kids who entered university at age 14 or whatever… he looked the same age as Leela.

We left him to his studies and adjourned to the hallway.

Yaz hissed, "Even if I want to, how can I move Leela with Romeo hanging around?"

"Okay, forget making her walk. We'll just have to wait till he leaves, get a wheelchair… No, wait. There are security cams all over, we'll be spotted. Hmm." I came to a reluctant conclusion. "We need to enlist Gunnar to be on our team."

Yaz crossed his arms. "We're not a team. We're a duo."

"Okay, sweetie, but Gunnar could be useful. He knows this place, all the schedules and stuff, he can turn off the cams and help us get her out of here."

"And *how* exactly do we enlist him?"

"Uh, we could catch his attention, firm up, and appeal to his scientific interests?"

"You're so cute." Yaz shook his head. "The whole idea is too risky. Also, as soon as Mom and Dad find out she's 'awake', they won't let her out of their sight."

"Why would they find out?" …D'oh.

Yaz rolled his eyes. "You wanted her to initiate an investigation, remember? That means cops, lawyers, the media… She'll be followed every second."

"Okay, okay." There went my idea, but I held it stubbornly close in case of future reference. I rubbed my neck. Strangulation had not been all shits and giggles, I was pretty sure. A flash of memory went by too fast to grab. Something that had happened between when I got yanked into the van and when I woke up dead. *Big eyes. A flicker in the back of my mind…*

Yaz said, "Can you get hold of one of Olive's pills? Maybe we could get it analyzed."

"See, that's the sort of thing we could get Gunnar to do."

Yaz growled. "I don't trust him. He makes googly eyes at my sister."

"He's in love, the poor sap. We need to figure out what Cloris the Science Gal is up to." I paused, watching Yaz's expressive brown face. Which at this moment expressed sadness. "Yaz… do you want to tell me more about the trap you were in? Like, do you think it's still there? And how *did* you get out?"

He shrugged. "I dunno. I was in this weird space with fronds flapping around, getting in my face. I… kind of freaked. A little. Suddenly I was twirling again, and it seemed to last a long time. Eventually I ended up at my urn."

"Hm. Well, first of all, be careful how you twirl, okay? No more trying to go anywhere you aren't sure of."

Despite my motherly advice and genuine concern, he still looked sad.

I really wished right then that Yaz could make himself known somehow to his mom and dad. Without destroying their hip, urban worldview. I was sure they didn't believe in ghosts—I mean, who does? But did anyone really hang onto skepticism when their kid died? And their daughter was as good as dead. Everyone wanted to believe their loved ones were still out there, somehow. Somewhere in the sky, happy and content.

But what about the loved one, floating around vainly trying to solve a stupid mystery? Yaz was really hurting. He needed reassurance as much as they did.

"Listen," I told him. "You stay here and keep an eye on Gunnar. You have my permission to scare the crap out of him if he tries anything with Leela. I'm going to Big Pharma and check out the lab."

He nodded, looking extremely dispirited for a spirit.

The Super Secret Science Lair

I poofed back to the lobby of Thane-Yeager and checked the directory. All the labs were on the lower levels. "Of course," I muttered. "The basement. Where else."

I had to follow the security guard around until he got me downstairs through the many code-locked doors. He shook his head and looked exasperated when he spotted Science Gal through the glass walls of her lair. Oops, I mean, state-of-the-art medical research facility. It seemed as if he hadn't expected her to be there.

He didn't open her door, just walked on by. I had to peer through the glass willing her to open up... Then I slapped myself on the forehead. I could see every detail in there. *Poof.*

Cloris was hovering over an array of screens, connected to several CPUs tangled together by wires. Lots of electronic stuff seemed to be crammed under her desk or teetering in stacks around a very cursory chemistry setup. If she was developing drugs and medications, it wasn't in the petri-dish and bubbling flask way, it was via sheer number crunching.

She was muttering to herself, alternately perching on a stool in front of the screens, and pacing around looking grumpy, which I understood was her natural expression. Resting Bitch Face. On one of the screens was a photo of Olive. Beside that was another photo, of a grinning pre-teen wearing a messy blonde braid and a saucy expression, caught in a casual shot with a sunlit lake behind her.

It had to be a young Olive—but I could barely imagine MDG smiling and carefree. Had something happened, and now she was depressed, confused and just plain nutso? Was that why Thane-Yeager was monitoring her—so they could feed her drugs until she tried to off herself?

Or... suppose she'd been partially zombified, and now they were tracking her. Or maybe she was in on it. Maybe Olive was recruiting *other* hopeless losers. Maybe she'd been trying to recruit me in some backward way. But why?

I drifted around not touching anything in case Cloris managed to spot me. There must be a ghost trap around here… but what would one even look like? Wasn't there something called… um… like, a faraway cage? I had a vague memory of physics class, something about faraway cages. They blocked rays or something, and were made of magnetism. Or magnesium.

Nothing resembling a cage lurked in a shadowy corner, dang it. There was a metal box the size of a microwave oven, perforated by thousands of teeny holes, like something you'd keep a husky rat in, but nothing that could hold someone the size of Yazeed. Did Cloris have a secondary lair somewhere?

She wandered away from her screens and started to fiddle with some knobs or whatever, and I took the opportunity to scroll down from the Olive pix. The younger one was dated, and would have made her ten when it was taken. Cloris came back before I could find more info.

This sleuthing gig was harder than it looked on TV.

I poofed back to Leela's bedside.

Yaz was hovering over Gunnar's shoulder, reading his laptop screen. He looked at me and said, "No porn. So far."

"Only a matter of time, right? Hey, I need your help. Something's going on with Olive. Do you know where she lives? I need to talk to her."

"Why would I know where she lives?"

"You know everything. At least that's what you keep implying."

"I know you can poof to the principal's office and take a look at the student files. You've been there often enough to know the lay of the land."

If he was trying to shame me, he was failing. "You're right! I can do that! Hang on—"

In about two minutes I was back. "'kay, she's at apartment 201, 5576 Wilbur Lane." I looked at him expectantly.

Yaz gave me the look my mom used to give me. "Number 39 bus. Every twenty minutes."

Less than an hour later I found myself standing outside apartment 201 with my thumb up my ectomorphic bum. Now what? Should I try, like, knocking? Why not?

My hand firmed up after a long, dirty look. I knocked. It worked. The door opened and a middle aged woman with a church-lady hairdo peered out. She was holding a Mountain Dew, which of course she was. She frowned, clicked her tongue and closed the door.

I could hear her say, "One of your school friends is playing a trick, Olive. Knocking and running away. I do *not* appreciate being taken away from Survivor Ultimate Smack-down to answer the door!"

"Sorry," Olive muttered. "Won't happen again."

In another two seconds she emerged, shutting the door behind her. "What are you doing here?" she hissed.

"I need to ask you a question. What happened when you were ten?"

She turned even paler than usual. Leaning against the door as if she was holding back the armies of Mordor, she quavered, "Do you mean… at the lake?"

"The lake. Yes! What happened at the lake, Olive?" I moved close, being intimidating.

She closed her eyes. "Oh, god! I… I…"

"You have to tell me."

She closed down totally. Her expression went blank and she turned and went back inside.

Something tugged at the hem of my t-shirt. Oh-oh. Some kid who lived on this floor had spotted me. I looked down to see a girl, who looked exactly like the picture of young Olive I'd seen on Cloris's screen, except she was faded around the edges. She wore a bathing suit, and her hair was wet. I held very, very still. A flickering, big-eyed image popped back into my memory. This ghost kid had been there, shortly before my death in the van. Had she been trying to tell me something? Warn me?

She stared at me wistfully, then closed her eyes and sank to the floor. After a while her eyes opened, staring at nothing. Then she began to float above the floor, limp as a corpse. Just like a drowned body in a lake, floating in water.

Then she vanished.

My body was crawling with icy goosebumps. I thought I couldn't get any colder, but this was just too creepy.

Okay, then. I pounded on the door, not letting up until I heard Olive's mom scream at her to get the fudge-brownie door.

Olive opened up, and would have looked steaming mad if she wasn't crying.

"You drowned," I stated firmly. "You drowned at the lake."

"No. I swam to shore. Do I look dead to you, Holly?"

"No, but I happen to think you *are* dead, you just don't know it."

"You're not making any sense," she sobbed. "Nothing makes sense!"

I touched her shoulder gently. She flinched and I drew back. "Sure it does. Just not in the ordinary, socially accepted way. Something traumatized you so badly at the lake, that you kind of... split in two. Dead and alive."

She gave me a disgusted look.

I continued. "That's why you can see me. You're partially in the land of the dead." I crossed my ephemeral arms. "Have you noticed a little girl hanging around? Bratty kid in braids?"

"No," she stated stonily. "I have never—"

Her mom threw the door open. "Olive, what are you doing out here? Are you talking to yourself again, sugar pie?" She looked up and down the hallway, not seeing me.

This was getting ridiculous. Time I used my initiative, as my history teacher, Mr. McKay, used to hiss at me, fed up with the futility of it all. I reached out and ran my cold, dead hand along Olive's mom's cheek. She yelped and swatted at herself. I grabbed her hand and squeezed. Admittedly not hard, I hadn't begun firming up yet. She still couldn't see me. She began to flail. I hung on, getting right up in her grill, calling, "Hey! Look at me!"

"Stop it!" Olive yelled.

"Oh Jesus, oh Jesus!" OM howled.

I saw the instant that she spotted me. She slammed her eyes shut. "This isn't happening! Oh Jesus!"

"Open your eyes. It's me, Holly. Olive's friend."

Olive sneered at me.

"Just how many other friends do you have?" I snapped at her.

"But Holly's dead!" OM wailed. "You're *dead*! Why can't you just go away to heaven?"

"So many ways I could respond to that, but I really need to ask you a couple of questions, okay? Won't take long."

"Please, let go of me," she whimpered.

"Sure, but first—was there some kind of… incident? At the lake, when Olive was around ten years old?"

OM's whole body stiffened. She turned a gaze of pure ice directly at her daughter. "I told you never to talk about that. I warned you! Now you're spreading lies about my brother? Your uncle Alan, who loves you?" She wrenched her hand free and slapped Olive across the face. "I *told* you to keep your lying mouth shut!"

Olive cringed to the floor. "I didn't tell anyone! It never happened! I swear I—"

"*What* never happened?" I plastered as much of my ghostly cold body up against OM's as I could get, twining my arms and legs around her like a snake. She shuddered and twisted, cussing like someone who needed her mouth washed out with soap. "What did Uncle Alan do to Olive?"

Olive moaned, holding her head.

People up and down the hall were opening their doors, taking a look, and quickly slamming them again. Pretty soon the cops would show up.

The little girl appeared again, and she had her mouth open in a silent scream. She was naked, with her bathing suit bunched around her knees. A blue, frilly, little-kid bathing suit.

I looked at Olive's mom, who had her mouth clamped shut and her eyes wide open like a spooked horse. She saw the girl too. She wrestled free of my grip. With one last horrified look at her daughter she scuttled back into her apartment and slammed the door.

Olive and I, and little fading Ghost Olive, huddled in silence for a while, hoping no one else would come out to check on things. So that was it—Mountain Dew Girl had been molested as a child. I felt sick, and thought about giving Olive a hug. She saw it coming and held up a hand.

"Forget it, Holly. It was a long time ago, and anyway, nothing happened."

"That's not what I'm picking up. Maybe you repressed the memory."

She held her head, tears leaking from her eyes. "There was nothing to remember." Her voice had become a monotone. "I knew Uncle Alan couldn't swim so I ran to the lake and swam out as far as I could."

This was getting really disturbing. I said, "*Something* caused your spirit to leave your body. Look, you don't have to try to remember anything right now." The girl needed actual therapy, not just me trying to prove a point.

Olive took a deep breath and hugged her knees. "I don't want to go back in the apartment. My mom is really losing it. You got some kind of ghost crypt I can stay at?"

"Unfortunately, no. But we have to get out of here in case cops turn up, or your mom drags you back inside and starts beating you up." I hauled her to her feet. "C'mon! Chin up! Now, march!"

Little Ghost Olive floated back in, wearing the look of a dog who never gets to go on walks. "Follow us, GO-girl," I said encouragingly. "C'mon!" Would she do it?

She did, fading out but always there in the corner of my eye as we left the building.

Olive, being a smart cookie despite all evidence to the contrary, pulled out her phone and held it to her ear while talking to me. Thus avoiding the "talking to herself like a crazy person" thing.

"I hope you know what you're doing, because I've got nothing," she muttered, as we hustled north along Wilbur Lane. "I don't even have an overnight bag."

"Never mind that. You are going to stick with me. I have an idea how you can get your soul back."

She sighed. "I've told you—I didn't die."

I gestured at Little Olive. "Then how do you explain your own mini-me over there?"

"Well… but… I…"

"You drowned, your soul left your body, but was unable to get back in when you stopped fearing for your life. Do you remember swimming to shore?"

"Of course I do. Are you trying to tell me that my soul just fell off? Like… like a lizard tail?"

"Oh, I like that! Cool. But it isn't going to grow back. You have to reunite with it. Until then, you are neither dead nor alive. I think it's why you're so nuts." And, I reflected, maybe why my theory about what was going on might pan out.

"Really? Okay then." She dug in her heels, turned and beckoned to Ghost Olive who was bobbing along a few feet behind us. "Come here! Now!" She actually slapped her knee, like you do when calling a dog. Surprisingly, it worked. Ghost Olive drifted closer, looking shy but hopeful. Olive made a lunge for her, and GO disappeared. She just popped right out. Maybe she poofed.

"Now you scared her… look, Olive, I may not have an actual *plan*, but I do have a viable course of action."

"Whatever." She slouched along beside me down the night-dark street, toward the office park of Thane-Yeager Pharmaceuticals, and one Cloris the Science Gal who toiled within.

The stars were white and cold above us, too far away and indifferent even to make a wish on.

Gunnar's Big Adventure

As we trailed along I realized I needed Yaz. Righteous indignation can only carry you so far, and I was starting to feel a little overwhelmed. Olive, being the only visible person on the street, was open to any kind of trouble that might walk or drive up and spot her. Even though Yaz wasn't any more visible than me, he'd be great for emotional backup.

I guess I didn't really *need* him. I just wanted him.

"C'mon," I said. "First we're going to Sunset Shores."

"What the heck is Sunset Shores?" She narrowed her eyes. "It better not be one of those club places where everyone dances naked."

"Oh, you've heard of those. Yeah, they're so awesome." I gave her a look that would have shut her up had she still been talking. Resuming her Resting Bitch Face, she kept marching.

*   *   *

Olive was in charge of getting us into the nursing home. I could poof in, but she and little GO couldn't. "I'm here to see my Gramma Mumble," she mumbled. "Room mumble." The attendant yawned and said, "Visiting hours till 11. No alcohol or tobacco allowed."

I led the way to Leela's room, Olive and Ghost Olive trailing. Once there, we were treated to an interesting tableau.

Gunnar, who didn't notice Olive wander in, was leaning over Leela's comatose form. Tenderly, he reached out to brush a stray lock of hair off her untroubled forehead.

Leela's hands whipped out, clenched around Gunnar's pencil-neck and squeezed. Gunnar emitted panicked squeaky noises.

Yaz saw us enter. "Hey, Holly," he said, through Leela's lips. "You brought friends."

"I did. Need any help?"

"Nah. I got this."

Gunnar flailed, whimpering. I felt a surge of sad affection for him, knowing in my heart that his one-sided romance with Coma-girl was doomed. Yet I had to admire his persistence.

Olive halted, looking scandalized at the scene on the bed. "What the fudge?"

"Leave it, Olive. I'll explain later. First…" I floated to Gunnar's side and began to pull his hair and generally freak him out. Leela's full, pouty lips curved into a smile. She, or rather, Yaz, let go of Gunnar's neck. He slid to the floor, hacking and wheezing.

I whispered in his ear. "You lack upper body strength."

"Augh! I wasn't… I just…"

"You just grabbed the wrong gal, dick-wad," Yaz said. Did it bother him that he sounded just like Leela, and not like an intimidating male?

"But… but… I thought I saw your eyes open… wait…" I could smell the wood burning as Gunnar tried to process conflicting information.

It's possible that Yaz had overreacted. After all, Gunnar hadn't exactly gone for the gusto. Yaz, however, had been spoiling for a fight ever since Erik killed his sister.

Yaz climbed out of Leela, letting her body sink back onto the pillows. Gunnar saw it happen. His eyes got big and white. His mouth opened. "G-g-ghost!"

"If you scream, I will enter your brain and explode your head," I whispered in his ear. Those little voices that come from nowhere can be so compelling. I really can be kind of mean.

But he surprised me. "This… this is f-fascinating. A third phase of being…" His big blue eyes started to gleam.

"Yeah, yeah, you're a smart guy. Now, crawl out of here like the worm you are and never touch this woman again! Um, except when administering necessary medical attention."

He nodded and scurried to the door on all fours, Olive watching in fascination. He looked over his shoulder at her. Their eyes locked. He stopped scurrying. Oh, for Pete's sake. Had he already forgotten his love for Leela?

"Gunnar! Keep moving. Olive! Pay attention!" I pointed at Yaz, who was pacing around in the minimal open space. "Can you see that guy?"

"The shirtless wonder? Sure. Uh, Yazeed, right? From school. So… who was the cutie that just left? He works here, right? He seemed kinda sweet. D'you think—"

"Keep it in your pants! All this is for your benefit, unless you have forgotten." She only liked Gunnar for his inability to overpower a petite woman in a vegetative state. And Gunnar probably found Olive's pasty skin, dazed eyes and trailing grey garments intoxicating.

Young Ghost Olive, floating over the orange vinyl chair,

looked confused. And exasperated.

I said, "You can come back and hit on Gunnar some other time, my friend. We have a mission."

Yaz, cocky from all the Gunnar intimidation, said, "Mission?" He rubbed his hands together.

"We're putting the little gal in the bathing suit back where she belongs—in Olive. We need to get into the Thane-Yeager labs."

Yaz thought about this for a second, looking back and forth between Olive and the kid, noting the resemblance. I love how quick on the uptake he is. "So, if this ghost can go back in Olive's body… maybe doctor what's-her-name could tell if Leela's still out there, maybe trying to get back in *her* body? Maybe?"

Wow. I hadn't thought of that, but… wow. "You've reached your lifetime limit on maybes. But, yeah. Maybe."

"So, we need to take Leela along. Make it happen."

Olive chimed in, sounding tentative. "So… could Gunnar disable the security cams I saw on the way in? And wheel Leela out of here? Me pushing a brain-dead lady around this late would be asking for trouble, with only you invisible guys beside us." Her chin went up. "I want Gunnar."

"He really isn't bodyguard material." Then I sighed. "But I guess he's better than nothing… Okay, go get Cutie-pie."

Turned out Gunnar was delighted to get on board. His shift had ended, and he'd been hanging around trying to Google Olive.

"I have an intense interest in the paranormal," he stated, bouncing up and down on his toes and whipping his gaze back and forth between Leela and Olive.

"How about that," I said. "So do we."

We headed out.

*   *   *

The night was chilly. Olive shivered, and Gunnar put an arm around her as they both pushed Leela along. She was tucked under a blanket, her head lolling. None of them looked weird or scary enough to repel drunk and/or horny denizens of the night, and I fretted until we made it to Thane-Yeager.

I poofed in, ascertained that Cloris was in her lair, then poofed back outside where the live ones were lurking behind the shrubbery.

"What about security?" Olive asked. "We can't just walk in there!"

"Actually, that's part of the plan. You do just walk in there."

"No! We don't!"

"Trust me. This should work, I think." Gunnar rolled Leela up the handicapped ramp as Olive sidled toward the big glass doors and started pounding and waving. After a while the security guard noticed, frowned, and ambled over to the doors to get a closer look at the freak show. "What can I do for you folks?" he asked through the comm panel. "Are you in trouble? Lost?"

I whispered to Olive, "I'll feed you your lines. Just go with it."

"Uh…" Olive said to Security Guy. *We're here to see Cloris,* I hissed. "We're here to see Cloris."

The guard's eyes narrowed. "You mean Doctor Roem? It's after 10 o'clock, young lady. She isn't here. Call tomorrow and make an appointment."

"She is here," Olive recited, like the world's worst amateur horror film actor. "I'm her… intern. I'm bringing… a test subject."

"Sure you are." He whipped out his phone. "Doctor Roem? Oh, you *are* here!—okay, I got some teenage girl out front claims she's your intern." He held out the phone and took a picture. "Check this out."

As I had been 85 percent sure would happen, Cloris recognized Olive, but showed no hint of surprise at her "intern's" sudden appearance in the late hours. Her eyes had widened but her pale, cranky little face remained mostly expressionless. Ha! My theory was panning out. Immediately she stated, "Let them all through, Bruce. I'll meet them at the elevator."

Olive, looking green around the gills with nerves, followed the guard, who was obviously not happy at letting them in at all. Gunnar manoeuvred Leela through the lobby and onto the elevator, and pushed the button labelled "This Way to Hell."

When the door opened onto the basement level, Cloris was there with a hand up, her cheeks pink and her eyes glittering. "Hold it right there!" she barked.

She held up a device, some kind of tricorder doohickey, and waved it around. It beeped and tweedled, as they do. "All right, you can come forward."

Olive looked about to cry, or giggle. Gunnar resembled a space cadet going on his first away mission—i.e., thrilled. No red shirt, fortunately. Leela drooled.

"So," Cloris said, rather smugly, as we made our way along a sterile, brightly lit corridor. "Three living humans and three ghosts."

"You can *see* them?" blurted Olive.

"No. But I know they're there." She opened the door to her lab. Once inside, there would be no escape for the living among us. "Step in, all of you."

Was I right to trust her, just because she had a tattoo of the cartoon Tasmanian Devil on her neck? Did this mean she was actually cool, or just crazy with a tendency toward violence? But she was our best chance to learn what was really going on. If we could get her on our side.

Gunnar parked Leela and immediately began scoping the place out, *almost* touching this and that enticingly flashing machine, but drawing his hand back. I swear he was humming under his breath. Olive tracked him with her eyes, seemingly oblivious to poor little Ghost Olive rising and falling in her ghoulish dance of death.

Why was GO unable to communicate in any useful way? Yaz and I could talk, why not her? Could it be because she was only half a person, ripped from her human body and forced to hang out in some kind of limbo? She was so young, so traumatized. We *had* to help her, no matter what Cloris's nefarious plan might be. Even if we couldn't get her back in her rightful body, there must be something we could do. Therapy? A trip to Disneyland? Were there ghost puppies around somewhere?

Cloris stared in my general direction, squinting and gnawing her lip. After a few seconds her eyes lit up and she sidled closer. Dammit, she was starting to see me. I moved behind a filing cabinet. She followed.

"Hold still. You know," she said, "I could tell when you were here before. I have no proof, unfortunately. The readings were ephemeral and sporadic, though perhaps reproducible in a controlled experiment."

Oh-oh.

I came out from behind the cabinet and crossed my arms. She ran her tricorder up and down my body, cackling to herself. Then she turned it in the general direction of Yaz.

"Look, Cloris," I snapped, "we're not here to participate in your research. We're here to put Olive's soul back in her body. And to find out what the hell has been going on with all the so-called *suicides* at my school."

She paused for just a second, weighing her options. "Understandable," she admitted. "What do you want me to do?"

"Kinda hoping you'd have a plan, lady. I know you're up to your pierced eyebrows in all this." I stared at her menacingly. "Look, I know about Essence, and I know Olive is Prime, whatever that is. Whatever you think you're doing, it's time to stop."

"And," Yaz said, taking my hand, "I need to know who murdered Holly."

Cloris perked up her ears and homed in on Yaz.

"I'd like to know too, actually," I said, squeezing Yaz's hand. This situation was so much more bearable with him by my side.

Though Yazeed's allegiance was split between me and Leela, he'd got less paranoid about protecting his sister now that Gunnar had a new enthusiasm. Two new enthusiasms: Olive, and Cloris's super-secret science lair.

Cloris rubbed her forehead and sighed. Theatrically. She was loving this, the bitch. "Yeah… sorry about that, Ms. Eddols, but according to Kyle, you were getting too close to the truth. In fact, you were running rings around him. He merely panicked."

"How do you know my—"

Yaz yanked his hand from mine. Cloris obviously could see it, because she tracked it right up to her own neck, where it was joined by Yaz's other hand. He squeezed. "Holly was strangled to death! How do *you* like it? Poor little Kyle *panicked*? Are *you* gonna panic?"

I think what most surprised Cloris was that ghost hands could pack such a surplus of constrictive force.

Yaz was getting pretty good at the grab-someone-around-the-neck gambit. I let him keep at it for a while. "Well, at least I know who killed me. Stupid Kyle the wonder boy. One murder solved." I spent a few seconds contemplating the upcoming gruesome haunting that Kyle was about to experience. It would be lots of fun to scare the accumulated crap out of him. Might make up a little for how sad my mom and dad were.

Yet something nagged at me. Was Kyle really the type to actually off someone? In cold blood? Trying to reconcile my image of the V.P. of Sales with killer-van-guy and me in a dumpster was something I'd think about later. More important things were on my mind. "So, Yaz, you admit I'm your girlfriend? In the context of an incorporeal lifestyle, what does that even mean?"

"Whatever you want it to mean, baby," Yaz said, grinning.

"Ack!" Cloris said, plucking at Yaz's fingers.

"Let her go. We need her, remember?"

He did, and began to stomp around the lab, his footsteps making no sound. So, not really stomping at all.

Cloris massaged her neck, scowling at Yaz, who I'm sure was fully 3-D to her by now. "I know your name, Holly Eddols, because you have been in the news, due to your murder. No other reason," she croaked. "Kyle was in charge of procuring subjects, not me. We need to get down to business. Yes, Olive is Prime."

"What does that m-mean?" Olive quavered, suddenly overtaken by a weepy phase.

"It means you were a serendipitous anomaly in a series of test runs I was doing. I almost deleted you from the data set, since your readings were completely outside established norms. I had to reconfigure my algorithms, test all my equipment, and get a new and better coffee maker. But once I realized your readings were valid," she waved a hand dismissively, "well, you can deduce the rest."

Gunnar raised a finger. "Well, I can certainly—"

"Shut up, Gunnar!" Yaz and I barked simultaneously.

Olive clung to Gunnar's arm, scowling at us. Gunnar handed her a Kleenex.

Cloris gave Olive the once over with her tricorder, then went to a small fridge and took out a Mountain Dew and a green pill from a bottle. Essence. She handed them both to Olive, then turned her attention back to her tricorder. Soon she had located GO, bobbing above Olive's head.

"Aha!" she crowed. "Sub-Prime!"

"Is that what you call her? So sweet."

Gunnar had spotted the metal box I'd noticed last time, the one with all the teeny holes. "Is this what I think it is?" he asked Cloris.

"Obviously."

Gunnar nodded in satisfaction.

Yaz said, "Excuse the hell out of me, but what is it, and does it have anything to do with getting some answers?"

"I know!" I chirped, suddenly remembering physics class. "It's a faraway cage!"

Cloris and Gunnar chuckled warmly. "Ha, ha! No, dear," said Cloris, "it's a *Faraday* Cage. And not an ordinary one. I've spent months tuning and augmenting this particular unit."

"Huh?"

Olive, perked up by the bubbly sugar rush from her drink, and whatever magic the Essence pill was working, chimed in. "It's a screen to block electrostatic and electromagnetic influences. Invented by the English scientist Michael Faraday in 1836."

Betrayed by smarty-pants Mountain Dew Girl. "How do you know all that? Also, were you pouring that soda on my grave to try to revive me?" If so, gosh. How nice of her.

She shrugged. "We were in the same physics class. I thought everyone knew that stuff. And no, I wasn't trying to revive you. I wouldn't be so delusional." She looked away and shuffled her feet.

We were getting off mission. "So what does a Faraday Cage

have to do with ghosts? Hey, Yaz—could that be the trap you were in?"

"Nah. Way too small. The place I saw was huge."

Cloris's eyes darkened and focused intently on Yaz. "So, you're the one I entrapped..." She glided closer to him. "I see that you tend towards translucence when not observed. Could this be a quantum phenomenon? An effect of the observation itself?" She shook her head. "I'll look into that at a later date. The cage's physical size doesn't matter, since it is not of this phase of existence. That is, in layman's terms, it occupies our space but also other adjacent universes, and therefore has more apparent volume."

Yaz said, "It also has apparent tentacles."

Cloris cocked her head. "Interesting... I wish I could become a ghost. I could see so much, do so—"

I cracked my knuckles. "We can arrange that. No problem."

"Idle threats will not intimidate me." Cloris looked at Olive and said, "Prime, you stated upon arrival that you were bringing me a test subject. I assume you were referring to this comatose woman." She nodded toward Leela.

"My sister is not a test subject," Yaz said testily. "You got my girlfriend killed. You owe us!"

Cloris frowned. "Owe you what, exactly?"

Yaz yelled, "Get Leela's soul back! Put it in her! Jeez, do I have to spell it out?"

"Hm," she said, tapping a finger against her lips. "It's not quite what I had in mind at this time. However... I will attempt it. But let me be clear: this is a quid pro quo situation."

"Huh?" Dratted Latin again!

"I means that if I am to attempt this, I need something in return."

Yaz brightened. "Sure! Yeah—whatever you—"

"You must re-enter the Cage."

The Faraway Cage

"Go back in there? No way, lady." He stalked up to her and stood glowering down, looking really tall. "It was freakin' grim in that thing. I don't know how it works and I'm betting you don't either."

Gunnar spoke up. "Actually, it's not very compli—"

"Shut up, Gunnar!"

"I understand your trepidation." Cloris said. "But, consider this: you could be the most important factor in my experiment. I'm not sure what inducements I could offer to prompt you into agreeing, but if you return to the cage, then report back—"

This time I stepped up. "No. Just no. Unless you can absolutely promise Leela's in there somewhere."

"Oh," Cloris purred. "She's in there. Everyone is. Everyone who's dead, that is. Or dead-ish."

"I'm not in there," I pointed out. Take that, Miss Queen of Science.

"Yes you are. You just don't know you're in it."

"What the hell is that supposed to mean?"

"Remember when I said the Cage is not of this phase? The phase Gunnar and myself are in is of the living. The other phases occupy the same space-time continuum, but they hold the dead, as well as the not-quite-dead who are among us yet discernible only in certain circumstances. We can interact because our phases have been… let's say, shuffled together."

"Are you trying to tell me I'm *not* dead?"

"Oh no. You're dead. However, Prime is only dead-ish. Leela as well, if my intuition is correct."

"Being in a coma makes you dead-ish?"

"That's what we are going to find out."

"Like I said, lady, not going back in there." Yaz folded his arms.

Cloris paused, eyeing him, then walked over to Leela in her

wheelchair and peered at her. "So, this is your sister. So lovely. Mouldering away, mindless and forgotten in a hospital, her beauty eroding, her muscles atrophying. You loved her once, did you not? You have already deduced that her spirit might still exist on another plane."

"Not on a stupid other plane! Like, in *heaven*!"

"An *accessible* heaven. One which I believe we can penetrate."

Really? Yaz believed in heaven? Well, why not? How was that any weirder than ghosts?

"Hang on, guys." I held up a hand. "What I hear Cloris saying is that if you scratch her back by going in the cage again, she'll find Leela and stick her back in her body. You could just man up, Yaz, give it a try. Win-win." God, I sounded like a soccer coach. "Or I suppose *I* could try going in the cage…" A passive-aggressive soccer coach.

"No! Absolutely not!" Yaz took a deep breath, probably just a reflex action since he really didn't need to breathe anymore. He ran his hands through his hair. "Okay. Let me get this straight. I'm a ghost with no body to return to, because it's all crumbly in my urn. Holly's the same—unless you plan to have her crawl out of her grave."

That was something I hadn't considered, and wanted to pretend I'd never heard. I bit my cold, dead lips to keep from making retching noises.

Yaz marched over to the little box and glared at it. "But Olive's and Leela's bodies are still alive. They have a chance. Right?"

Cloris and Gunnar nodded sagely. I wanted to slap them both.

Yaz squared his naked shoulders. "I'll do it."

"Excellent," Cloris said briskly, and began firing up computers, activating sensors, and grinding coffee beans.

I pressed my mouth with my hand to keep from begging Yaz

not to go in the cage. Unfortunately my manipulation had worked. So conflicted. Yet, what if… what if all the souls of all the dead *were* in there, somehow existing in an unknown realm? Trying their best to communicate, to reunite with the living? Millions upon millions of ghosts. In all the time Homo sapiens had been around, how many souls had accumulated? And what about the Neanderthals?

This was totally nuts. What were we even doing here? Cloris was evil!

Then I had a wild and crazy thought. Naturally, I blurted it out. "Yaz and I could go in together."

"No!" Yaz yelled. "I forbid it!"

"Yes," Cloris whispered. "*Yesss*… two viewpoints… less chance of subject loss… more data…"

Subject loss? Um, wait.

No, I told myself. I taunted my boyfriend into going in the cage. I couldn't chicken out now.

I poked Yaz in his strikingly attractive belly. "You *forbid* it? Really?"

"Think about it," Cloris said, in her most persuasive voice. "You two are the only dead I've been able to bring into focus and communicate with. Your psyches are intact. In fact, Olive's sundered spirit is right here with us in the lab. You located her and brought her to me. You are obviously adventurous and brave individuals—"

Olive snickered, gasped out a sob, then snickered again.

"Hey, Olive, you wanna try going for actual dead status instead of kinda dead?"

She shut up. Gunnar patted her hand. She burrowed into his shoulder and wept.

Oh good grief. "Sorry, Olive. Didn't mean it." I grabbed Yaz's hand. "Let's go, boyfriend. Cloris—tell us what to do."

"Just stand there without moving."

"That's it?" Anticlimactic. "Hey, what about Olive's ghost? Should she be coming too?"

Cloris shook her head, squinting at her computer screen. "Actually, she *has* been inside the cage, which acts more as a… funnel, shall I say, than a realm unto itself. Unfortunately, she still couldn't or wouldn't talk when she came back. All I need right now is a coherent overview of what you experience in there. Please don't try to do anything that may upset the equilibrium of this phase space."

"Um, sure." What if Cloris was planning to just leave us in there? What if she really was in thrall to Big Pharma? Was this all an elaborate ruse to eliminate us? I started to ask, but my words were drowned out by the rising hum, whir and gurgle of equipment. My hair lifted away from my head. The rich odour of espresso filled the air.

Yaz took my hand, and I looked down at it. Our linked digits were vanishing, no matter how much I concentrated. Then our arms began to go. I opened my mouth to say something smart-assed, but at that instant I got the same feeling of vertigo that you get when a roller coaster plunges into its descent. If there had been ghost food in my tummy it would have come up. I think I made a short *yawp* noise, and then we were in the cage.

It *must* be the cage. My arm had become a flapping strand of something like kelp, vainly groping for Yazeed's kelp-arm. Silky green fronds stroked my body, or my soul, or whatever I was experiencing as "me." It tingled. Much the way that amazing kiss had tingled. I began to shiver, in a good way, like when you're at a really good horror movie. Was Yaz feeling it too?

In the distance—or was it in my own eyes?—were thousands of tiny points of light. Like the stars, or like sparkles on a vast dark ocean. I felt vanishingly small and at the same time as if I could spread my arms and encompass the universe.

I liked it. The whole thing, rather than being scary, was

incredibly freeing. Being a ghost floating around town regretting my past sins seemed mundane next to this. After a while I remembered that Yaz was in here too, and the last time he'd been freaked out. Was it different for him now, or was this sensation of euphoria just me? "Yaz! Where are you? Yaz!"

A flapping bundle of kelp, trimmed with sparkles, launched toward me and hit me with a soft slap. I almost expected to feel wet.

"Holly! Is that you?"

"Yaz!" I grabbed for him. We clung together in the manner of seaweed, looking around with our strange new senses. Sparkles everywhere. The sound of rushing wind or crashing waves, or perhaps the howling vortex of the hereafter.

I could not believe all this was in that stupid little microwave-y cage. However, Cloris had said it was like a funnel. A funnel leading to where all the ghosts, from all of time, dwelt.

"We have to report back," I hollered. "What are we looking for? Anything other than fronds and sparkles?"

"Beats the hell out of me. Other ghosts? Are they the sparkles? Are we sparkly too?"

"I sure hope so! Some bling in the afterlife would be nice."

Another kelp bundle lurched toward us. It was small, and it came out of nowhere to cling slimily to my leg-fronds. Could it be Ghost Olive? What was she doing here? I heard a little echoing voice inside my brain. *Help me! I'm so c-cold. I don't want to be alone.*

It had to be little traumatized kid Olive. If I was picking up what Cloris was putting down, it was a special feature of the phase realm. A frill, so to speak. Our phases, once separate, had intersected, and she had found the ability to ask for help. *It's gonna be okay,* I assured her. *Don't be scared. We'll get you back inside your body.* Her ghost self finally had a voice here in the phantom realm, and I wasn't going to ignore it.

I *was* going to ignore Cloris and her instructions.

I was tired of simply reacting to what had happened. My death, Yaz's death. All the others who had been caught in some crazy experimental nightmare. If we went along with Cloris and her quest for knowledge, or power, or whatever she was after, more innocent lives would be lost or permanently damaged.

Little ghost Olive and her weird seventeen-year-old self—the one who hadn't been able to admit she'd been killed.

Leela, destroyed by a no-good boyfriend and left to rot.

Yazeed, murdered by a greedy drug corporation.

But I really didn't know what to do. I had an idea, but ideas are a dime a dozen. It's all in the follow through, like Dad used to say. Well, Dad, I hope I can make you proud… somehow.

The cage could be escaped, we knew that. Cloris expected us to return to ordinary space-time, like good little lab rats. Hmm.

After some flailing, I hauled in my fronds, leaned to one side and *shoved*. Yaz and Ghost Olive clung to me, their energy augmenting mine. Our conjoined bundle made its way as if through jelly toward the edge of the cage, coming close to what looked like a giant computer screen. It filled the whole sphere around us, really a superior 3-D effect. On it was a wavering image of Cloris, Olive, and Gunnar, in the Secret Science Lair, all with their mouths open as if they were shouting. But they just stood there, frozen. Not moving at all.

Stasis, dammit! I'd seen this sort of thing before. Lots of TV shows and movies did it. Obviously time was moving much faster within the Faraway Cage Realm than in the outside world. I could see Leela sagging in her wheelchair, drool caught in mid-stream.

I admit that Yaz's older sister had been the pinnacle of cool to me. She was smart, sarcastic, hot as hell. She didn't just follow trends, she set them. I wanted to be her, knew I couldn't. And now look at her. A brainless husk, mouldering away just like Cloris had said.

But then something changed. A darkness blew in from somewhere outside the cage, like the tornado from The Wizard of Oz. Black, coiling, powerful.

It was Leela. Over, around, and through the sad, sagging form in the wheelchair whisked a ghostly presence: herself in spirit form. She firmed up in my vision.

She wore a skin-tight black dress, funky leather wrist cuffs and a lot of makeup. It must be what she'd been wearing when Erik choked her. Her long hair coiled around like wind-driven storm clouds. No wonder she'd been popular at clubs. She wasn't caught in the stasis, she was owning the whole lab and all its phases. So was her mouth. I lip-read many colourful expressions, making it pretty obvious that she wanted back in her body. But something was standing in the way. Something most people guarded and cherished.

Life.

Ah… the incomprehensible divide between life and death. How could a soul cross it, except one-way? The usual way, into the dark mystery.

I wanted to reverse that. I had to, to save Olive. And Leela.

From death back into life. So, if you hadn't completely made it through that doorway to the afterlife, perhaps you could be shoved back the other way? Reporting back to Cloris was useless at this point. I was sick of her know-it-all jabber and suspicious of her motives. And I knew what to do.

But would it work? If it didn't, I'd have some serious amends to make…

Cloris had told us that the phases of life and death intersected. In fact, that we all existed, in some weird form, in the same area of the space-time continuum. By implication, this indicated that I was becoming a lot smarter. I was starting to get it.

Though it would make sense to try my idea on an adult—Leela—Olive was ahead of her in line. And Ghost Olive was much less scary to deal with.

With all the focus I could muster, I sent a message to Ghost Olive. *Hang in there, kid. Watch, and be ready.*

Then I focused on Yaz. *I'm going to try something. Just go with it. Hold on!*

Their sparkling fronds melded with mine in a messy swirl of black, green and brilliant flickers of light. We edged toward the boundary between the Faraway realm and reality. When I felt their combined energy ripping through me, I whipped out a frond and let it burst into the normal phase that existed right next to us: the laboratory. The twisting length of eldritch flame I emitted lashed across the gauzy barrier between normal time and phase time, life and death, and sought its mark: Olive's heart.

With an ear-splitting crack and a flash of light, it smacked her chest. Instantly she dropped to the floor. Not merely dead-ish any more.

It was now or never. Ghost Olive's stunted consciousness throbbed with fear and hope. *Now's your chance, kid,* I said. *Go to her! She's you. She needs you, and you need her.*

A pulse of something like heat went through me, and probably Yaz too. Felt good. I was sick of being a cold, empty ghost. Little Olive's fronds peeled away from ours, she firmed up into something like a swimming octopus and darted directly for Olive's dead body. In an instant she had slipped in, like bong water soaking into a pillow.

The wavering edges of the Cage vanished. The stasis ended. Regular noise and movement resumed. I smelled something electrical burning.

Olive twitched, gasped, opened her eyes and sat straight up. "Son of a bitch!" She scrambled to her feet and began to pat herself all over. "What just happened?"

Her entire demeanour had changed. Her posture was aggressive, her eyes glowed and her cheeks were pink. Even her hair had gained body. She looked down at herself. "What the hell am I wearing?" She stripped the baggy grey sweater off to reveal a baggy grey t-shirt underneath, and squared her shoulders, looking around for someone to fight.

It was a joy to behold.

One thing I realized instantly: We needed to go shopping, stat.

The Faraday Cage had released us, or had maybe just burnt out, and all of us were shuffling back into our normal phases. My fronds were morphing back into arms and legs. Yaz's too. The sparkles were fading as the Phantom Realm retreated.

Cloris, hunched over her equipment, muttered and cursed. "Dammit! The field has collapsed."

Yaz launched himself at her. "What does that mean? What about Leela?"

The smell of burning metal and wiring made my nose wrinkle. Pops and hisses sounded from under and around Cloris's desk, and several of her computer screens blinked out. She swatted Yaz's hands away. "Look, there's nothing I can do until I rebuild, and it *won't* be here at Thane-Yeager."

Gunnar circled warily around Olive as she scowled down at her ugly pants, and said, "Now that you have proof of concept, Doctor Roem, I can certainly see—"

"Shut up and let me think," snapped Cloris. "Once Dick and Kyle find out about this breakthrough, they'll confiscate my data and get rid of me."

"Uh, *get rid* of you? Does that mean…" I made a throat-cutting motion.

"Probably. Therefore, we can't let them find out about any of this." She pointed at Gunnar. "You! You seem to have a brain.

Help me dismantle my equipment and purge my files."

Gunnar, surrounded by bossy women and literally smokin' hot computers, sprang into action. I wondered how Olive would adjust to having a boyfriend whose allegiance was torn. From what I could tell, that girl could handle anything now that her soul was back.

Yaz was by Leela's side, holding her unresponsive hands and sobbing. "I swear to God," he bawled, "I'm going to get you back! Cloris, you better come through or, or…"

"Or what? Don't worry, I have a backup plan. If you all help, we can successfully relocate."

"Do you have a backup *lair*?"

She eyed me. "Of course I do. And while I'd love to stand around and chat, we need to get out of here and leave no trace."

"Other than all this melting equipment."

"They can have it." She grabbed her espresso machine and headed for the door. "Nothing useful will be left."

I had to admire her style.

Olive pushed Leela in her wheelchair. Gunnar, laden with a big box of assorted data storage devices, followed them. Smoke rose, setting off the alarms.

As the automatic sprinklers came on, I grabbed Yaz by the hand and together we poofed outta there.

And Then What Happened

It was three days later.

Olive had gone home, quickly browbeaten her mother into submission, thrown out all her old clothes and medication, and gone shopping. With me floating by her side, telling her what not to wear.

I had to yank her hand away from anything animal print. Or with fringe. She displayed a tendency to go for the slutty stuff, probably in compensation for her anger over being molested all those years ago. She'd been repressed during her formative shopping years.

Cloris, armed with multiple degrees, blonde hair and an evil disposition, had secured herself a cushy research grant from a rival drug company, and was busy freshening up her backup lair in the university's derelict Biology Complex, which had sat half-vacant for months now that a new one had been built. She offered Gunnar a position as her assistant. Surprisingly, he declined.

You could tell it was a hard decision for him, but he did the right thing after wrestling with the tempting offer. "Who will take proper care of Leela?" he pointed out. "None of those idiots at Sunset Shores gives a crap. I can only imagine what her hair will be like without me there."

Gunnar had reverted to his adoration of Coma Girl once Olive had regained her soul and become feisty. Boy, would he be surprised when Leela got back in her body. And there lay a problem.

Leela was nowhere to be found, in any of the realms of life, death or kinda-death. Her spirit, which had seemed eager to get back into her body, had vanished completely.

Yaz simply refused to believe it. He blamed Cloris, but Cloris now had enhanced security and opaque walls, so he couldn't get into her new labs to scream at her.

"My sister is out there," he stated grimly, seething in our old spot next to the compost bin. "Somehow she got scared away, or driven off by Cloris and her stupid cage. Why didn't we grab her when we had the chance?"

"We'll find her," I assured him, though I had no idea how. There was plenty of universe out there for a spirit to roam— maybe she just didn't want to rejoin the crazy circus that is human life. "We will figure out a way. We'll get some Essence pills and give them to her. And some Mountain Dew."

"Like, put it in an I.V. drip? God, Holly, you make me insane sometimes."

"Fine. I can see you really don't want me around. I'll just leave then. Outta here. You can beg me to stay, but I won't. Go on, beg. You won't see me any—"

He snarled and poofed out, probably to Leela's bedside. Gunnar had been great, sneaking her back into the nursing home after our escapade. The whole nighttime operation had probably been the highlight of his life so far. I'd found out his real age, and it was not the one on his job application at Sunset Shores. He was twenty. Barely older than Yaz and me! And already a fuddy-duddy.

The old gang would never be the same. The past was gone, never to return. So crazy that time worked the way it did... people were born, lived and then died, and those left behind in the stream of time didn't even know their loved ones were still out there. I sighed, moped a bit, and twirled to where the swing-set used to be, so I could mope harder. My familiar spot, forlorn and empty—

But the swing-set was there. Right where it had always been.

Huh? Had Dad and Mom bought a new one? 'Cause this swing-set was shiny and rust free. I hung there gawking at it, feeling completely betrayed. What the hell? Had they no respect for all the years I had played on that old swing-set? Licked it when it was frozen to see if my tongue really would get stuck (it did), bonked my head on the upper bar, scraped my little knees on the slide? It had my DNA all over it!

After a while, I heard a screen door slam. A familiar sound, part of my childhood. And you know what else was part of my childhood? Me. As a child. There I was, skipping over to the dopey little slide next to the swing, and climbing up.

Whoosh, down I went. Gosh, I was a cute kid. But how could

it be me? I looked around. Everything was the same but different. The maple tree was more like a sapling. And then I spotted Silly String, asleep on the back porch, an orange ball of shouldn't-be-alive. I so desperately wanted to grab him and pet him and hug him… but I didn't want to scare my kitty. On the other hand, you know the way cats stare at nothing sometimes? As if, maybe… there's a ghost nearby that only they can see? I cruised over to where he lay in his patch of sun.

"Hey," I murmured close to his ear. "Silly String! Goofy Guy! Nutty Nuts! It's me."

He opened his eyes and looked right at me. My heart did a flip, then went back to lying there in my chest like a dead fish. Silly String knew I was there. Then he closed his eyes and went back to sleep. He saw me, and he simply didn't care.

Typical feline. I drifted back to watch myself play on the swing. I knew boredom would set in soon for little me, and I'd go back inside to read comics.

No doubt about it—I had somehow twirled myself into the past.

This was a fine state of affairs. My first impulse was to find Yaz, tell him all about it, and have a good laugh. However, little six-year old Yazeed might not appreciate a teenage ghost hassling him, if he could even see me.

I watched myself pumping away on the swing, going higher and higher. I showed athletic promise that never manifested itself in later life.

I contemplated the meaning of time and life for a while.

Wait—what if I couldn't get back to my own time? What benefit to me would there be in existence in the past? But… I thought for a while, remembering sci-fi stories I'd read. What if instead of the past, I was in an alternate universe? Gunnar would know. He liked to ramble on about stuff he'd read online, and some of it involved the multiverse. If Gunnar was here now, he'd be a know-it-all kid and would enjoy explaining to me that even if I did return to the "present," it wouldn't be *my* present, but an entirely different timeline.

Crap.

I decided to ignore Gunnar's imaginary lecture and try twirling back to the Tuesday I'd left. But first… I peeked in the kitchen window. It must be the weekend here, because both Mom and Dad were there, drinking coffee and reading the paper. Dad liked to read articles of interest to no one but himself aloud while Mom did the crossword.

I sighed. In just over a decade I'd be dead. I wanted to whisper in little me's ear: Hey kid. Don't be a bitch when you get older. Don't be selfish and thoughtless. Cherish life while you have it. Tell Mom she's pretty. Accompany Dad on his trips to the hardware store.

Contemplate the brevity of your time on this plane of existence, damn it!

Instead I closed my eyes and twirled.

Publishing credits

"Speaking Sea"
Originally published in *Tesseracts 8*, edited by Candas Jane
Dorsey and John Clute, Tesseract Books, 1999

"Softlinks"
Originally published in *On Spec* Vol. 3 #1, Spring 1991
Reprinted in *ComputorEdge*, December 1992
Reprinted in *On Spec, the First 5 Years*, Tesseract Books, 1995

"The Queen of Yesterday"
Originally published in *Realms of Fantasy*, January 1998
Honourable mention in 16th Annual *Year's Best Science Fiction*

"The Emperor of the Half-Garden"
Originally published in *House of Zolo's Journal of Speculative
Literature*, Vol. 1, Jan 2020

"The Fragrance of Orchids"
Originally published in *Asimov's Science Fiction* magazine,
May 1994
Won Canada's Aurora Award for short fiction in 1995
Reprinted in *Northern Suns*, Tor Books, 1999
Reprinted in *Aurora Awards: An Anthology of Prize-Winning
Science Fiction & Fantasy*, edited by Edo Van Belkom, Quarry
Press, 1999

"Hello, Jane, Goodbye"
Originally published in *Northern Frights 4*, edited by Don
Hutchison, Mosaic Press, 1997
Reprinted in *Wild Things Live Here: The Best of Northern
Frights*, Mosaic Press, 2001

"It's the Elemental Spirits!"
Originally published in *Untethered*, edited by Rhonda Parrish, Poise and Pen Publishing, 2022

"As Far As Is Feasible"
Originally published in *Polar Borealis*, Vol. 23, edited by R. Graeme Cameron, 2022

"Totem"
Originally published in *Tesseracts*, edited by Judith Merril, Press Porcépic Ltd. 1985

"There Is a Violence"
Originally published in *Tesseracts 5*, edited by Robert Runte and Yves Meynard, Tesseracts Books, 1996

"The Paisley Snow"
Originally published in *The Cockroach Conservatory*, #1, July 2018

Sally McBride has lived in Toronto, Calgary, Edmonton, Vancouver, Victoria, and (briefly) Florida (her cat didn't like it there). These days she divides her time between life in the mountains of Idaho (with her American husband) and city living in Toronto (close to Canadian family). In all these places, she has found supportive friends and fellow writers who get what it means to stare into the abyss trying to interpret what-ifs, if-this-goes-ons, dreams and wishes, and all the random stimuli that feed a writer's creativity. Sally has two amazing children and some equally amazing grandchildren. She enjoys skiing, reading (of course), and zipping around on her electric bike.